TO RULE IN AMBER

ALSO BY JOHN GREGORY BETANCOURT

TO RULE IN AMBER

BOOK THREE OF THE NEW AMBER TRILOGY

JOHN GREGORY BETANCOURT

ibooks

new york

www.ibooks.net

DISTRIBUTED BY SIMON & SCHUSTER

An Original Publication of ibooks, inc.

Copyright © 2004 Amber Ltd. Co.

An ibooks, inc. Book

Distributed by Simon & Schuster, Inc.
1230 Avenue of the Americas, New York, NY 10020

ibooks, inc.
24 West 25th Street
New York, NY 10010

The ibooks World Wide Web Site Address is:
http://www.ibooks.net

ISBN 0-7434-8709-5
First ibooks, inc. printing September 2004
10 9 8 7 6 5 4 3 2 1

Edited by Howard Zimmerman

Interior design by Gilda Hannah & John Betancourt
Typesetting by Wildside Press, LLC.

Printed in the U.S.A.

This one is especially for
KIM

ACKNOWLEDGMENTS

The author would like to thank Byron Preiss for making this project possible; his editor Howard Zimmerman, who has done a superlative job through a sometimes grueling schedule; and Theresa Thomas, Warren Lapine, and Lee F. Szczepanik, Jr. for providing commentary, criticism, and advice on the early drafts.

ONE

rayness surrounded me. Gray the color of morning twilight. Hours and days and years and centuries of gray. A featureless, all-consuming, all-encompassing gray that sucked the strength from your limbs and the will to live from your heart. So much gray that you couldn't take it all in no matter how hard you tried.

I fell through that gray, thinking of my crazy brother Aber, who had run out on me. Then I thought about my crazy father, Dworkin, who had left me guarding his back while he destroyed the universe.

For a while I wanted to kill them both. That lasted a long, long time. Then I wanted to hurt them. That lasted even longer.

Finally I didn't care.

And still I fell.

Uncountable ages passed. My mind wandered; I dreamed unhappy dreams. Now and again my father's voice spoke to me.

"Be patient," it would say. "The end has come, and the beginning lies ahead."

"What's in it for me?" I asked warily.

"Nothing," he said. "You were a tool, nothing more, used and discarded."

"No!"

I jerked around and tried to grab him, but my arms windmilled through nothingness. He hadn't really been here. I had imagined it.

Dreams, nightmares, hallucinations, imaginings. Call them what you will. They were one and the same.

And still I plunged through that gray, a never-ending sea of it. Forever passed. At least twice.

The end came with no sense of motion. Had I really been falling? Aber would know, some distant part of me remarked. Aber knew everything about magic.

Frowning, I tried to remember something important. Something about having to kill someone . . .

I couldn't recapture the thought. My head hurt. My muscles seemed to groan and my bones to creak, as though they hadn't been used in a long, long time.

Lurching, I almost fell. Suddenly I had direction again: a clear sense of up and down, left and right, forward and back. Thick, impenetrable grayness still surrounded me, but something had definitely changed. Something big.

"Aber!" I shouted. The air seemed to swallow my words.

"Aber! Where are you?"

No reply.

Besides, I knew my brother hadn't done anything to save me. He would have gone . . . where? I frowned. Back to the Courts of Chaos, probably. Who else could help me, then?

A face, a name on the tip of my tongue . . .

"Dworkin?" I whispered. That sounded right. "Dad?"

Memories suddenly flooded back. Our flight from Juniper to the strange Courts of Chaos. Someone named Lord Zon trying to kill my whole family. My half-brother Aber, who painted magical cards called Trumps that could be used to travel between worlds . . . my half-sister Freda, who saw the future . . . and most especially our father, the dwarf I'd grown up calling Uncle Dworkin. It turned out he'd been lying to protect me. He really *was* my father, and he commanded magical powers I had only just begun to understand. Someday soon I too would command those magics. I knew it.

Dworkin had created his own universe, a huge sprawling place of Shadow-worlds, and in so doing had weakened the powers of the sorcerers who lived in the Courts of Chaos. So someone from Chaos — probably Lord Zon — had sent hell-creatures to kill our whole family and destroy the Shadows, along with the magical Pattern that cast them.

My head hurt just thinking about it.

Fleeing the Courts of Chaos, Dworkin, Aber, and I came to a secret place that contained the Pattern at the center of the new universe. Unfortunately, Dworkin hadn't understood the Pattern fully when he'd created it, and its very essence held a flaw. To fix things, he had destroyed the old Pattern and retraced it from scratch using his own blood. He had collapsed after finishing it, and I had fallen into a void.

Had it worked? Did a new and correct Pattern really exist now? I didn't know. How could I find out?

First things first. I needed a plan. Mentally, I made a list:

1. Get out of the fog.
2. Find the rest of my family.
3. Stop everyone from trying to kill us.

If I had time, I'd add:

4. Beat my father to a bloody pulp for getting us all into
   this mess in the first place.

The air flickered around me, brighter then darker, brighter then darker. Stretching out my hands, I squinted into grayness, trying to see my fingertips. Nothing. Was I imagining things?

The light flickered again, subtly. I couldn't tell whether I had dreamed it, but somehow it felt *different*.

I fought back a rush of excitement; no sense in raising my hopes. I had been disappointed too often. And yet a small part of me wondered — could dawn finally be approaching? Had something else happened?

Anything would be better than this gray fog.

Slowly I inched my hands closer to my face. Dim shadows appeared. I wiggled my fingers; the shadows wiggled. The gray really *had* begun to lift. I could see again, if poorly. There's nothing more useless than a blind swordsman.

Hunkering down, I waited impatiently. The grayness seeped away slowly, like a morning fog lifting as the sun grows high. A long time later, I could see my hands clearly. A heartbeat later, and I could see all the way down to my boots. Another heartbeat, and I could see ten feet in every direction, then twenty, then fifty —

Rising, I looked around, but saw nothing but rock and sand and sky. No trees, no bushes, no blades of grass broke the desolation. Not even lichen grew here.

Gray fog continued to rush away from me in all directions, an outgoing tide revealing hills and valleys and distant mountains, all as barren as the land around me. I had never seen a place as dry and dead before.

The staff I had been carrying when I fell lay a few feet away, mostly hidden by rocks. Strolling over, I picked it up and leaned heavily on it, feeling old and tired. All I needed was a long gray beard and I'd be set.

The last of the gray vanished, but it didn't leave a promising world behind. Even on the distant mountains I saw no trees, bushes, or even grass — not a single living thing of any size, shape, or kind. No birds chirped or winged past; no insects *brred*. Not even a breeze stirred the dust on the ground.

I had never felt so alone in my life. Where *was* I? Where had my fall left me?

The sky overhead turned blue, the deepest, purest azure I had ever seen, without a single wisp of cloud. I gaped up into the vastness of it all.

At last, forcing my gaze back down to land, I sighed and resigned myself to work. My first job would be rescuing myself. I had to get off this Shadow — if Shadow it proved to be. If nothing else, I had begun to feel the first gnawing pangs of hunger.

I took a quick inventory. Sword, knife, boots, deck of Trumps — all where they belonged. All my limbs; all my fingers. I had not so much as a single bruise. My mental faculties seemed as sharp as ever.

If the Trumps still worked, I could use them to call any of my half-brothers or half-sisters for a way out. Or I could use one of the Trumps that showed a place, such as the Beyond or the Courts of Chaos, and bring myself directly there. The only problem was, I didn't know how safe any of those places would be. Too many people were trying to kill me right now to go blundering off to unknown destinations. At least, not without taking proper precautions — an army, for instance.

Removing the deck of Trumps from the pouch at my belt, I flipped through them until I came to the image of Aber. I liked Aber best of all my siblings; he was the only one who seemed to have a sense of humor, and he had been the only one to really take me in and make me feel as though I belonged. I hesitated. Should I contact him and ask to be rescued?

No . . . not Aber, not yet. I liked him, but I didn't quite trust him. He had his own problems and his own agenda. He had betrayed us to King Uthor of Chaos, though under duress. I could forgive him for that . . . but my trust would have to be earned back.

Moving his card to the bottom of the deck, where I could find it again easily, I kept going. My dead brother Locke . . . he couldn't be of any help now. My brother Conner . . . my sister Blaise . . .

Then I came to our father's card. It showed a dwarf dressed in a ridiculous jester's outfit, with bells on the toes of his pointy purple slippers and an idiotic grin on his face. Aber had painted Dad this way on purpose. He never missed a chance to secretly mock anyone who slighted him, our father most especially.

Raising Dad's Trump, I concentrated, envisioning him before me. But his image failed to come to life. I didn't sense so much as a flicker of consciousness when I concentrated on it. Dead? Unconscious? Just ignoring me? All seemed equally likely, and I had no way of finding out the truth right now.

It also could be that my Trumps no longer worked. Dad had destroyed the Pattern they were based on, after all. No, I'd have to assume they worked. Dad could easily be unwilling or unable to respond. I'd try another card.

Who was left? Just my other siblings, and I didn't know most of them well enough to decide how much I could rely on them. Any of them could be in Lord Zon's employ. Someone in Juniper had deliberately let an assassin into the castle to kill me. The plot had failed, but I still didn't know who the traitor had been.

Putting Dad's card on the bottom of the deck, next to Aber's, I pulled out my sister Freda's Trump. I trusted her more than most of the family. She might be a mystic and have visions of the future, but she had always been honest about her scheming: she wanted to be in charge of the family.

As painted by Aber, Freda looked gorgeous and sexy, with her red hair up, accentuating her high cheekbones and pale skin. Her shimmering reddish-purple evening gown accentuated her dark eyes. She had a cat-with-bird-in-mouth expression, which I found somewhat intriguing.

As I stared down at her, the stars behind her began to twinkle, and I felt a stirring consciousness. Good — the Trumps still worked. Then her picture moved, but oddly, with jerky movements. I couldn't quite see her face clearly. A veil seemed to hang between us.

"Who . . . it?" she asked. Words seemed to be missing. *"I . . . see –"*

"It's me — Oberon," I said.

"Who?" she cried. *". . . again!"*

Before I could reply, the ground trembled underfoot. An earthquake? I leaned on my staff for support and tried not to lose my balance. The vibrations grew stronger. Pebbles on the ground began to hop and jiggle. Rocks slid, and when the ground gave a sharp convulsion, I almost fell.

Freda was saying: *"–swer . . . ! Who is . . . ?"*

"Not now," I said to Freda. I covered her card with my hand and abruptly lost contact. I would try again once the earthquake passed. Before I could lose my deck of Trumps, I shoved them back into their pouch.

A distant rumbling began at the very edge of my hearing and grew steadily louder. Not thunder — it reminded me of stampeding horses. But there were no horses here . . . were there?

I turned slowly, hunting for the source of the noise. There — coming up from the valley — raising a cloud of dust — it really *was* horses!

No, not horses . . . *unicorns*. Dozens of them, a hundred or more, all running at breakneck speed toward me. Their silvery-white coats flashed in the sunlight, shiny with sweat. The horns on their heads bobbed up and down in rhythm to their strides. Their hooves blurred with the speed of their movement. I had never seen anything so magnificent before. What could they be doing here?

They swept across the land like a wildfire. Behind them came a tide of color: greens and browns and pinks and yellows, flowing across the mountains and valleys. Oceans of grass surged from the earth. Trees sprang from the ground; first seedlings, then towering oaks and maples and pines and so many more. Bushes heavy with ripe berries sprang full-grown from the ground. Meadows — forests — green from trees and grass; pinks, yellows, and purples from flowers; reds and golds from ripening fruit —

The herd approached my position rapidly. The jarring force of their stampede made everything loose bounce across the landscape like so many children's toys. I staggered but, with the help of the staff, kept to my feet.

Still the unicorns rushed forward — hooves pounding like hammers on anvils, the sound of their passage growing to a deafening roar. A hundred yards away, and I saw the wild, fierce looks in their eyes. They ran with a mad abandon, savage, fierce, unstoppable.

Panicking suddenly, I looked around for cover but found none. If the whole herd ran me down, I'd never survive their hooves. Where could I go? What could I do? My thoughts raced through the possibilities.

Fifty yards —

I'd never get a Trump out in time, even if I could contact someone to save me.

Thirty yards —

Taking a deep breath, I raised my staff and faced the unicorns. I could never hope to outrun them. What if I treated them like a real herd of horses?

Bellowing a war-cry, though they never could have heard me over their own deafening noise, I twirled my staff and stomped my feet. If I could spook the leaders enough to make them shy away —

Ten yards — five —

It wasn't going to work. I saw it now. Their nostrils flared. Their jaws snapped. Their eyes rolled wildly. They ran with no thought or reason; a terrible madness seemed to have come over them all.

I steeled myself. My heart hammered in my chest, but I set my feet and held my ground.

Three yards — one —

At the last instant, the lead unicorns veered aside, one to my left and one to my right, and the others followed right in their paths. Like a river flowing around an island, they separated just enough to avoid hitting me.

The rushing, pounding noise of their passage deafened me. The heat of their bodies washed across me in a burning wind. The cloud of dust raised by their hooves filled my eyes and mouth. Flecks of foamy sweat hit my face and arms.

Coughing and choking, half blind, I held as still as I could. They would pass me safely. I could live through it if I just kept still —

And then they were gone. The sudden silence and stillness was overwhelming.

But before I could relax, the ground underfoot seethed and churned. What now? I teetered, off balance. A moment later, thick blades of grass popped out under my boots, growing rapidly until it was waist high. I braced myself with my staff, trying desperately to keep my balance.

As my staff touched the ground, it ripped free from my hands and took root. Branches burst out along its length, several almost skewering me. Then a hideous, tortured face appeared in the center of the trunk. Two orbs flickered, then opened . . . showing familiar blue eyes . . . eyes I had looked on with admiration and respect a thousand times before.

Now, though, they glared down at me. I had seldom seen such hate and loathing. It wanted me dead.

"No. . . !" I whispered. My heart seemed to skip several beats. No matter how hard I tried, I couldn't tear my gaze away. "No. . . !"

Those eyes — that face — belonged to King Elnar of Ilerium. King Elnar had died because I abandoned him, despite my oath to serve both king and country for all my life. He had died — murdered by hell-creatures — what now seemed a lifetime ago.

The wooden mouth opened. A groaning, moaning squeal of pain came out.

"Please," I begged. "Not this! Not again!"

I swallowed hard. The lump in my throat felt as large as my fist. I couldn't believe this was happening to me.

Elnar had been almost a father to me. I had worshipped him . . . done everything I could to be just like him. Of all the things that had befallen me — of all the horrors I had seen since leaving Ilerium — his death struck me the hardest.

After murdering him, hell-creatures had mounted his head on a pole outside of Kingstown. When I had returned there, the king's head spoke to me. Somehow, impossibly, magic kept it alive. It had called me vile names and shouted for hell-creatures to come and kill me.

That had been one of the worst moments of my life.

Of course, I knew deep inside that it hadn't really been King Elnar speaking — not truly — but the words still hurt like no others could have. I *knew* I had betrayed his trust. I *knew* I had deserted him in his time of greatest need. Because of me, he had died. Horribly.

No, I forced myself to think, not because of me. Because of the foul magics of the Courts of Chaos.

I took a deep breath, forcing down my shock and repulsion. Hell-creatures had created a grisly parody of what King Elnar had once been. The head on the pole had not been my liege and friend. Nor was this face in this tree King Elnar. It was an abomination, created by magic — an abomination to be loathed and destroyed.

And yet — it was King Elnar's face —

As I watched, those familiar blue eyes stared down at me. The wooden mouth parted, twisting into a half snarl.

"You!" it moaned at last, with Elnar's voice. "I know you! You are the one who did this to me! Murderer! *Traitor!*"

TWO

 took a deep breath, then let it out explosively.

"You're wrong!" I said. The severed head on the pole in Ilerium had uttered pretty much those exact same words. "Think back to what really happened. Look inside yourself. You will see the truth."

"Traitor!" it cried. Its lips pulled back in a pained grimace. *"Murderer! Butcher!"*

I turned away. My eyes burned and my head pounded. I couldn't believe my luck. Why had the unicorns done this to me? Were they trying to punish me for some reason?

No, not the unicorns . . . the blame lay with Aber. Understanding came on me suddenly. I had returned to Juniper with the pole upon which King Elnar's head had been impaled. Aber had taken the pole. Later, at the Pattern, when I asked him for a staff, he had summoned one for me . . . and it was my bad luck that he had given me back the one which had held King Elnar's head.

The unicorns, with their life-giving magic, had somehow brought both the staff and King Elnar back to life, but joined together. It made a certain amount of sense. King Elnar's head had been growing *into* the pole, as I had discovered when I smashed his head to a pulp in Kingstown, what now seemed a lifetime ago.

"You deserve to die!" the face in the tree screamed. "No — death is too good for you! *Torture!* A thousand years of torture!"

I pressed my eyes shut and turned my face away. How much more of this could I take? Still King Elnar called down abuse. What could I do to stop him? What could I do to make it up to him?

"Enough!" I said. Drawing a deep breath, I whirled. My temper flared; I could not put up with his abuse any longer.

"Oh, the coward speaks!" he mocked. "Enough! Boo-hoo! Did I cry when you killed me?"

"I mean it!" I said. I drew my sword and took a step forward, raising my blade menacingly. Would it be soft like human flesh, or hard like a tree? "Shut up, o —!"

"Or what? What are you going to do, kill me again?" It actually laughed at me. "You always were a fool. A fool and a traitor! Look how you respect your oaths of allegiance. Will you kill me by your own hand this time? Or will you leave that to the hell-creatures?"

I sucked in an angry breath and raised my sword.

"Assassin!" it shrieked. *"Assassin!"*

"I'm only going to say this once," I said in a dangerously quiet voice. I owed it to King Elnar's memory to try one last time to make peace with whatever part of him remained alive here. "Believe me, I could not have done anything more to help you. Had I stayed in Ilerium, we would both be dead now. That is the truth."

"You *should* be dead!" it cried. "Thousands perished because of you! *Murderer! Traitor!*"

"Enough!" Rage swept through me.

Without a second's hesitation, I stabbed the face with the tip of my sword. Steel bit into its nose with the dull *thump* of metal hitting wood. It didn't penetrate far, but it seemed to hurt.

"Assassin!" the face howled, its voice rising in panic. Its eyes crossed almost comically as it tried to see the wound. *"Help me, someone! Help me! Save me from the assassin!"*

I jerked my sword free, leaving a long gash in the wood of its nose. Slowly, a sticky-looking black sap oozed out. It had the consistency of blood. And, like blood, it slowly beaded.

Still the tree cursed at me.

"Enough, I said!" My voice rose to a roar. If I couldn't out-fight or out-reason it, maybe I could out-shout it. "Be quiet, or I'll carve out your tongue!"

"You wouldn't dare!" it cried. "Oath-breaker! Liege-killer! *Murderer!*"

On and on it went.

I forced myself to take a deep, soothing breath. Clearly the hell-creatures had taken all of King Elnar's rational mind, leaving behind a creature that could only parrot human speech. Nothing remained of my old friend.

It was all too ridiculous. I couldn't allow hell-creatures to waste my time and energy. I would *not* fight a tree.

Shaking my head at the morbid humor of this whole situation, I turned away. I could easily waste all my time and energy trying to reason with this monstrosity. And maybe that's what the hell-creatures wanted. Maybe it was supposed to keep me busy until they could capture or kill me. Unfortunately for them, they were nowhere close. They would never find King Elnar again . . . never use him against me.

Clearly this *thing* wasn't my old liege. I didn't have to treat it with any special deference or respect. Nor would I fight with it. After all, what could I possibly accomplish by hitting a tree with a sword? Maybe I could claim "first sap" instead of "first blood" in our fight. Not that anyone would call striking an unarmed tree with a sword a fight . . .

Then the answer came to me suddenly.

I didn't have to do anything at all. If I wanted to win, all I had to do was walk away. If I abandoned it here, forever howling insults and cursing my name, it had no power over me.

Turning, I headed up the valley. And why not? With so many Shadows to choose from, I had no reason to ever come this way again. Let it scream. Let it curse my name. What did I care?

"Come back!" it yelled. "Coward! Simpering weakling! *Traitor!*"

I paused. Despite the soundness of my own advice, I discovered I couldn't just leave. I *did* care.

Maybe it was my oath to King Elnar. Maybe I owed something to his memory. Or maybe the hell-creatures had put a spell on the head, a compulsion to make me stay and argue with it against my own better judgment. Whatever the reason, I *needed* to make peace with the tree.

But how? Threats hadn't worked. Reason hadn't worked. What else remained?

"Assassin!" it continued to scream. *"Murderer!* Someone help me! Avenge my death! *To arms! To arms!* He's getting away!"

What else? Perhaps . . . reality?

With a sigh, I took a deep breath and faced the tree again. What did I have to lose? Things couldn't get any worse, after all. King Elnar had already died. Hell-creatures had already cut off and ensor-celled his head. Maybe, if he truly understood what had happened to him . . .

I seized on that idea: *make him understand.* If I could make him see his own grim predicament . . . or shut up for a minute to let me explain it . . . maybe that would be enough.

"Let m —" I began.

"Assassin!"

"Le —"

"Murderer!"

"— me explai —"

"Traitor!"

"— it to you!"

"Oath-breaker!"

I paused. The abuse didn't stop for a second.

A human being who talked and screamed and shouted non-stop would rapidly lose his voice. What about a tree? I didn't know. But I intended to find out.

"Liege-killer!"

"Uh-huh," I said. "Tell me about it."

And he did, calling me every sort of vile name imaginable — and some I never would have imagined. Through it all I just stood there and nodded, smiling now and again, making encouraging noises at all the right places. Maybe all he needed was time to talk himself hoarse.

Well, let him! His words couldn't hurt me.

Finally, as he began to repeat himself, I decided to take a rest. I sat beneath its spreading branches, stretched out my legs, and gave a wide yawn. Wriggling my back, I found a comfortable spot against the trunk, leaned back, and shut my eyes.

Abruptly the abuse stopped. I opened one eye.

"Go on," I said. "Don't stop."

"What are you doing?" he cried.

"Taking a nap."

"Stop it! Murderer! *Help me, someone!*"

"Go on," I said sarcastically. "I love the sound of your voice."

If anything, that seemed to enrage him. He screamed, shouted, threatened, and insulted me time and again.

Despite the constant stream of abuse, it actually *did* feel nice to relax. I could even fall asleep here . . .

Closing my eyes again, I pretended to snore.

After ten minutes, the cursing and name-calling came to a stop. Now the tree muttered the vilest of threats under its breath, promises to disembowel, behead, and boil me in oil — sometimes all at once.

Minor progress, but progress nonetheless. I continued to snore.

The muttering lasted another ten minutes or so. At last it grew silent. Had I outlasted it? Had its murderous rage finally passed? Would it talk civilly to me now?

Cautiously opening one eye, I peeked up at King Elnar's face. He stared down at me, frowning severely.

"Don't stop," I said with a chuckle. "The music of your voice soothes my sleep."

"What are you doing?" it demanded.

"Resting."

"Why?"

"I felt like it."

"Traitor!"

"Scream all you want," I said, folding my arms behind my head and closing my eyes. "It doesn't bother me a bit."

"Why not?"

"We're far from Ilerium. I don't have to worry about hell-creatures finding and killing me here."

"Why not?"

"It's just you and me, old friend. No one can hear you, so go ahead! Scream all you want! Curse. Call me names. It doesn't bother me. No one can hear you. After all, we're alone in this world."

"I don't believe you."

"And I don't care." I closed my eyes. This time, I almost *did* fall asleep.

When at last it spoke again, suspicion hardened its voice. "What do you mean, alone?"

"We aren't in Ilerium anymore, old friend. We're in a new world . . . an empty world. No people. No hell-creatures. Just you and me. And you're a tree."

"You're a liar!"

I actually laughed. "I wish I had a looking-glass. You're not even a tree — you're a face stuck *in* a tree. Now that's funny! King of Shrubbery, I'll call you!"

"Liar!"

"Shrub!"

When it didn't reply, I squinted critically up at the twisted, gnarled trunk. Had my words finally sunk in?

"You're not even a very good looking tree," I went on. Why not add insult to injury? "You're lucky I don't have an axe. I have a feeling you'd make better kindling than anything else."

"Liar! Liar!"

"Don't you believe me?" I streched one arm up, caught a low-hanging branch, and broke off a handful of leaves with a twist of my wrist.

"Ow!" it cried.

"Look! You really *are* a tree, whether you want to admit it or not!"

"That hurt!"

"What hurt?" I demanded.

"My . . . my leaves?" A horror-struck look came over the face, as it realized what it had said.

Leaves. *Its* leaves.

I smiled grimly.

"That's right, Your Highness," I said. "As I already told you, you're a tree now, complete with roots, trunk, branches, and quite a nice bunch of *leaves.* Everything I've said to you has been the truth."

Casually, I reached up and snapped off a small branch just above my head. I got a shriek in return.

"See?"

"Stop that!"

Perhaps I'd found the negotiating tactic I needed.

I said, "You need to keep a civil tongue, O King of Shrubbery.

Set a good example for your people." I nodded to one side. "The blackberry bushes over there are watching, after all."

"Do not mock me, traitor!"

"Why not? It's fun."

"*Woe!*" cried King Elnar's voice. "I am lost! I am a tree, and I am lost!"

"Be quiet," I said, reaching for another branch, "or I will have to do a fair amount of pruning . . ."

The face closed its mouth with a snap. The silence seemed unexpected — almost unnatural. If it had enough sense left for self-preservation, what else might it be capable of? Maybe more of King Elnar remained than I had dared to hope.

Slowly I lowered my arm.

"If you're going to be reasonable," I said calmly, "we can work things out between us."

"You are trying to trick me!"

"Why would I do that?"

"I . . . I don't know. But you will! That's what traitors and murderers do!"

"Here's a thought. Maybe I won't trick you. I have no reason to, after all. And I'm neither a traitor nor a murderer. Don't call me that."

"But —"

"But nothing! Everything I've told you has been the truth. You really *are* a face stuck in a tree. Hell-creatures killed you, not me. They put those words in your mouth and made you say them. The man I knew, the man you once were, would never have believed their lies.

We fought them together, side by side."

The face and I stared at one another. I didn't know what else to add; apparently, neither did he. We had reached an impasse. At least he had stopped yelling and calling me names.

Then a bird flew past, twittering loudly. I sat up, startled. A bird — the first animal I had yet seen in this world! It seemed the unicorns had left more than mere greenery and magical trees in their wake. I watched the bird land twenty feet away. It picked up a piece of grass, then flew to a nearby tree, where it seemed to be building a nest. If this world had animals, what else might there be? Perhaps . . . people?

Rising, I turned slowly, searching for any sign of civilization — houses, smoke from cooking fires, anything that spoke of a human presence. My gaze lingered a long time in the direction the unicorns had gone.

A perfect stream, surrounded by cattails and thick green reeds, burbled happily through the picturesque little valley. Iridescent dragonflies buzzed over the water, and a frog hopped from the bank into a blue-green pool with an audible splash.

"What are you looking for?" asked the tree.

"Shh!" I held up one hand for silence. Something felt subtly different . . .

Stealthy movement caught my eye. A single white unicorn moved with dainty steps from a copse of trees beyond the stream, lowered her head, and drank deeply from the frog's pool. She had something around her neck . . . something that looked like a giant ruby on a chain.

I gaped. It had to be the jewel my father had shown me in Juniper . . . the one he used to trace the new Pattern. This unicorn had to be the one that had helped Dad and me.

When she raised her head and she saw me staring at her, she stamped her right forefoot and tossed her head. I took a step in her direction. As I did, she turned and slipped into the trees. There she paused long enough to glance over her shoulder.

Follow me, she seemed to be saying. *Follow me to your destiny.*

THREE

ll right," I called. "I can take a hint. I'm coming!" I started after her.

"Do not leave me!" cried the tree.

"What?" I demanded, looking back in surprise. "I thought you couldn't wait to be rid of me!"

". . . Please?"

I hesitated. King Elnar might be dead, but my sense of duty remained. Almost reluctantly, I turned back to the tree. That unicorn could wait another minute.

"What is it you want from me?" I said.

"I . . . I think I know you."

"You'd better, after all those accusations you made." Then I paused, as a horrible suspicion bubbled up inside me — what if he really *didn't* know me? I had to ask: "What's my name?"

"I think . . . Ar . . . Orl . . . Erlock?"

"You called me Obere," I said gently. "But my real name is Oberon."

"Obere . . . Oberon . . . yes. Yes, that sounds right. I *know* you. Obere. Oberon."

"What happened in Kingstown? Do you remember?"

"I . . . cannot remember. You said I was a tree. But I think I used to be a man. Was I a man?"

"Yes, long ago," I said. The hell-creatures had done their work well if he couldn't remember such simple details. Everything he had said, everything he had done since his death, must have been due to their foul magics. Only now had he begun to recover.

I went on. "Do you remember anything about me? Do you remember fighting hell-creatures in Ilerium? Do you remember anything more of your old life?"

It gnashed its wooden teeth, but made no reply. Apparently it didn't remember. Considering how I'd destroyed King Elnar's head the last time we met, the tree's lack of memory probably shouldn't have surprised me. With his brains scattered across a battlefield on another Shadow, how could he remember much of anything?

"Do you know your own name?" I asked. If I pressed him for information, perhaps he would recall more.

"Ev . . . Agg . . . Ygg. . . ?"

"You don't remember," I said sadly. I had hoped, for a moment, that more of King Elnar remained. "Do you recall anything of your days as a man? Do you remember your kingdom?"

"So much darkness . . ." it whispered. "Shadows fill my mind . . . there is nothing left . . ."

"Think!" I cried.

It gave a sob. "I cannot! My memories are gone! I cannot recall anything before I awoke here!"

I glanced at the unicorn. She stamped her feet impatiently and slipped into the trees. Time to go. She wanted me to follow.

Hurriedly, I said, "I have to leave. If you'll talk to me instead of calling me names, I promise I'll return when I can."

"I agree . . . Oberon."

"Thank you, old friend."

Giving it a brief salute, I took a deep breath and faced the stream again. Snorting, the unicorn moved farther into the trees, dark gray on black beneath a canopy of leaves, drifting away. The reddish glint of her eyes seemed almost catlike as she watched me now. I knew she hadn't enjoyed waiting, but after all, she and her kind had brought King Elnar back; what could I do?

Briskly I hiked after her, splashing across the stream and entering the cool, moist-smelling forest. No birds sang here, nor did any insects chirp or buzz or wing through the air. Each leaf, mushroom, and splay of sunlight filtering down through the treetops took on a special sharpness, as though each line had been carefully etched with a needle-sharp tool. We were cutting across Shadows, through world after world after world. The air almost sang with power.

When I reached the spot where she had been standing, a faint flash of white, ahead and to the left, drew me farther into the trees. The faintest of trails wound among the ancient oaks and pines, skirting rocks, twisting and climbing into low hills.

So it went. Over the next half hour, she lead me through the forest, then into grassy hills dotted with the round shoulders of ancient boulders. We crossed lush but empty valleys where wind sang a single mournful note, and then again entered a long stretch of primal forest where a peaceful, hush hung over everything. I could not tell if we were traveling through Shadows, but I didn't think so.

Finally, we pushed through a thick hedge and entered a broad clearing. Here, in its center, on top of a huge stone slab that must have been a hundred and fifty feet wide, shone the Pattern that my father had inscribed with his own blood. It glowed with a clear bluish-white light, cold and beautiful . . . more beautiful than the last Pattern, perfect this time in every way.

Slowly I approached it. Waves of energy came off its sleek lines, humming deep inside me. It felt *good*. Strange, unlike anything else, but good.

I basked at its edge, eyes shut, just *feeling* its nearness. Warm all over, strong and more alive than I had ever felt before, I might have stood there for days had a snorting bark of sound not jarred me from my half-sleep.

The unicorn. It still wanted something. Almost reluctantly, I forced my eyes open.

As my gaze swept across the length of the Pattern, searching for her, I noticed a curious lump in the exact middle. Aesthetically, it didn't belong. I stared at it, puzzling, and slowly realized it was the body of a man. Dark shirt and pants, graying hair . . . my father?

Panic surged through me. The longer I stared, the more certain I became. It had to be him.

"Dad?" I called, taking a step forward. "Are you all right? Can you hear me? *Dad!*"

He didn't so much as stir. How had he gotten there? I'd watched him disappear after creating the Pattern, teleported off to gods knew where. Why had he returned? Had he left something undone and returned to finish, only to be attacked? Or had he been hurt somewhere else and fled here for safety?

35

Or maybe it wasn't him.

Swallowing hard, I drew up short. Considering how powerful our enemies seemed to be, this might be a trap of some kind.

I glanced toward the place I'd last seen the unicorn, but she had disappeared again — probably watching from cover. Clearly she had brought me here for a reason, though. Why else but to save my father?

I didn't think she would lead me into a trap, but nevertheless I circled the Pattern warily, keeping a close watch on the body. When I finished my circuit, I found myself no closer to an answer. Nothing unexpected had happened. No hell-creatures had jumped from the hedge with swords raised. No barrage of arrows had flown at me. No sorcerers had hurled flames or lightning-bolts in my direction.

My every instinct said it wasn't a trap. If someone wanted to kill me, the perfect opportunity had already come and gone.

And Dad still lay unmoving in the middle of the Pattern.

I took a deep breath. Nothing to do now but investigate.

With a last glance around, I stalked toward the body. As I reached the edge of the Pattern, though, I seemed to run into an invisible wall. As much as I tried, I couldn't force my way through. The wall wasn't *physical*, as far as I could tell. But I couldn't get past it no matter how hard I pushed.

Circling to the right, I tried several more times to get to my father but met the same impenetrable barrier. I couldn't cross onto the Pattern no matter how hard I tried.

I stepped back to think. Dad or the unicorn must have put the barrier in place to protect the Pattern. It made a certain amount of sense. If King Uthor, Lord Zon, or anyone else from Chaos found a way to get here, we didn't want them destroying the Pattern.

Only that didn't help Dad or me right now. If I couldn't get to my father, how could I help him? For all I knew, he might already be dead.

I frowned. *Think, think, think!*

Dad always said every problem had a solution — you just had to find it. I tried to look at the situation from a different point of view. If I couldn't get to him . . . perhaps he could get to me.

"Dad!" I called again, as loudly as I could. "Listen carefully! It's Oberon! Can you hear me? Can you stand up? Give me a sign! *Dad!*"

No answer. He didn't so much as twitch.

He might have been lying there for days or weeks. Time moved strangely from Shadow to Shadow. How long had I been trapped in that gray fog, anyway? I had no way of knowing.

Until I found out otherwise, I had to assume he was alive but merely unconscious. Perhaps creating the Pattern had done something to him — exhausted him to the point of collapse. Maybe the unicorn had brought him back here for his own safety. I couldn't rule anything out.

I paced around the Pattern, trying to figure a way through. If I had a Trump showing the center of the Pattern, I could use it to travel there. I supposed I could always try to draw one . . . but with what? I had no pen, no ink. I could use my own blood, I supposed — but then I didn't have any paper or vellum.

"Dad!" I called again. "Wake up! *Dad!*"

Still no response. I looked around for the unicorn. Never a divine being when you needed one . . . she seemed to have abandoned me here.

I recalled how I had once traveled across an image of the Pattern inside the unicorn's ruby. It had been difficult, but not impossibly so. If this version worked the same way, maybe I could work my way through it to reach him.

I headed toward what seemed the obvious starting point: the place where Dad had begun tracing the Pattern with his blood. Here, when I stretched out my hand, I felt a curious pins-and-needles sensation in my fingertips . . . but no barrier blocking the way. Apparently I could enter the Pattern here, treading its long, convoluted line like a path.

"Hesitation is for cowards," I told myself with more courage than I felt. Taking a deep breath, I stepped forward. No turning back now.

The moment my foot touched the Pattern, my peripheral vision flickered faintly. The tingling sensation spread from my fingers through my entire body, and I shuddered involuntarily.

With my second step, a needle of pain shot through my head. As a low drumlike throbbing began in the back of my skull, a curious ache spread through my head and into my eyes.

I can do this.

I took a deep breath.

Keep moving.

Once more the Pattern seemed to radiate power in waves. A strange giddiness ran through me, and I almost giggled. It actually felt *good* in a way I couldn't properly explain. Strength coursed through me. I took another step, and then another.

Suddenly everything got harder. Keeping my head down, I had to concentrate on moving my feet one at a time. With every step, a strange and slightly unpleasant jolt shot up each leg and into my thighs.

Don't stop.

One foot after another.

Keep going.

My gaze followed the sweep of the path as it wound into a series of long and graceful curves. I knew every twist and turn already, just as I knew the battle-scars on the backs of my hands. The pattern was a part of me, forever seared into my mind. Blindfolded, I could have followed the Pattern's line without missing a step.

I entered the first curve and suddenly walking got really hard. My legs dragged; I forced myself to pick up each foot and put it down again. Sparks swirled around my boots, rising to my knees, and every hair on my body stood on end.

Don't stop.

One step, then another, then another.

Things got easier at the end of the curve, and I let out my breath in an explosive gasp. My head pounded. My shirt clung to my back, uncomfortable and clammy with sweat. Nothing I could do now, though. I couldn't exactly turn around and go back. Besides, I had come at least a third of the way.

After a brief period of easiness, the path started to grow hard again. Sparks swirled up to my waist. I seemed to be slogging through mud.

Another step. Then another. Then another.

My legs went numb. Then the numbness spread to my chest, and I had to force myself not only to walk, but to breathe. It would have been all too easy to give up, but I refused to take the easy way out. Dad needed me.

Rounding another curve, the numbness passed and I could move easily again. Blue sparks ghosted across my clothes and skin. I had the sensation of thousands of insects crawling over my body. I had never felt anything like it before.

Not much farther now.

Keep moving.

Halfway there.

I tucked down my head and pressed on. The path curved back upon itself, then straightened. Still I slogged on through what felt like miles of heavy mud that sucked and pulled at my feet.

Slowly, the end grew near. I could see my father's face clearly now. His open eyes stared up into space. Dead? Had I come for nothing? Then his eyes blinked — he *was* alive!

"Dad?" I gasped. "Dad — can you — hear me — ?"

A crunching sound filled my ears. The hair on my neck and arms rose again. I had to force myself to take each step forward. If I stopped, I didn't think I would be able to get started again.

The path curved sharply, and all of a sudden I found I could walk almost normally. Gathering my strength, I strode forward as quickly as I could, but then a heaviness grew on me. I found it harder and harder to advance, as though chains now dragged on my arms and legs and chest. I might have been pulling a ten-ton weight.

Gritting my teeth, I pressed forward. One step. A second. A third. Each took more effort than the last. When I raised my hand, sparks poured like water from my skin.

Through!

Suddenly, I could walk again. Sparks dashed and flew all around me. I felt hot and cold, wet and dry, and my eyes burned with a fire that could not be quenched. I blinked hard many times.

One more curve.

Almost there.

Dizzy, I reeled through another curve, a short one. Then straight, then another curve.

It was the hardest yet. I could barely move, barely see, barely breathe. My skin froze, then boiled. Sparks blinded me. The very universe seemed to beat down upon my head and shoulders.

I concentrated on one foot at a time. As long as I kept moving, I drew closer to my goal. Just another inch at a time — anything to *keep going* —

I could barely see the Pattern. Unable to breathe, I used the last of my strength to take a final step.

Then I was through. I had made it.

My legs felt weak. Drawing on final reserves of strength I didn't know I had, I staggered to my father's side.

"Dad?" I said. It came out barely a whisper. "How about helping me out here?"

He didn't move. Somehow, I managed to kneel, then roll him over. I checked him for wounds, but he seemed whole — nothing worse than a slight bruise on the back of one hand.

"What's wrong, Dad?"

Slowly his lips moved. He seemed to be trying to speak.

I leaned close, straining to hear. He kept saying what sounded like, "Thellops . . . Thellops . . . Thellops . . ."

"Thellops?" I demanded. "What in the seven hells is *that*?"

He stared blindly off into space. His lips continued to move. Clearly he hadn't heard me. What could be wrong with him?

"Come on, Dad!" I said. I shook him. "Wake up! I can't get you out of here by myself! *Dad!*"

Still no response.

Grabbing him under the arms, I hauled him to his feet. Maybe he'd come out of it if I got him up and moving. His head lolled forward. When I draped his arm across my shoulders, he was so much dead weight. He made no effort to support himself.

"Attention!" I barked like a drill sergeant. "On your feet, soldier! *Move!*"

That would have gotten me up, no matter how hard or painful — as a soldier in King Elnar's army, obedience to orders had been drilled into me. You didn't make Lieutenant without it.

"Dad!" I said, urgently. "I need you awake now! *Dad!*"

I shook him again, but all he did was drool. Just great. Could things get any worse?

With nothing left to try, I slapped his face. He blinked and moaned. Then his eyes closed and opened several times in quick succession. He seemed to come out of his stupor enough to turn his head toward me.

"Can you stand?" I asked him.

"Not . . . real . . ." he mumbled.

"Of course I'm real. It's me — Oberon."

"Imagining . . ."

I slapped his face again, just enough to sting. That seemed to bring him around a bit more.

"Look at me!" I said. "Can you stand, Dad? Do you need help walking?"

Mumbling, he shrugged away my hands. For a second he wobbled, but then he seemed to draw on inner reserves of strength. He straightened his back and stood rigidly upright, and an odd, slightly bewildered expression flickered across his face.

"Where . . . ?" he whispered.

"You're back at the Pattern," I said. "Do you know how to get out?"

"The Pattern . . . yes . . ."

"Good. You do remember." I turned and gazed along the shimmering path I had just walked. With all those twists and turns, it seemed a lot longer than I had first thought. "Is it easier when you're leaving?" I asked. "Can you walk? I'm not sure I can carry you back out."

The faintest hiss of steel leaving a scabbard sent a shiver of alarm through me. Instantly, I threw myself to the left, tucking into a quick roll. I came up on the balls of my feet, fists ready.

I'd acted just in time — my father had drawn his sword and lunged at me. If I hadn't been fast, he would have run me through.

"Thellops!" he roared, advancing on my position. He had a half-crazed look in his eyes. "Never again!"

FOUR

ad!" I cried, backing away desperately. Had he lost his mind? Didn't he recognize me? "It's Oberon — your son! *Dad!*

Howling, he lunged again.

Fortunately, he barely had enough strength to hold his blade. Batting his sword aside with my arm, I closed fast and punched the side of his head as hard as I could. The force of my blow sent a shock of pain the length of my arm and sent him reeling.

That blow would have been enough to knock out or even kill a normal man. Not my father, though. Dazed, the tip of his sword dragging across the stone, he gave a low groan and rushed me again, slashing.

"Dad, look at me!" I said, dancing back to safety. Somehow, I held my temper. I knew he wasn't thinking clearly. I just had to make him understand.

Staggering back, he raised his sword with a grunt and seemed to be gathering his strength for another rush.

"Why are you doing this?" I demanded. "Think about it, Dad! Reason it out!"

Clutching the hilt of his sword with both hands now, he rushed straight at me. It was a clumsy move that no master swordsman in his right mind would have tried.

Dancing easily to one side, I gave him another punch to the head. He stumbled, then reeled back, slashing at me. He missed by several feet.

"Damn Thellops," Dad muttered.

"What is Thellops?" I demanded. "Talk to me, Dad!"

Staggering, he almost fell. I took the opportunity to draw my own sword. He might be my father, but I wasn't taking any chances. I couldn't stand here and let him attack me again and again. It only took one lucky swing.

"Won't do," he muttered. "Won't do."

"What won't do?" I demanded.

Shaking his head, once more he charged straight at me.

This time we met with a clash of steel on steel. I had planned to disarm him quickly, but as our blades locked, his strength returned. He hurled me back with a powerful surge of his muscles, then launched into a blistering series of double-feints and lunging attacks that I barely managed to turn aside.

"Dad! Stop it!"

"No more tricks!" he cried.

"It isn't a trick! It's me, Oberon!"

"Thellops!"

Not that again. Backing away warily, I kept my gaze on the tip of his sword. It darted from side to side like a wasp looking to strike.

"I don't want to hurt you," I said, "But if you keep this up, I'm going to have to!"

He feinted, then slashed at my head. I parried, giving way, then parried again as he pressed the attack. This time he used a complicated series of feints and thrusts. Even crazy, he was the greatest swordsman I had ever seen.

He got first blood. On a swift feint-and-riposte, he came in under my guard and nicked the back of my right wrist. I never saw it coming. A second later, he gashed my right forearm. Nothing life-threatening, but blood poured down my hand. In a few seconds I wouldn't be able to grip my sword properly.

He threw back his head and howled with laughter. If I fell down, would he think he'd won? I would have to keep that as a backup plan, in case he hit me again.

Before the blood ruined my grip, I switched sword-hands. Clearly I couldn't fight him on even terms. If I didn't do something fast, he'd kill me.

"This is your last chance," I bluffed. "Put up your sword, or I won't hold myself back!"

"Thellops!" he growled. "Never again!"

So much for diplomacy.

He might be a better swordsman than I, but in the real world, I knew the best didn't always win. The smartest did. And if I couldn't out-think a madman, I didn't deserve to live.

He attacked again. I fell back before him, yielding ground quickly, concentrating on fighting defensively. There had to be a weakness in his attack. I just had to find and exploit it.

His sword blurred and darted, testing my defenses, trying to find a way past my guard. Still I parried frantically, retreating in slow circles. His every attack seemed perfect. He fell into a rhythm now: attack, rest, attack, rest.

The next time he paused to catch his breath, I took a moment to study him carefully. That's when I noticed the huge bruise purpling around his left eye — at exactly the spot I'd punched him twice. I figured the swelling must have cut into his field of vision. If I played to his left side, taking advantage of that injury . . .

He launched a blistering attack again. This time, though, I circling to my right. He kept blinking and shaking his head. The faster I circled, the more I noticed his pauses and hesitations.

He started to tire again. As he drew up short, his sword dropped out of position.

My turn.

I came in low and from the right, hitting him fast and hard. I hammered at his blind side. He reeled back, turning my sword frantically. Then I deliberately over-extended my reach, letting my sword's point drop. He never saw it coming — the swelling blinded him — and even if he had, I don't think he had the strength left to stop it.

My sword's point bit deep into his right foot. I jerked it free, and blood spurted.

Yowling, he slashed wildly. His blade whistled through the air, missing my eyes by inches. When he landed on his bad foot, his leg started to give way. He staggered and almost fell.

Got you! Leaping forward, I caught his frantically windmilling free hand, whirled, and heaved in one smooth motion. He sailed over my shoulder and landed flat on his back ten feet away. The breath whooshed from his lungs. He lay there stunned.

I leaped, pinning his sword-hand beneath my boot. He released his weapon, gasping. He couldn't move, could barely breathe. I kicked the sword away, sending it skittering twenty feet across the stony ground to the very edge of the Pattern.

"This is your last chance," I said with more calmness than I felt. "Yield, Dad, and we'll have a drink and a laugh about it later."

Tired and hurt as he was, he tried to throw me off. I had to give him credit for that — I wouldn't have had the heart to continue the fight. Unarmed, how could he hope to continue?

Suddenly he rolled to one side and made it to his feet in a convulsive movement. Before I could react, he whipped a knife from his belt.

"Die!" he roared. He dove forward and tried to stab me in the chest.

"Dad," I said in a warning tone, dancing back to safety, "give it up! You don't have a chance!"

He growled, so I clouted the right side of his head with the hilt of my sword. It made a meaty *thunk*. He fell to his knees, stunned.

"Enough!" I kicked the knife away, then booted him in the stomach. He doubled over, gasping hard.

"Sorry, Dad," I said, more heartsick than angry. "But you brought this on yourself."

I punched the side of his head with the hilt of my sword again. He fell face-down, struggling to rise.

"Thellops!" he cried.

Without hesitation, I threw myself onto his back. I got a knee between his shoulder blades and pinned his arms behind his back.

He couldn't possible attack me now — or get up, for that matter.

"Tell me what I did to piss you off," I said in his ear. "What in the seven hells does 'Thellops' mean, anyway?"

Still growling, he turned his head and bit deep into my left wrist. With a yelp, I jerked free, then punched him twice in the back of his head. He started to whimper again.

"Dad," I said in a hard voice, "I'm going to help you. But you've got to stop trying to hurt me. Do you understand what I'm saying?"

He tried to bite my hand again.

After that, I lost my temper. I punched him until he passed out. Father or not, I would only put up with so much. I'd given him more than enough chances.

When I'd caught my breath and regained control of my temper, I tied his wrists with strips of cloth torn from his shirt. I wasn't sure how well they would hold, so I searched him for weapons and removed a second knife, this one with the head of a unicorn worked into the hilt. Very nice. I tucked it into my own belt for safekeeping.

Finished, I stood. The cuts on my hand and forearm had already stopped bleeding; I had always been a fast healer. The bite marks on my wrist would leave a half-moon shaped bruise, but nothing worse. He had gotten far worse than he'd given.

I picked up my sword, sheathed it, then sat down cross-legged next to him to think. What should I do with him? I couldn't cart an unconscious — or worse, wide awake — homicidal lunatic around with me.

He moaned and twitched suddenly. When I glanced over, I found him staring at me through slitted eyes. Great, not a moment's rest. With his face bruised and his nose bloody, he looked more pathetic than dangerous, but I knew better. His jaws slowly worked up and down, but no words came out.

"What do you have to say for yourself?" I said.

"Thellops," he whispered.

"Don't start that again." I'd had just about as much of this "Thellops" as I could tolerate.

Taking a deep, cleansing breath, I stood and stretched the stiffness from my neck and back. Then I retrieved his sword, sheathed it, and slung the second swordbelt across my shoulders. No point leaving it here.

"Thellops . . . kill . . ." he muttered.

I sighed. First things first . . . I had to get us out of here. How?

In Juniper, Dad had somehow projected me into the unicorn's ruby. I had walked the length of the Pattern inside the gem. At the end, when my thoughts turned to Ilerium, the Pattern had sent me there.

Maybe the same thing would happen after walking this version of the Pattern? If it had the power to somehow read my mind and send me wherever I wanted to go, that would be our surest way out.

No time like the present to find out. I climbed to my feet.

"Come on, Dad."

I picked my father up and threw him none-too-gently over my shoulder. He weighed less than I'd expected. If this worked, if the Pattern really could send me to another Shadow, I didn't want to leave without him.

Now — where to go? Ilerium and all the other Shadows I'd

known were gone . . . destroyed when Dad destroyed the first Pattern. I needed someplace safe. A Shadow close to this one, but protected from the worst of Chaos's influence. A warm, comfortable world like Juniper had been . . . but more easily defended.

"Ready?" I asked.

He moaned again, but made no protest. Lucky for him, he didn't try to bite me again. I didn't want to have to pound him back into unconsciousness.

"Then let's go!"

I visualized the Shadow in my mind, took a step forward — and the Pattern vanished.

FIVE

found myself standing on a grassy mountainside, gazing down at a sparkling blue sea. An inlet with a ribbon of white sandy beach lay directly below, as beautiful as that at any seaside resort I had ever seen before. All it needed was a line of brightly colored canopies and pavilions. A warm, steady breeze carried the smells of salt and brine up to me as the low murmur of surf mingled with the raucous cries of gulls and other sea birds. As sunlight danced and sparkled on the waves, I glimpsed dolphins leaping a hundred yards out from shore. A good omen.

Setting Dad down on the ground — he moaned and grunted several times, but lay still — I continued to turn, studying the terrain around me. To my right the mountain rose higher, strewn with the occasional boulder and oak tree; to my left lay a dense old forest, ready for logging. Behind me lay miles of open grassland, ideal for a town or perhaps farming — or both.

"Thellops . . ." I heard Dad whispering faintly. He struggled to free himself, but I ignored him for now. He couldn't do much while tied up. "Not in time . . . Thellops . . ."

I frowned. What exactly *was* this Thellops? Not in time for what? It might prove important. I'd have to find out as soon as I knew this Shadow would be safe for us.

Turning, I picked my way among the boulders, climbing toward the top of the mountain. I remembered how the rocks had moved in Chaos, but thankfully these seemed perfectly normal and completely stationary.

At the crest, I shaded my eyes and peered into the distance. I could see for miles in each direction. Dense forests lay to either side, then distant snow-capped mountains. The sea below sparkled endlessly.

All in all, a very pleasant world, full of promise. It had everything I had wished for . . . except an insane asylum. A castle could easily be built here.

If this Shadow had a flaw, it had to be the lack of inhabitants. We wouldn't be able to draw on the locals for help. Well, workers could always be brought in from other Shadows; there was very little gold couldn't buy, if you have enough of it. I had seen Aber's tricks with the Logrus often enough that I now knew anything could be found, and fairly fast, if you knew where to look for it in other Shadows.

I sat down on a large sun-baked rock to consider my options with greater care. Dad came first. I looked down at him with a measure of concern — at least he had stopped struggling to free himself and lay quietly. Clearly he needed real medical care. That meant doctors.

Where to start? The Courts of Chaos? Doctors there (did they have doctors in Chaos?) might be able to help him. Unfortunately, we would undoubtedly be arrested if not killed on sight.

I supposed I could carry him to other Shadows looking for help . . .

Then I felt a flicker of mental contact. Someone was trying to reach me through a Trump. Aber? Freda? I would take whatever help I could get.

Opening my thoughts, I found myself gazing at my half-sister Blaise, but uncertainly, as though through a hazy, flickering tunnel. I saw part of a bed over her left shoulder. Her private chambers? I noted a smudge of dirt across her right cheek, and her normally elegantly coiffed hair now hung in disarray. I had never seen her looking this bad before.

"Oberon!" she gasped.

"What's wrong?" I gave a bitter smile. That might easily become our family greeting.

"You *are* alive!" She smiled in relief.

"I could say the same thing about you. How are you? What's going on there?"

She smoothed her low-cut gown. Its shimmering green material, which accentuated her stunning figure, looked as though she'd slept in it for many days in a row.

"I have been better. Where are you now? Safe?"

"Yes," I said. "I'm in a Shadow with Dad."

"Good. I had given you both up for dead." She glanced almost casually over her shoulder. I heard a distant pounding noise and the clash of steel on steel. Swordplay?

"What's going on there?" I said sharply. "Where are Freda and Aber?"

"I'm about to be arrested by King Uthor's men," she said with calmly measured tones. "I don't know what happened to the others. I haven't seen Freda in two weeks, and I haven't seen Aber in a month. Are you going to bring me through or not?"

A loud banging noise, metal striking on wood, carried to my ears. She glanced over her shoulder again. The door behind her suddenly splintered.

"Where are you?" I asked.

"In the Courts," she said. "Visiting Aunt Tana and Uncle Snoddar." I had never heard of them. At my puzzled look, she went on: "They are all that's left of my mother's family. Unfortunately, things are not going well. Uncle is dead, and I think Aunt Tana just fled to the Beyond without me. I heard her carriage racing outside. Now, if you don't mind —"

"Does Uthor have anyone else?" I asked.

She nodded, eyes growing wide. "He ordered our whole family arrested. They already have Titus and, oh, I don't know how many others!"

"And I'm your last hope for rescue," I said with a sigh. It figured I'd be the last one she'd call.

"Who else but the family champion?" She smiled almost desperately. Behind her, the door snapped in two; the top half sagged off its hinges. "Don't make me beg. Bring me through like a good brother."

Why not? I had nothing against her. In fact, my original low estimates of her had proved quite wrong. She had more of steel than lace in her blood, a true daughter of our father.

"All right," I said.

She swallowed visibly. "And, if you wouldn't mind *hurrying u —*"

I reached out to her. "Come on!"

She seized my hand with bone-crushing force, and I pulled her through to join me on the mountaintop. The bedroom scene behind her disappeared just as the first of Uthor's snake-faced troops came through the door.

Blaise gave a cry and collapsed into my arms. A jolt of alarm went through me. Had she taken a knife or crossbow bolt to the back?

Gently, I eased her onto the grass, searching for any sign of a wound. I couldn't find so much as a scratch. And yet she lay there gasping.

"Are you injured?" I asked.

"No . . ." she whispered. "I just feel . . . very strange . . . it hurts . . . all over . . . very sleepy now . . ."

Mental alarms went off. The same thing had happened to me the first time I entered the Beyond, the part of Chaos where Dad had his lands and keep. I had not been prepared for it, and I lay unconscious for most of three whole days as a result.

Her head fell back and her eyes closed. She snored softly.

"Oh, no you don't!" I cried. I shook her until her eyes opened blearily. "Stay awake!"

"Wha — why — ?" she murmured blearily.

"This Shadow is affecting you," I said. "Fight it. Talk to me, sing to me, curse at me — anything! Just stay awake."

Her brow furrowed. "But I've been in a thousand Shadows before —"

"Not like these," I said. "Dad redrew the Pattern that's casting them. It's all different now, but subtly. Can't you feel it?"

"Different?" Her eyes widened. "How? Where is this Pattern?"

"Uh-uh." I shook my head, smiling. "It's best if you don't know. Safer for you, too. Uthor would kill to find out."

She sighed. "Everyone's already trying to kill me . . . what can one more secret hurt?"

"Not everyone."

"Need to sleep . . ." she whispered, head sagging toward her chest.

"No! No sleeping! On your feet! *Now!*"

I lifted her easily, and she slipped one arm around my waist for support. For a second she looked up at my face. Then, seemingly against her will, her eyes closed and her chin slowly lowered again.

"Blaise!" I shouted.

"I'm awake!"

Her eyes blinked fast several times, then closed. She couldn't help it, I knew.

No more fooling around — this time I slapped her as hard as I could, leaving a scarlet handprint across her left cheek.

Her eyes flew open. A wolfish snarl came over her usually smooth features, and she twisted away from me.

"How dare you!" she snapped. She punched my chest hard enough to stagger me back a foot. Like everyone in my family, she had a temper to reckon with. And fists of steel.

I had the strangest feeling I might have gone too far. I had never seen her so furious. Still, it was too late to back down now, though not too late to apologize.

"I'm sorry," I said quickly. I rubbed at my chest. "Keep in mind, though, that I was only trying to keep you awake and alive!"

"That's not good enough! *Never touch me!*"

She caught my hand. Her grip tightened painfully.

"That hurts!" I said, trying to keep my own temper. "Let go. We shouldn't be fighting among ourselves."

"I've killed men for less than that," she said. Her voice had a dangerous edge.

"I'm sure you have." I smiled my most charming smile, which had been known to melt the heart of the iciest widow back in Ilerium. "It was the only thing I could think of to wake you up. I won't do it again if you don't go to sleep, okay? It's important."

"Explain it to me." Yawning, she let go of my hand. At least she managed to keep her eyes open this time.

"The same thing happened to me in the Beyond — I slept for three whole days. Dad and Aber finally got me up and wouldn't let me go to sleep. Dad was afraid I might never wake if they left me alone. I don't want that to happen to you."

"Where is Dad? You said he was here."

"Down the mountain." I jerked my head toward him. "He's sick, too."

"Everyone in Chaos is looking for him. He has to go back. Is he asleep?"

"No, tied up."

"What!"

"It couldn't be helped." I shrugged. "He isn't well. Not sleepy, really, but . . . kind of crazy."

"Crazy?" She stared at me. "What do you mean? What's wrong with him? If you did something —"

"No, no, nothing like that." I hesitated. "Maybe you'd better see for yourself. I think it might have something to do with the Pattern. It's obviously affected you. Maybe it's affecting him, too."

"Show me."

I escorted her down the slope, one hand on her elbow to keep her steady. When we reached our father, she gave a mew of unhappiness and bent to untie him.

I held her back. "Don't. It isn't safe to let him go. He tried to kill me."

"He's hurt —"

"He'll live. I was just about to find him a doctor. I don't suppose you know anything about medicine. . . ?"

"A little." She knelt beside him, pressing one hand to his forehead. Then, with the hem of her gown, she wiped a line of drool from his chin.

"He's been badly beaten," she said. "Who attacked him? King Uthor's men?"

"I'm afraid it was me." It came out apologetic. "I didn't have a choice, though. He was trying to kill me."

"Why?"

"I don't know." Shrugging helplessly, I knelt beside her. "He was acting crazy. He attacked me with a sword when I turned my back, and if he had been a little stronger, he would have killed me. He's a better swordsman than I am."

Her eyes narrowed, studying my face intently. "What did you do to him? He never does anything without good reason. Did you say or do something to make him mad? Did you threaten him in some way?"

"No, I didn't do anything. I found him unconscious and was trying to help."

She touched the red handprint on her cheek. "Like you helped me?"

"No. I shook him, but . . ." I shrugged.

"Hmm." She fumbled with the bindings on his wrists. "Help me get these off. Maybe —"

"Don't do that!" I pulled her hands back. "I told you, he's dangerous. He fought like a demon. Next time, he might get lucky and kill me — or both of us!"

"You have to let him loose. He's the only one who can save us."

"Save us?" I stared at her, puzzled. "Save us how?"

"He caused the Shadows," she said urgently. "Everyone in Chaos is talking about it. If he gets rid of them, maybe the king will let us go home agai —"

I drew back. "Impossible."

"Why? Don't you want to go home?"

"This *is* home. I need the Shadows like you need the Logrus." I thought back to the unicorn and the Pattern, and suddenly the half-formed suspicions in the back of my mind came out: "Besides, the Pattern can't be destroyed. It isn't Dad's creation."

She stared at me. "Of course it is! Everyone knows he made it!"

"He drew it, but it existed long before him. It's in me . . . and it's in other places, too." I thought of the ruby hanging around the unicorn's neck. "There are forces at work which I don't understand yet. I think they used Dad to create the Pattern. If he hadn't done it, they would have found someone else . . . me, probably."

"So it was inevitable?" she said, gaze distant. "Is that what you're saying?"

"I think so. Yes."

"But *why* did it have to be my family?" Her voice rose in a wail. "Why must we suffer for it? I just want to go *home!*"

"Look around!" I said, taking her hand and pulling her to her feet. I took in the whole of this virgin world with a sweep of my arm. "Here is a kingdom ripe for the taking. I'm going to build a city here. If you're not happy, there are more Shadows than you can possibly visit in your lifetime. Anything you can dream up exists somewhere out there. You just have to find it. You want to be a queen, or a goddess? Go ahead! You want jewels or riches? Take them! It's your right. You are a creature of the Pattern, just as Dad is . . . like I am. It's in you, too, at least partly. It's in *all* of us. I can feel its presence. You might as well enjoy your true heritage."

"No!" she cried. "That's not what I want! I didn't realize how much I missed the Courts until I went home!"

"The Pattern is in your blood!" I said emphatically. "Look within yourself. Can't you feel it?"

"No!" she cried.

More gently, I said, "The Pattern is here to stay whether we want it or not. If that means you can't go back to the Courts of Chaos — well, we'll make our own version here. Call them . . . the Courts of

Dworkin."

"Don't make fun of me."

"I'm not," I said. She just needed time to get used to the idea of living in Shadows for the rest of her life.

"Chaos is beautiful . . . a tide of unending change . . . music made flesh — and the powers we command there . . ."

"Used to command."

"You don't understand," she said bitterly.

"You're right," I said, letting a hard note creep into my voice. "I *don't* understand. I hated every minute of my time in Chaos. The only way you'll get me back there is if I'm dead!"

"That's why you tied Dad up, isn't it?" she demanded, turning on me suddenly. "He wanted to destroy the Shadows, and you wouldn't let him —"

I actually laughed at her.

"Stop that!" she cried. "It's not funny!"

"Don't be a fool, Blaise. Everything I've told you is true. You can see it, if you'll let yourself. Dad has gone crazy in a dangerous way. He can't help us now. We have to help *him.*"

"He must have had a good reason to kill you. You did something to him, or he knew you were a danger to Chaos, or —"

I sighed. She didn't want to listen to reason.

"No," I said slowly and calmly. "As I told you, it wasn't like that. I found him lying unconscious in the middle of the Pattern. He kept saying the same strange thing over and over . . . 'Thellops.' Does it mean anything to you?"

She looked startled. "Thellops?"

"Yes." I saw the recognition in her eyes. "You know what it is, don't you?"

"It's not a what, it's a who." She licked her lips. "Thellops guards the Logrus."

SIX

Lord of Chaos." I snorted. It always came back to our enemies. "I should have guessed."

"He is more than that," Blaise said. " He takes care of the Logrus. It's a sacred trust. After the king, he is the most important man in the Courts."

"So he attacked Dad?"

"No. He's harmless . . . old and doddering. His mind drifts. Everyone says he's crazy, but no one does anything about it."

"He's crazy?" That caught my attention. "How? Like Dad?"

"He . . . he talks to the Logrus. Treats it like a person. Wanders around mumbling to it all day long. I've seen him do it. It's . . . unnerving."

Dad hadn't gone quite that far around the bend yet. At least, I knew who Thellops was now. Perhaps the answer lay somewhere close at hand, and I just didn't see it yet.

"How well do you know Thellops?" I pressed. Maybe she could get him to come here and help us. "Would he take a look at Dad, if we asked? Or would he betray us to King Uthor?"

"I don't know. I never paid much attention to him before."

"But you've met him," I said. "He knows you?"

"Yes."

"And Dad?"

"Of course. We've all met him. Everyone in Chaos has. He decides when — and if — you can enter the Logrus. And sometimes he gives you advice, whether you want it or not."

That piqued my interest. If magically powerful objects were anything alike, maybe Thellops's advice about the Logrus could be applied to the Pattern, too. If I could only master the Pattern and its powers, I had a feeling everything would be a lot easier for all of us.

"What sort of advice?" I asked. "What did he say to you about the Logrus?"

"When my turn came to enter it, he told me to bring a mirror with me. I did, and it became enchanted." Her voice grew husky. "Though I've lost my mirror now, of course."

"Can't you get it back?" Aber, after all, could summon almost anything across vast distances using the Logrus. Something as small as a mirror ought to be fairly easy. And an enchanted one might prove very useful to us here . . .

Blaise shrugged. "I will try later. I miss her."

"Who — the mirror?"

"Yes."

"What did it do?"

"She showed me the truth, always. Even when it hurt."

Interesting. Unfortunately, truth didn't strike me as particularly useful right now. I already knew the truth: we had a lunatic for a father and no clear way to help him.

What I needed more than anything else was a plan of action. If there was even a chance that Thellops could help Dad, we had to find

a way to get him here. But how?

I took a deep breath and slowed myself down. It never helped to rush into things. I tried to take a mental step backward. It always helped me to try to look at problems from a different angle.

Instead of bringing Thellops here . . . might we somehow bring Dad to Thellops? King Uthor might have a price on our heads, but I could change my appearance at will. From what I'd seen, others in Chaos had that ability, too . . . maybe even Blaise? If we could disguise our father and smuggle him back to the Courts of Chaos for Thellops to cure. . . .

Then I almost chuckled out loud. Ridiculous — we couldn't just walk into our enemy's stronghold with a vague hope someone might be able to cure our father. We might as well stroll up to the palace gates and ask to be captured or killed.

I chewed my lip thoughtfully. Again I tried to take a mental step back. There had to be another way.

"Tell me more about Thellops," I finally said. Understanding him better might provide a third solution.

"Everyone says he's a harmless old man. I don't know what else to add."

"Is he Uthor's man?"

"I don't think so."

"Why not?"

She hesitated. "It's just a feeling I have. The way he's always looked at the king . . . with more annoyance than respect, I'd say."

"If I wanted to talk with him, how would I go about it? Is there a place I might find him alone and unguarded?"

"Maybe at the Logrus . . ."

"Does he ever leave the Courts?"

"I don't think so." She hesitated. "He's old. And crazy. Where would he go? Nobody wants him."

I started to pace. "Tell me more about the Logrus. Is it guarded? Could I get to it?"

"It's not guarded . . . it doesn't need to be."

"What about Thellops?"

"He doesn't carry any weapons, if that's what you mean. Maybe, if you caught him by surprise, you could bring him here before he could stop you. He doesn't look very strong."

"You never know. Appearances can be deceiving, especially with creatures of Chaos." I shook my head. "No, kidnapping him wouldn't work, anyway. We need him in a cooperative mood. Might we appeal to his sense of duty? Or friendship? How well does he know Dad?"

"Not well, I think. I have never heard Dad mention him before, except off-handedly."

"Thellops!" Dad suddenly muttered, as if on cue.

I glanced down at him. He seemed to be asleep. His arms and legs twitched like a dog chasing dream-rabbits.

Then another thought struck me.

"What if Dad was trying to warn me about something?" I said slowly. "Could Thellops have done this to him? It might explain Dad's behavior. He called me Thellops before he tried to kill me."

"I don't know . . ." Blaise hesitated. "Freda might be able to tell. Was Dad ever out of your sight? Could they have met without your knowing it?"

I remembered how Dad had vanished from the center of the Pattern. Where had he gone? And how long had he been there? I had no way of knowing.

"It's possible," I admitted. "We got separated."

"How long were you apart?"

"I don't know. Time got weird." How long *had* I been trapped in that gray fog? After Dad redrew the Pattern, I fell and lost all sense of time. It could have been an hour. It could have been days or weeks. I had no way of telling, especially since time ran differently among all the Shadows. At least a month had passed in the Courts of Chaos, according to Blaise.

With a sigh, Blaise continued, "Thellops *is* very powerful. He has to be, since he works directly with the Logrus. But, assuming he really is to blame for what happened to Dad, I have to ask — *why?* It doesn't make sense to me. Why would he attack Dad? And why would he make Dad crazy?"

Good questions. I wished I had an answer.

She went on, "Thellops has never been involved in politics, as far as I know. He doesn't carry a sword or fight duels. Why would he interfere? Why wouldn't he let King Uthor and the *lai she'one* take care of Dad? It doesn't make sense to me."

"How about revenge?" I suggested. "No one but Dad and me seems to want the Shadows."

"And Aber," she said, pulling a sour face. They had never gotten along. "And Freda, of course."

I nodded. True, they both seemed to love the Shadows as much as I did. We were all more alike that I'd thought . . . children of the Pattern, all.

Blaise said, "Besides, many people in the Courts have grown up with the Shadows and enjoy playing in them. But the rest of us . . ." Her voice trailed off. "The Shadows just don't seem right to me, somehow. They don't belong. I think everyone feels that way now. When the storms came —"

"But that was years ago!" Aber had told me about the terrible magical storms that swept in from the Shadows after they first appeared, wrecking havoc on the Courts of Chaos and killing thousands.

"No," Blaise said firmly. "More storms struck Chaos — a lot more — over the last month."

"They must have happened when Dad drew the Pattern again," I said.

"I don't know." She sighed heavily. "They were horrible, Oberon, pounding at the Courts and the Beyond until we thought the universe itself was coming to an end. I never want to experience anything like that again!"

"I'm sorry about the Shadow-storms," I said, "but they're gone and nothing can be done about it now. You survive —"

"No thanks to you!" she said with a snort

"— and I find it hard to care about anyone else in Chaos, beyond our immediate family. In fact, I wish the storms had killed off Uthor and Lord Zon and everyone else who stands against us. I'd send *more* storms, if I knew how!"

"Don't even think that!" She looked horrified. "You have no

idea how horrible they were! I wouldn't wish it on our worst enemy — think of the thousands of innocent people who would die!"

I snorted. "You have a soft spot in your heart. I would kill our enemies in one quick swipe, if I could. No matter the cost."

"You would only make more enemies." She shook her head. "We're a hardy lot, we Lords and Ladies of Chaos."

"Almost as hard to kill as Dad and me."

"You'd be surprised at how much it takes to kill a Lord of Chaos." She shrugged. "The Pattern storms served as a wakeup call. When the Courts are weakened and Chaos itself is threatened, everyone will put aside their differences and join the king."

"Against Dad and me."

"If you want to put it that way, then yes. Everyone blames Dad, but they want us *all* dead. You, me, Freda, Dad — everyone. It's in our bloodline, they say . . . traitors breed more traitors. If we are dead, the problem goes away . . . or so the reasoning goes."

"I think I'm finally beginning to understand," I said. In a sudden flash of inspiration, the truth came to me. We weren't *really* fighting over the existence of the Shadows or the devastation caused by Pattern storms. We were fighting over *power.*

The Pattern rivaled the Logrus . . . might even be *more powerful* than the Logrus. Sure, purebred Lords of Chaos could change their appearance, move through Shadows, and summon objects from far away. But I could do most of that already using just the Pattern. And, unlike Chaos, the Pattern cast a seemingly infinite number of Shadow-worlds across the universe.

I had to ask myself, *If the Pattern holds such power, why would anyone need the Logrus?*

Dad was like the first Lord of Chaos, the one who discovered and experimented with the Logrus, mastering its gifts to forge an empire. This first King of Chaos must have wielded powers unimaginable to all who came before him. And he had used that power to conquer his enemies and create the Courts of Chaos, which he and his descendants had ruled for untold thousands of years.

A shiver of excitement and anticipation ran through me. I wondered . . . could the Pattern do the same? Once mastered, would it make Dad — and me! — the undisputed rulers of both Shadows and Chaos?

I swallowed hard. No wonder King Uthor wanted us dead. He feared not only the Pattern and its powers, but what we might become if we mastered it.

And he had good reason to fear. If I had the ability to strike, I would have used the Pattern against him without a second's hesitation.

I had missed part of what Blaise was saying and forced my attention back to her.

"— can you blame them?" she said. "Those Pattern storms killed hundreds and destroyed a dozen keeps! The Pattern is a menace and must be destroyed for everyone's safety!"

Half amused, I smiled down at her. She suddenly seemed almost childlike, prattling on about insignificant details in the mistaken belief they might somehow be important.

"Forget about getting rid of the Shadows," I said. "I told you, it isn't possible now."

"King Uthor will destroy them. And the Pattern."

"He can try."

She snorted. "Do you really think you can stand against the king?"

"If necessary. I'm not going to roll over and give up."

Blaise shook her head wonderingly. "You're either incredibly stupid or incredibly brave."

I grinned. "Maybe a bit of both. Now, about Thellops . . ."

She rubbed Dad's forehead gently. "It doesn't make sense. If Thellops wanted Dad dead, why not kill him outright? Why make him crazy?"

"Maybe Dad escaped. Or maybe Dad won . . . we have no idea what happened. Or Maybe Thellops thought madness was a better punishment."

She shook her head. "Maybe . . . but it doesn't feel right. I think there's another answer. Something that hasn't occurred to either of us yet."

I had to agree. None of it quite fit. Somehow, I had the feeling we had missed an important detail or two.

Blaise stifled a small yawn. "Anyway, it's best to do nothing if you don't know what the problem is. You might make it worse."

"I don't think it can get much worse."

"I'd say death is worse. Dad *is* still alive."

"True." She had me there.

"Wait and see if Dad recovers his senses," she said. "Then you can ask him why he keeps saying 'Thellops.' Maybe he's dreaming of old friends."

"I don't think Thellops is a friend." I had to smile. "Dad wanted to *kill* me. And he put a lot of effort into it. Old friends don't generally go around trying to murder each other."

"It could be something you said or did to Dad." Blaise yawned again. "It's nothing a good night's sleep can't fix. Speaking of which . . ."

"No!" I raised my hand as if I planned to slap her again, and her eyes flew open.

"All right, all right!" she snarled, eyes narrowing to slits. "I'm awake now! Honestly, Oberon, you can't go around hitting people. The next time you try, I'll break your arm!"

"Promises, promises." I smiled and shrugged. "As I said, you have to stay awake. I can only carry one unconscious relative at a time."

"I'm not going to fall asleep."

"Uh-huh. Not with me on watch, anyway."

I studied her face carefully; her eyelids already drooped. What could be causing her sleepiness? Our proximity to the Pattern?

Maybe she would feel better if we moved farther away from it. It was worth a try.

"Come on, let's get moving. We'll find a place where you can rest safely."

"All right." She climbed unsteadily to her feet. "What about Dad?"

"If you can walk, I'll carry hi —"

"I *will* walk." She sounded determined.

"All right. Follow me. Shout if you can't keep up. I'll slow down."

"Don't worry about *me*, brother dear."

"Fair enough."

Picking Dad up, I started for the forest at a brisk pace. A clear destination filled my mind. As I walked, I let my imagination soar, and the landscape around us began to flow and change: a hint of pink around the sun, bunches of white flowers at the curve in the path, a covered bridge spanning a creek. A tame fawn paced us, nuzzling our pockets for treats.

Blaise laughed in delight. I glanced back and smiled. We didn't have enough laughter in our lives.

Then, letting my stride lengthen, we left the deer loping through the underbrush, playing hide-and-seek in the bushes with rabbits, skunks, and other forest creatures.

Forest, to grasslands, to gently rolling hills lush with ripening wheat and rye, and on through pastures of fat cows and rotund sheep. Here and there prosperous-looking farmers worked the fields with sons. All waved and drawled the friendliest of welcomes. Two boys came running, carrying packs. They both eyed our father curiously. Neither asked why I had a tied-up old man in my arms; that would have been rude, and they weren't the prying types . . . a restful Shadow indeed. We needed calm natives who wouldn't try to kill us or betray us . . .

"May we offer you a drink, sir?" they asked. "Or a sandwich, ma'am?"

"No, thanks." I paused and looked back as my sister caught up. "Blaise?"

"A drink would be lovely," Blaise said. She brushed a dangling strand of hair off her forehead. Without makeup, with her hair in disarray, she had a harder edge to her face. I remembered the strength behind her punch and wondered not for the first time if I had somehow underestimated her.

"Here." The oldest of the two fumbled a clay jar from their pack and poured water into a cup held by his brother. They both handed it to her.

"Thank you." She drank deeply, coughed, gasped, and handed it back quickly.

"Good?" I asked with a grin.

"It was . . . *water.*" She gave a horrified shudder.

"More?" Both boys grinned up at her, thinking she had enjoyed it.

"I'm fine now."

They looked at me again. "Sir? Perhaps for the old gentleman?"

"We're both fine," I said. I glanced up the road and frowned. There would be an inn just ahead, beyond the grove of trees over the hill. . . a rambling old inn with a railed porch around the front. Dad could rest easily there. A brilliant physician lived on an estate not far beyond. He could help us.

It had to be so. My vision made sure of it.

SEVEN

ure enough, the small town came into view when we topped the hill. As places go, it was nothing fancy, perhaps two dozen buildings, but a sprawling old inn sat facing us. Smoke drifted lazily from a pair of tall brick chimneys, carrying smells of fresh bread and roasting meat. Three gray-bearded old men sat on the porch in rocking chairs, whittling away at wooden blocks. As we approached, they all looked up and called cheery good-mornings.

"Somethin' wrong with that fellow?" one of them asked me idly. He stared without concern at our father's bruised face and bound wrists.

"He has seizures," I said. It came out sounding more exhausted than convincing; it *had* been a long day. "I tied him up to keep him from hurting himself. That last seizure almost killed him."

"Ayah." Nodding sagely, he settled back into his chair and began rocking slowly once more. "You'll be wanting Doc Hand, then."

"Not Young Doc Hand," said the second old-timer, still whittling. "The one you need is *Old* Doc Hand."

"Ayah," said the third whittler. "Old Doc Hand, he's the best for seizures, sure enough. He lives over the short hills, nearer to

Haddoxville than to Barleyton, at Manor-on-Edge."

"Thanks," I said. Old Doc Hand would be our man.

The first whittler said, "Have Young Jamas fetch Old Doc Hand for your daddy. Young Jamas ought to be inside, behind the counter more'n likely. He won't mind the trip. His girl's in Haddoxville, right enough."

"Ayup," said the second whittler rocking slowly. "Young Jamas won't mind 'tall."

I glanced at Blaise. "How are you doing?"

"I feel *much* better," she said, giving me a look that said the worst for her had passed. "Though after that foul farm beverage, I need a real drink."

"Jamas has the best wine in seven counties," said the third whittler.

"Thanks," I said. "When you're thirsty, come in and I'll buy you all a round of drinks."

"Thank you kindly!" said the first. "We'll be along presently, once Jamas has you settled in, sure as you're standin' there!"

I carried Dad inside. As my eyes adjusted to the dimness of the low-ceilinged common room, I saw scattered tables and a long counter. A pot of something hearty-smelling simmered in the fireplace.

Behind the counter stood a red-haired man of middling years. He looked up from polishing the thick oak slab used as a bar and gave a friendly nod. Could this be Young Jamas?

"Mornin'," he said with a pleasant smile. "Somethin' wrong with that fellow you're carryin'?"

"He's ill — having seizures." I decided to stick with that story.

"Need a room, then?"

"Three of them."

"Have your pick upstairs." He nodded to the steps at the far end of the room. "There's no one else stayin' here at the moment. It's nothin' fancy, mind you, but the beds're warm and the food's good and plentiful."

"That's all we want." I started for the stairs, then hesitated. Better take care of Dad first. "The men outside said to ask for Young Jamas. That wouldn't be you, would it?"

He chuckled. "I haven't been Young Jamas in nigh on twenty years. That's my eldest boy. I'm just Jamas now."

"Not Old Jamas?" I joked.

"Nope. Old Jamas is my Da."

"Pleased to meet you, Jamas." I nodded politely. "I'm Oberon. This is my sister Blaise. We were hoping your boy might go to Haddoxville for Old Doc Hand."

Jamas nodded. "Old Doc Hand is the one you want, sure enough, for somethin' like seizures. Always go with experience, I say. My boy's out back getting wood for the kitchen. He'll be back in a few minutes. I'll send him straight for the doc. He won't mind."

"Thanks."

"Don't mention it."

Turning, I carried Dad up the narrow flight of steps to the second floor. I pushed open the first door on the left with my foot, finding a small chamber with mismatched pieces of furniture: a high-canopied bed, a narrow armoire, and a battered wash-stand with a chipped blue basin. It would do quite nicely for Dad.

"Here, let me get the bed."

Blaise hurried around me and drew back the patchwork quilt. I slid Dad between the sheets. He was drooling again. I sighed and wiped his mouth on his shirt.

"Can I untie him now?" she asked. "I don't think he's dangerous."

"All right. But be careful — if he wakes up, he might get violent."

"He wouldn't hurt me."

"You can't trust a madman."

Silently she untied our father's wrists, rubbing at the deep red marks they left. Dad stirred a bit and murmured softly. Then, to my surprise, she reached down and removed a knife with a unicorn-hilt from his right boot. I hadn't known he carried one there. It matched the one I'd taken from him earlier.

"I keep my eyes open," she said with a grin, as if in answer to my thoughts. She passed the knife to me, and I tucked it into my belt, next to its mate. "Not that it will do much good — he can always get another one with the Logrus."

I hadn't thought of that, and I frowned. What use to disarm someone who could get a new weapon any time he wanted?

"Maybe we *should* leave him tied up . . ." I said.

"If he gets loose, he gets loose. I'll help you catch him next time, if it comes to that."

I raised my eyebrows. Again, I sensed the warrior within her that she kept so carefully hidden behind silks and lace. I did not doubt her word: if she said she'd help catch him, she would do it.

"Come on," Blaise said. "I want that drink now."

"Me too."

We started for the door, where I drew up short.

"Wait!" I felt a sense of contact from a Trump.

"What's wrong?" Blaise asked.

"Someone's trying to reach me —"

I concentrated, and through a strange, flickery tunnel I saw a shadowy figure. He — I thought it was a man — seemed to be saying something. I couldn't quite make out the words, though.

"Who is it?" Blaise asked.

"I can't tell," I said.

"Oberon . . ." The man's voice echoed faintly.

"Aber?" I said. His image flickered, then grew clearer. It definitely was my brother — but much thinner than the last time I'd seen him. His cheekbones stuck out and dark circles rimmed his deep-set eyes.

" . . . alive!" he said. His voice faded it and out. "I've . . . to reach you . . . days!"

"Time runs differently here. Where are you?"

"About . . . killed!" he howled. He sounded desperate. "Get . . . before . . . ! *Hurry!*"

EIGHT

ere!" Without hesitation, I reached toward him.

He glanced over his shoulder, eyes growing wide, then seized my wrist with both hands. It felt as though he weighed a ton, but I gritted my teeth and hauled him forward. He tumbled into my arms.

"O –!" Aber stretched out his hands and staggered. He couldn't seem to get his balance. "There's something wrong here —"

He would have fallen if I hadn't supported him. Could the same thing that happened to Blaise be affecting him, too?

"You just need to get your Pattern-legs," I said wryly, with more confidence than I felt. When he didn't so much as smile at that private joke, I knew he had to be in pretty bad shape. More concerned now, I helped him sit on the bed next to Dad.

He had lost a lot of weight, and his face had a desperate, hunted quality I'd only seen in game animals before the kill. Although he wore his usual blue pants and shirt, yellowish dust covered him from head to toe. The knees of his pants had been torn to shreds, like he'd just crawled through a rock garden . . . which, for all I knew, might have been trying to eat him. Rocks had strange properties in Chaos.

"What's wrong with Dad?" he asked, staring at our father. "Did someone attack him? Is he all right?"

"He's sick," I said.

"Great," Aber muttered, putting his head down in his hands. He took a deep shuddering breath and let it out slowly. "I figured he'd be able to fix everything."

"Let me guess," I said. "You want him to destroy the Pattern."

He glanced up. "No! But . . . maybe if he gave himself up, Uthor would spare the rest of us."

"Self-sacrifice? That doesn't sound like Dad."

"No, I guess not," he said, a note of bitterness creeping into his voice. "Though, of course, we could always sacrifice him ourselves. Maybe the king would make a deal . . ."

"No," I said flatly. "We're family, and we're going to stick together."

"You and your idealism! Dad would sell you out in a heartbeat if he thought it would save his own skin."

"You aren't doing him justice," I said. Dad had gone to great lengths to protect me during my childhood. "Take a minute to catch your breath. Then you can tell me all about what happened in the Courts. Maybe I can help some other way."

"I don't think anyone can help now." He studied the floorboards. "They're after us all. I think Uthor's caught everyone but you and me and Dad."

"And Blaise, of course," I said. "She's free."

"Blaise? *That's* just great!" he said sarcastically. I remembered there was no love lost between them. "Of *course* she would be the one to get away."

"Thanks for caring, Aber," Blaise said coolly from behind me.

He glanced up in surprise.

"I thought you were dead," he said to her.

"Sorry to disappoint you."

"Why didn't you answer my calls?"

"I must have been busy."

Aber opened his mouth for an angry retort, but I waved him to silence.

"Go downstairs," I told Blaise. "We'll join you at the bar in a few minutes. I need to talk to Aber alone."

"Oh, very well. I need that drink anyway. Especially now that *he's* here." She stomped off into the hall without another word.

"Bitch," Aber muttered under his breath. To me, he said, "I tried to reach her five or six times over the last few weeks, when I really needed help. She didn't answer. I assumed she had been captured. It figures she wouldn't bother to answer *me*."

"She had her own problems," I said. "I got her out of the Courts of Chaos just in time — hell-creatures were breaking down the doors to her room."

"You should have left her there." He folded his arms stubbornly. "Some people aren't worth rescuing."

"She's still family," I said. I tried to look stern. We couldn't let arguments divide us, not with so many enemies after our blood. "If what you say is true, there are few enough of us left now. And I'm sure Blaise will prove useful once we're settled in again."

He gave me an odd look. "She wouldn't help in the Courts when I needed her. I'm not going to forget that!"

"I didn't say you should. Be aware of her limitations and know you can't count on her. She may be difficult, and you may not enjoy her company, but we have to stick together whether you like to or not."

"That's a good way to get us all killed," he grumbled. "I keep telling you not to trust anyone!"

"Except you."

"Of course!" He laughed, a bit of his old spirit returning. "And Freda, of course. But Blaise? Certainly not! I wouldn't be surprised if she turned out to be the traitor who almost got us all killed in Juniper."

"Don't worry." I shook my head. "I don't trust anyone right now. She wants me to destroy the Pattern, after all."

"What!" He gaped. "And destroy the Shadows?"

"Don't worry, I won't do anything so drastic." I chuckled. "Even if I knew how to destroy it. Which I don't."

He sank back. "Good."

"You said Uthor has everyone else?"

"I think so. As soon as those storms came, he issued orders to arrest everyone in our family."

"I'm not surprised." I would have done the same thing, in his place.

"How were the storms created?" Aber asked. "Did Dad really send them to destroy Chaos, the way everyone says?"

"If he created them, it was by accident." I shrugged. "When he retraced the Pattern, it destroyed all the old Shadows and made new ones. The force of that destruction must have carried as far as Chaos. I can't think of any other explanation."

"The Pattern — are you sure he made it correctly this time?"

"Yes. I can feel it in the back of my mind, the way you must feel the Logrus."

"Really?" he brightened. "That *is* good news! Since you're determined to keep it, there's only one thing to do."

"What's that?"

"Learn to control its powers. Maybe Dad . . ."

His voice trailed off as he looked at our father again. He leaned closer, studying the bruises, cuts, and split lip. At least the swelling had started to go down.

"What happened to Dad?" he asked. "It looks like a ton of rocks fell on his head."

"Making the new Pattern did something to his mind. He's been acting crazy. He tried to kill me this morning, and I had to defend myself."

"So you did this?"

"Afraid so," I said half apologetically.

He whistled, then looked at me with new respect. "Except for Locke, Dad was the best swordsman in the family. You must be even better."

I didn't deny it. Let him think so . . . a dangerous reputation never hurt anyone.

Aber continued, "All I can say is — good for you! About time someone put Dad in his place. I only wish I'd been there to see it. Do you really think he'll be okay?"

"Sure," I said with more confidence than I felt. "He just needs time and rest. We've already sent for a doctor. Just a matter of waiting for him to show up."

"Good."

"How about you?" I asked. "Are you feeling better now?"

He thought for a second. "Actually, yes."

"Up for a drink?"

"Almost." Aber stood unsteadily and began straightening his clothes and brushing himself off. Clouds of yellow dust puffed out from his pants and shirt. "So, where *have* you been, Oberon? I've been trying to reach you for weeks. I had just about given up!"

I shrugged apologetically. "Time runs differently here. I don't think it's been more than a few hours since I last saw you. At least, that's what it feels like. How long has it been since you've seen me?"

"I'm not sure." He frowned. "At least four or five weeks. Maybe longer. I've been on the run most of that time just trying to stay alive. The *shai le'one* finally cornered me in the Beyond, right after the last of the storms let up. That's when I started trying every card I had left."

"Did you reach Freda? Anyone else?"

"No. I couldn't reach anyone except you."

I felt my heart plunge.

"If Freda's been hurt or killed . . ." I said.

"I imagine King Uthor has her, but . . ." He shrugged. "I don't know. She wasn't publicly executed, at least. Not like Mattus and Titus."

"What!" I stared at him, shocked. "When? How?"

"Uthor put them to the sword about two weeks ago." At my horrified expression, he went on grimly, "Their heads are on pikes outside the palace gates. I'm surprised Blaise didn't tell you."

"No, she didn't say anything." I swallowed hard. Two brothers, dead. Freda, my favorite sister, probably captured. And all the others. . . . Right now, Uthor might be torturing them . . . or worse. I remembered how Lord Zon had used my other brothers' blood to spy on Dad in Juniper.

My thoughts turned back to Freda. Just a few hours ago, as these Shadows reckoned time, she had tried to contact me through my Trump. Had I missed my chance to save her? By not answering, had I gotten her captured or killed?

Unfortunately, there was nothing I could have done at the time — those unicorns would have killed us both if I'd tried to bring her through to join me. I sighed.

"Let me try her now," I said.

"I just did. But go ahead."

Quickly, I pulled out my deck of Trumps, riffled through them until I got to her card, and held it up. I concentrated hard, staring at her picture.

Nothing.

"Well?" Aber asked.

I just shook my head. Lowering the card, I returned it to my deck. Until I saw her body, I refused to believe anything bad had happened. I'd try again later . . . and as many times as it took to reach her. If that failed, we would have to find a way to rescue her. I couldn't leave her in Uthor's clutches.

"What about Conner?" I asked quietly.

"I don't know. I couldn't reach him, either. Nor Fenn, Isadora,

Syara, Pella, or Leona. Have you heard from *anyone* other than Blaise?"

"No."

He shook his head slowly. "I'm not surprised. With the king's whole army out hunting for us, we didn't have much of a chance."

"You're still alive."

"By the skin of my teeth. What about you? Have you heard from anyone else?"

"From Freda a few hours ago. But time is running so slowly here, it must have been weeks ago in Chaos."

"A pity."

I nodded. Bad news, indeed. For now, I could only hope at least *some* of our siblings were alive and in hiding. After all, we came from a big family. If Blaise and Aber had escaped, others might have, too. We would work on contacting them as soon as we had a safe place to gather our forces.

Aber looked around the room. "Where are we, anyway? This isn't Juniper, is it?"

"No, Juniper is gone. This is a small tavern in a Shadow cast by the new Pattern. If it has a name, I don't know what it is."

"Are we safe?"

"As safe here as anywhere, at least for now. I wouldn't risk much magic using the Logrus, though, just in case."

"Fair enough." He stood. "I need to get cleaned up. I'll tell you everything else after a long, hot bath . . . I assume there *are* long hot baths here?"

"There you go." I jerked my thumb toward the small basin on

the washstand against the far wall. "Jump in."

He raised his eyebrows. "You're kidding, right? I want a *real* bath, with scented oils. Then a massage. Then a good hot meal — a light cream of mushroom soup, then salad and braised lamb chops, followed b —"

I couldn't stop laughing.

"What is it?" he demanded.

I said, "Do I look like I'm kidding? You aren't going to get any of those things here. If you're lucky, maybe the innkeeper can get you a bowl of whatever stew he's got simmering in the fireplace. You might be stuck with bread, cheese, and wine."

"I'll settle for a steak if there's nothing better. Or I can always get it myself."

"As I said, I don't think it's a good idea for you to use the Logrus here. What if Uthor has a way to track you when you use it?"

"Magic doesn't work that way."

"Humor me." I shrugged. "I never claimed to be an expert, just paranoid."

"No bath. No servants. No food." He shook his head glumly. "This isn't going to work, Oberon. There's nothing here. A Lord of Chaos could walk right in, kill us all, and destroy the Pattern."

"First he has to find us. Then he has to kill me. And then he has to find the Pattern. It's not as easy as it sounds. It's been hidden, just like last time —"

"Where *is* it, then?"

"Safe. And it's going to stay safe from now on. I'm not telling anyone."

"Even me?"

I chuckled. "*Especially* you. You were on King Uthor's payroll, re-member?"

"Unwillingly! They threatened to kill me, remember. And any-way, look where it got me — hunted through the Beyond and a dozen other Shadows of Chaos."

"Even so."

He shrugged. "Okay. It's not like I *need* to know. Or particularly want to." Rising, he started for the washstand. "If I'm going to avail myself of your so-called bath, the least you can do is find me some decent clothes while I'm getting cleaned up!"

"Would you settle for a towel?"

"I'll get my own." He reached into the air and plucked a towel from nothingness — using that Logrus trick again to summon what-ever he needed.

"I said no Logrus tricks!"

"Oh — sorry. It's instinct, I guess. I wasn't thinking."

I sighed. "Just don't do it again."

For the first time, I wondered if the Pattern would let me do the same sort of summoning-trick. I'd have to experiment with it later. Maybe I could get him to explain how it worked with the Logrus . . .

"I'll meet you downstairs," I said as he stripped off his shirt and began splashing water onto his face. "I want to hear about everything I missed. And I'm sure Blaise does, too, whether she admits it or not."

I carried Dad's sword downstairs with me and had Jamas put it away for safekeeping. Then Blaise and I passed a pleasant half hour sitting quietly at the bar, sipping a cool, fruity red wine and sharing a comfortable silence. We both had a lot to think about.

Jamas had just informed Blaise and me that his eldest son had left to fetch for Old Doc Hand when Aber trooped down the staircase and joined us. My eyes widened in surprise. He now wore a shimmering blue tunic, deep blue hose, and black riding boots with heavy silver kickplates at the toes. His brown hair, brushed straight back, glistened damply. With the dust and dirt scrubbed from his face and hands, he looked even more gaunt than before.

"Much better," I said. Then I sighed. "But you used the Logrus again, didn't you?"

"Uh . . . sorry." He gave a sheepish grin and pretended contrition. "Really, I couldn't help myself. I hate being dirty. Besides, no one can trace us when we use the Logrus. Ask Blaise if you don't believe me."

"Blaise?" I glanced at our sister.

"How would I know?" She shrugged. "I don't care how the Logrus works. I'm just glad it does!"

"Considering our enemies," I said, "I'd still rather err on the side of caution. They seem to know more about how magic and the Logrus works than anyone else here — including you and Dad."

"True . . ." He sighed. "I'll be more careful. Besides, we aren't going to be staying here long, are we?"

"Just long enough to get Dad well."

Aber took the stool next to mine, on the other side from Blaise. I caught a whiff of lavender — he'd even perfumed himself. I shook my head in disbelief.

"What are you drinking?" he asked, peering over the rim of my tankard.

"Stout."

"I'll have a pint, too," he said to Jamas.

"Aye." Jamas squinted at Aber as he drew a pint from a keg. "Didn't see you go upstairs, sir."

"I'm pretty quiet," Aber said with an half smile. "People don't notice me much."

"Not quiet enough," Blaise murmured to herself.

"Better quiet than blathering." Aber glowered at her. Blaise suddenly found it necessary to study her fingernails.

"Cut it out!" I told them both. "We don't have time for such childishness. If we're all that's left of our family, we *will* get along. Got that?"

"You're right, of course, dear Oberon," Blaise said. She put her arm around my shoulder and gave a not-so-subtle wink. "I'm sorry, Aber," she said. "You certainly *didn't* deserve that. I'll try to be more *kind*."

"You're not my sister," Aber said darkly. He drained half in stout in one long gulp. "The real Blaise would never apologize. It's not in her nature."

"You don't know anything about her nature," Blaise said. "*My* nature, I mean."

"Whose nature?"

"You're an idiot!"

He brightened. "Now *that's* the Blaise we know and love!"

I sighed. So much like little children . . . I half wished I could spank them both and send them off to bed without supper. But Blaise would probably break my arm if I tried.

Better to simply change the subject.

"Tell me what I missed in the Courts," I said to Aber. "What happened to you?"

"It's quite a tale."

"I'm not going anywhere."

"Neither am I," said Blaise somewhat contritely. She leaned on the bar, pillowing her chin in her hands. "Tell us of your heroic cowering in basements."

"Blaise . . ." I said warningly.

"Don't mind her," Aber said. "No one else does."

Chuckling, he drained the rest of his stout, then motioned for Jamas to refill his tankard. With a new drink in hand, he cleared his throat, leaned back, and launched into his story.

NINE

fter I left you and Dad at the Pattern," Aber began, "I returned to our home in the Beyond. A week or more must have passed while we were away. The house was strangely quiet — it had that echoey, empty feeling a place gets when there's no one left alive. Even the torches had gone out.

"'Hulloo!' I called several times. I got no answer. Where had the servants gone?

"I used a quick spell and sent several balls of light spinning toward the ceiling. Their glow revealed a dozen corpses up there — on the ceiling. Each one had been beheaded. From their uniforms, they all belonged to the household guard.

"After that, I moved cautiously through the house, looking at all the damage. Every piece of furniture had been smashed, and every door had been torn from its hinges — even the magically protected doors. That took a lot of power. Uthor's men — at least, I assumed it had been Uthor's men — had not been fooling around.

"I counted thirty-nine headless bodies on the ground floor. The second and third floors had also been trashed. In my own rooms, someone had poured all the paints, pigments, and inks onto the floor, then smashed the empty jars against the walls. It made a huge sticky mess. Of course, I could replace it all; what really hurt was the loss of my storage trunks — and, with them, my most treasured possessions, including hundreds of Trumps I'd painted over the years. Those Trumps showed places I'd been, friends and classmates, and, most of all, relatives. I could easily imagine Uthor's men using them to round up our family.

"Dad's workshop had been cleaned out. Everything, from the largest of his inventions to the smallest scrap of notepaper, had been taken away. Not so much as a piece of lint remained. That didn't particularly worry me, of course — Dad hadn't looked at any of those things in decades. His last ten years of work and research had taken place in Juniper, after all.

"Finally I made a methodical search of the building from attic to basement. It didn't take me long to determine that nothing of value remained anywhere. I counted ninety-four bodies in all, all guards. None of our servants lay among the dead — they must have either run away or been taken prisoner . . . or, considering how hard it is to find good help these days, perhaps they were, ah, shall we say — forcibly hired away?

"Finding a mostly intact couch in one of the spare bedrooms on the fourth floor, I flopped down and tried to rest. I didn't know what else to do. From the looks of things, the *shai le'one* had gone through the house so thoroughly, they wouldn't need to come back. I felt safe enough for the moment.

"Exhaustion overcame me. I fell asleep.

"When I finally awakened, hours must have passed. But instead of feeling rested and refreshed, a strange uneasiness settled over me. I had never felt anything like it before. An odd pressure filled my ears. My nerves jangled in warning. The very air itself seemed curiously charged, almost as though a lightning storm were about to break. More than anything else, I wanted to crawl into a hole and pull it closed after me . . . and yet I could not have told you *why*.

"Something was coming. Something *bad*. I felt it in my bones.

"It took more courage than I thought I still had, but I forced myself to go downstairs. Cautiously, I crept to the front doors — one lay flat on the ground; the other hung off its hinges at an angle — and I peeked out.

"The sky looked strange. Clouds boiled and churned, lit from within by constantly striking bolts of blue lightning. All across the courtyard, balls of fire rained down, smoking and smoldering. The air shimmered with odd hues of blue and gold. Then, as I watched, the ground shuddered and rippled like a lake in a windstorm. The rocks lay still.

"When I looked up, beyond the outside wall I saw a shimmering yellow-gold curtain of light slowly moving toward me. It must have been a hundred and fifty feet tall — maybe taller. I stepped outside to see better. Through the open gates to our estate, I saw the ground beneath it churning and breaking apart as it advanced.

"This was my first glimpse of a storm from the Shadows. I had heard tales of them before — they hit Chaos many years ago, I assume when Dad drew the very first Pattern and first created all the Shadows — but I had never thought I would see one this close.

"I backed up in sudden panic, then turned and fled into the house. The walls and floor shook; corpses slid across the ceiling.

Colors bled like ink in water, and that sense of pressure building in my head grew so bad, I could barely see straight.

"I fled deeper inside, looking for a place to hide. Small balls of light appeared everywhere, rolling across the floor and walls and ceiling, pooling in the corners. Where could I go? Underground, maybe?

"As I ran toward the kitchens and the nearest staircase to the basement, the walls started to bubble and dissolve. A rushing, ripping, grinding noise rose to deafening levels. I would never make it — the storm had caught me.

"The walls started to peel away and fly into the air. An odd tingling began in my hands and feet. When I raised my arm, I found my flesh had grown translucent — I could see through it. If I didn't do something fast, I wouldn't live through the storm.

"I pulled out the first place-Trump I could find — it showed Triffiq Square in the Courts of Chaos — and used it to jump straight there. I barely made it in time. When I came through, I collapsed and couldn't get up for a few minutes. My arms and legs wouldn't work. I must have been babbling incoherently — I remember strangers helping me up and asking me questions I couldn't understand — but everything else is jumbled and fragmentary.

"Someone there must have recognized me and reported my arrival to Uthor's spies. By the time I came to my senses, the *lai she'one* were on the lookout for me. I spent the better part of a day losing them. Of course, the Shadow storm helped — between earthquakes, lightning storms, and squalls of destruction like the one that hit our house in the Beyond, not even their urhounds made much progress that day.

"For two days, I hid out and watched and tried not to attract any attention. The storm-darkened sky continued to show spectacular light-effects. Now and then the ground shook — a lot more than it should have, anyway — but the storms that reached the Courts were nowhere near as bad as the ones in the Beyond.

"Over the next few days, I tried repeatedly to reach family members. I managed to contact Conner and Freda. Conner was in the Beyond, safely ensconced with Titus at their Uncle Clengaru's keep, which had been spared from the worst of the Pattern storms; Freda had taken refuge with one of her aunts in the Courts. Neither could take me in, so that left me in something of a quandary. With the Shadows gone, our ancestral home destroyed, and the *shai le'one* searching for all of us, I didn't have many choices left.

"Finally, in desperation, I returned to the Beyond. Our home had been devastated; what the *shai le'one* hadn't destroyed, the storm had. The walls had melted, the roof had been ripped away, and little remained beyond a misshapen puddle of melted stone, wood, and glass. Only one wall still stood from the main building, and at its tallest, it couldn't have been more than six feet.

"For a while, I searched among the debris, but found nothing of any possible use. Everything had melted and run together. It was a complete loss.

"I took shelter in one of the small guardhouses that had been part of the wall surrounding our keep. Miraculously, it had escaped unharmed — though I couldn't say the same for the three men whose bodies lay inside. The *lai she'one* had beheaded them and left their bodies rotting on the ceiling. I dragged them outside, released them, and let them drift into the sky. That took care of the worst of the stench.

"I stayed there for a week, hiding out and waiting to be discovered. Using the Logrus, I snatched food and drink — along with books and anything else I needed for comfort — from nearby Shadows. I talked with Freda several times a day. The one time I reached Conner, he told me he didn't think he and Titus would be alive much longer . . . people in his uncle's household were giving them strange looks, growing silent when they entered rooms, or just refusing to talk to them or dine with them. He said they blamed Dad for the Shadow-storms. He didn't know what to do or where else to go.

"Of course, I offered to bring them both through to join me, but he wouldn't hear of it. Better dead than living like an animal, he told me scornfully.

"Every day I watched as new storms came through the Beyond, each a little less severe than the last. Fortunately none of these hit near me, and I waited them out in relative comfort and safety.

"Two weeks passed. The towering Shadow-storms had all but ceased, though tiny squalls continued. When I tried to reach Conner, I suddenly got no response. Freda told me she feared what might happen if she ever left her aunt's house. An angry mob had tried to drive her out the day before.

"That was the last time I talked to her. The next day, I couldn't reach her anymore. I assumed she had been killed or arrested, too, like Conner. I would probably be next.

"Another week passed. Loneliness finally got the better of me. I couldn't hide in the ruins for the rest of my life. I had to go out and see what had happened.

"Shapeshifting has never come easily to me, but I changed my features as best I could. Disguised as an old man, I returned to the Courts to see what I could learn.

"When I arrived, a strange mood hung over the streets — anxious, apprehensive, and most of all afraid. People in the streets and plazas stood in small knots, talking and looking around apprehensively. I half expected guards and soldiers to appear, dispersing the crowds, but none did.

"And, as I walked, I couldn't help but notice all the damage. Many buildings had collapsed from the force of the earthquakes and the storms. Giant stones — the kind normally found in the wildest parts of Chaos — nosed among the wreckage like grazing cattle. Women cried and men searched among the debris for loved ones.

"I wandered slowly through the Courts, pausing now and then as I caught interesting bits of conversation. Everyone seemed to be voicing the same thoughts:

"*'Dworkin betrayed Chaos.'*

"*'How many more storms will Dworkin send to destroy us?'*

"*'Dworkin must be stopped.'*

"As I got closer to the palace, I noticed a distinct change in the tone. Instead of *'How will the king stop Dworkin?'* it became, *'The king can't protect us anymore. Someone else must!'*

"At any other time, such words would have been treason. And to hear well-respected citizens openly saying such things in the streets! Incredible!

"When I got to the palace, I found the gates shut and barred. Grim-faced guards stood at all the entrances, swords out. I tried not to stare, but they were so preoccupied with watching the crowds that they wouldn't have noticed me anyway.

"Then I noticed two severed heads hanging from the spikes to either side of the gates . . . Mattus and Titus. Signs hung from both — BORN OF A TRAITOR. A coldness touched my heart. King Uthor must have executed them to try to appease the crowds. Only it hadn't worked. Everyone wanted Dad's blood. Nothing else would satisfy them at this point.

"And, I realized, if anyone caught me here, I would probably share their fate.

"At least no other grisly trophies decorated the gates. Perhaps Freda and all the others were still alive in one of the dungeons. I could only hope.

"With no place to go and no plan in mind except to stay alive as long as possible, I went to a small tavern I knew and settled in at a corner of the bar. As I sipped a beer, I listened with interest to all the gossip and talk of Uthor's failings around me. No one mentioned any family members other than Dad — and they mostly cursed his name.

"Then they began to speculate about what the king would — or wouldn't — do to protect Chaos. Several people openly said King Uthor ought to step down in favor of one of his sons.

"'He's too old,' one man said.

"'He cares more for his palaces than his people,' said another, nodding.

"Everyone echoed those sentiments. Then talk turned to how Dad ought to be killed when he finally got caught. Slowly grinding him to mincemeat, starting with his toes, seemed the most creative solution.

"Finishing my drink, I left, and once more wandered the streets. If anything, the crowds had grown larger, and the mood had grown darker. A new storm seemed to be coming: the air had grown darker, and a strange pressure filled the air, just like it had back home in the Beyond. You could feel the people's tension mounting.

"Finally, the *lai she'one* appeared. They marched toward the largest groups of people, shouting: 'Clear the streets! By the king's order — clear the streets now! Back to your homes or you will be arrested!'

"No one dared protest, but many men gave them angry looks, and I noticed a few fingering their swords or knives. If any had dared start trouble, I think the crowds would have rioted.

"But everyone began to disperse. In twenty minutes, the streets grew relatively empty — the few people still out moving with purpose on personal errands.

"I turned away from the others and took shelter in the ruins of a once grand home. I found a corner where two corner walls and part of the second floor still stood and took shelter just as the storm struck.

"It wasn't nearly as bad as any of the storms I had seen in the Beyond. The walls and ground shook; colors ran into puddles at my feet, and lights played weird tricks on my eyes — glowing and pulsing, they came in waves that left me disoriented and confused.

"When stones fell from the crumbling walls, I crawled under a table. That kept me safe for the next hour.

"The storm passed quickly. By the time I felt well enough to crawl out from the wreckage of the house, criers wandered the streets, shouting the latest news and proclamations — fifteen thousand dead, the hunt for Dad going on, another son of Dworkin captured. I wondered who it could be.

"In Triffig Square, an angry mob burned Dad in effigy. I had never seen so many people out for blood. *Our* blood.

"I spent another week in the Courts, carefully keeping up my disguise. I listened to the news and kept to myself. Several times people tried to contact me by Trump, but I ignored them. With so many sets of Trumps now in King Uthor's hands, I could not trust anyone.

"Subtly, I made enquiries of old friends, feeling them out for their loyalties. They had all turned against us. I had no one to fall back on for help. At night, I tried several times to contact family members . . . you, Blaise, Freda, Conner. I even tried Dad a few times. I knew Dad was still free, from all the rumors circulating about him putting together an army to attack Chaos. But he never answered.

"Unfortunately, the stress of keeping up my disguise proved too great. My control over my new face slipped one day as I was walking through the streets by the palace — I tried to go every day, to see if any more family members had been executed. When my old face returned, someone must have recognized me. The next thing I knew, *lai she'one* were running toward me, packs of urhounds baying as they picked up my scent, and I had nowhere to hide.

"I fled into the wilder Shadows of Chaos. I used every trick I could think of to hide my trail. I crossed the Beyond, then passed through the Gates of Stygia and into Ellysiom. I rode the back of a wild stone through the Mad Lands, and passed through Lyric's Furnace. The heat seared me half to death, and still they followed.

"If not for the urhounds, I probably would have escaped. But they had my scent and wouldn't let go. No matter how far or how fast I fled, their baying voices came behind me.

"I crossed the Golgul Wastes on foot, doubling back several times through the Lesser Catacombs, but nothing worked. I gained a few hours' lead skirting the Abyss, but no more. Finally they cornered me at Draak-Bal Forge.

"That's when I began trying every Trump I had left. Finally I reached you, Oberon. Lucky for me.

"And that's the whole story," Aber finished. "Not very impressive, I admit, but thanks to you, I escaped Uthor's grasp, which has to count for something. No thanks to Blaise." He gave her a dark look.

"It wasn't safe where I was, either," she said. "If not for Oberon . . ."

I cleared my throat and motioned for more drinks from Jamas. He refilled our tankards silently. He had been listening to Aber's story with a bewildered expression, but like any good barkeep, he knew when to keep his mouth shut. I nodded to myself in silent approval. Perhaps he and his son could be persuaded to relocate to my future Shadow kingdom once we began recruiting settlers.

I turned to Blaise. "Did anyone try to contact you by Trump while you were with your aunt and uncle?"

"Yes, nearly every day." She shrugged. "I ignored them. I didn't feel like talking to anyone. Much good that it did — the *shai le'one* came for me anyway. Why? Is it important?"

I paused thoughtfully. "I think so. Uthor must have been using Trumps to find everyone in our family. Had you answered, he probably would have located you sooner. That must be how they captured everyone else."

The sound of horses' hooves came from outside. I glanced at Jamas, endlessly polishing the far end of the bar with a rag as he listened to our gossip.

"Your son?" I asked.

"Ayeh," he said with a smile. "Back with Doc Hand, I'll wager. He'll fix your Da up, right enough."

A loud crash came from somewhere upstairs. Aber and I exchanged a startled glance.

"Dad!" we both said.

I leaped to my feet and sprinted up the stairs with my brother at my heels.

TEN

rawing my sword, I came through the bedroom doorway poised for a fight. I found Dad next to the bed, looking around with wild eyes. He had knocked over the washstand — that's what had made the crashing sound. Its blue basin had shattered on the floorboards, scattering broken pottery and dirty water across the floor.

Aber drew up behind me.

"Dad?" I said. "How are you feeling?"

I stepped forward cautiously, lowering my sword. He hadn't summoned a weapon through the Logrus, which I took as a good sign.

"Where is he?" Dad said in a hard voice.

"Who?"

"Thellops, my boy! We were just arguing —"

"He's not here," I said quickly. "You've been sick. Unconscious for hours."

"Hours? No!" He sat heavily on the edge of the bed, shaking his head. "What did he do to me? How long has it been?"

"I'm not sure." I hesitated. He seemed a lot better, and yet . . . subtly different. I couldn't quite put my finger on what had changed. "I found you unconscious at the Pattern a few hours ago, Dad, and brought you here."

"Where is this place?"

"Just an inn in a Shadow."

"Time moves differently there . . . we may still have time." He stood again, looking around with some confusion. "You must come back with me, of course. And Aber, too . . ." He frowned, eyes distant. "And Locke. Where is he? I need him."

"Locke is dead," I said softly. He had to be very confused, if he'd forgotten his first-born son's death in Juniper.

"Was it Thellops?" He paused. "No . . . no . . ."

"That was a long time ago," I said quickly. Better to steer him back to the subject at hand. "What about Thellops? Has he done something? Is it important?"

"Yes. Thellops." He looked at me, and I saw a raw anger in his eyes. "The three of us together should be enough."

"For what?" Aber asked.

Dad stood, then looked down. "What have you done to my boots? The laces are gone. And where is my swordbelt? Thellops is a crafty devil. We must be prepared this time."

"I have your swordbelt. It's downstairs." I took his arm and eased him back onto the bed. "Sit down for a minute. Tell me how you're feeling. You took a few blows to the head. Do you remember anything from the Pattern?"

"The Pattern is fine. I drew it, after all."

"After that . . ."

He blinked and his eyes grew distant. "Tired. Hungry." He looked around the room as if seeing it for the first time. "Where am I?"

"At an inn," I said reassuringly. He was repeating himself . . . and not thinking too clearly. Then I glanced at the door. What was taking Old Doc Hand so long? Maybe he could help.

Dad frowned. "I . . . already asked that, didn't I?"

"Yes," Aber said, folding his arms. "Try to focus, Dad. What about Thellops?"

"Thellops?" He looked at me. "Did I kill him, Locke?"

"I'm Oberon, not Locke. I don't know if you killed him. Were you fighting?"

"Yes . . ."

"Then we'll find out soon enough."

Dad leaped to his feet. "He got away!" Pulling free from my grasp, he paced like a caged animal.

"Do you know who I am?" I asked.

He glanced at me. "No more games, my boy. We don't have time for nonsense. We have to find Thellops before . . ." He frowned. "It may be too late now. We will see, we will see . . ."

I glanced over my shoulder. I couldn't see the stairs, but now I heard a man's heavy footsteps coming slowly up them.

"The Pattern!" he said suddenly. His eyes suddenly widened. "You tried to kill me —"

"No, Dad." Quickly, I told him what had happened. I wasn't sure how much of it he understood, but he listened, shaking his head now and then. I glossed over our fight — no need to rub his nose in it.

"Sorry, my boy," he said. "I . . . was confused."

"You're better now," I said reassuringly.

"Yes."

Just then a short, white-haired man dressed all in black, from a round flat hat to his narrow pointy-toed shoes, came clumping into the room. He carried a small black bag in one hand and a cane in the other.

"Someone sent for me?" He smiled in a kindly way and nodded to each of us.

"Yes. You must be Doc Hand," I said.

"Ayeh. Are you the patient?" he asked. His watery blue eyes peered up into my face.

"No, our father," I said, turning to indicate Dad. "Lord Dworkin."

"Lord?" Doc Hand raised bushy eyebrows. "It's not often the noble-born call on me."

"Get out," Dad said brusquely, motioning toward the door. "I need you like I need a hole in the head. Less, in fact."

Doc Hand chuckled and set his bag on the bed. "Now, now, your Lordship, let me be the judge of that. Seizures, is it?"

"Oberon —" Dad began in a warning tone.

"He seems to be doing a lot better," I said almost apologetically to the doctor.

"I *am* fine," Dad growled.

"Nonsense." Doc Hand leaned forward and peered at Dad's eyes. "You are certainly *not* fine," he said. "You have a concussion, sir. I see it clearly in your eyes. You were beaten severely . . . twice, I would say, from the looks of that bruising. Once yesterday, once this morning. You got the concussion yesterday. Now, are you going to let me treat you, or do I get these strapping lads to sit on your arms while I do my work?"

Dad glared at all of us. I tried to look firm but menacing. A concussion explained a lot.

"Oh, very well," Dad finally snapped. He perched on the edge of the bed. "Get on with it!"

I looked at the doctor with new admiration. This was the first time I had ever seen anyone intimidate Dad. Aber seemed equally impressed.

"Hmm," said the doctor. He skinned back each of Dad's eyelids in turn, peering deep inside. Then he felt Dad's skull for bumps. Finally he stepped back.

"Seizures?" said the doctor. "I see no sign of them. You are quite the brawler, though. I see scars from dozens of swordfights over the years. But who gave you that concussion, eh? There was no fight. Something hit you from behind . . . a sap, maybe?"

"I . . . do not remember," Dad said.

"I'm not surprised." Doc Hand looked at Aber and me. "Lads? Any idea?"

"We weren't there," I said.

Before I could stop him, he reached out, grabbed my right hand, and turned it over. I still had two fresh sword-cuts from my fight with Dad, one on the back of my hand, one on my forearm.

The doctor tsk-tsked. "You've been fighting, laddie. Beating up your Da, or defending him — that's the question, ayeh?"

"You have a good eye," I said, pulling my hand back. I didn't enjoy being under the old man's exacting gaze. "But my father is the one who needs you, not me."

"Oh, I treat all who need healing." He chuckled. "You're next, laddie."

I sighed. What did I expect, when I had deliberately sought a Shadow with a doctor capable of treating Dad?

"Ayeh," said Doc Hand, grinning. He rummaged around in his black bag, pulling out needle and thread. "You need a few stitches, laddie. Your Da needs a week of bed rest. And maybe a good hot meal and a stiff drink. Not much more I can do today."

"I told you so," Dad grumbled.

Doc Hand carefully threaded his needle, then looked at me expectantly. Gritting my teeth, I stuck out my arm and let him stitch my cuts back together.

Once the doctor left, Aber laughed and couldn't seem to stop. I glared. Finally he managed to regain control of himself.

"You should have seen your face," he told me.

"It's not funny," I said. "I hate catgut stitches. The damn things always pull at me."

"Sorry," he said. "But . . . I've never seen you look so annoyed! You got it worse than Dad!"

"Feh," I said.

"Don't pick on poor Oberon," said Blaise. I hadn't noticed her arrival. She leaned against the doorway, looking radiant. A few drinks had done wonders to restore her self-conficence. "He meant well."

"Enough," said our father, climbing out of bed and looking around. "Where is my sword?"

"You heard Doc Hand," I said. "You're due for a week of bed rest."

"I cannot rest," he said, "until we have Freda back. I remember now. Thellops has her — and you and I are going to get her back!"

ELEVEN

our sword is downstairs," I said. I didn't know much about Thellops, but already I hated him. What could he be doing with my sister?

I turned to my brother. "Aber? Would you mind getting his sword?" Considering how fast time ran in the Courts of Chaos, we needed to move quickly. Hours here might mean days or weeks of torture for Freda. "I had Jamas put it behind the bar for safekeeping."

He rolled his eyes, but dutifully trotted out of the room and down the stairs. Much as he liked to complain, I knew I could count on him, especially when Freda's safety was at stake.

Turning back to Dad, I said, "Do you have a plan?"

"Yes. Go in fast. Take Freda. Run away before anyone can stop us."

I snorted. Well . . . it had a certain elegance to its simplicity. Unfortunately, I didn't think we would be able to simply walk in.

I said as much.

"Nonsense, my boy," he said, grinning. "You are a fair swordsman. Together, Thellops cannot stop us."

"He stopped you already," I pointed out.

He shrugged. "He caught me by surprise. I made the mistake of

trying to talk to him as a friend and an equal. We are neither."

"Don't forget it."

He grinned suddenly. "I still have one trick left, too. Something he has long forgotten . . ."

"Got it!" Aber cried, dashing in with Dad's sword. He passed it over, and Dad swiftly buckled the belt around his waist, loosening the sword in the scabbard and adjusting it to a comfortable position.

"Do you want to come?" I asked Aber. He might want to help rescue Freda.

"No!" Dad said firmly.

Aber swallowed. "Uh . . . not this time. I'm no fighter; I'd only be in the way. Besides, if I stay here, I can be your escape route. Call me when you need to leave and I'll bring you all back."

"Good." I knew I could count on him. "Then you'll definitely be staying here until you hear from us?"

He pulled a sour face. "If I have to. Any other Shadow *would* be a improvement over this dump, though. It doesn't even have a decent bath . . ."

I chuckled. "I don't care if you stay or not. Just make sure we can reach you at a moment's notice wherever you are, okay?"

He brightened. "Sure!"

Blaise appeared in the doorway. She had taken the time to wash her face, fix her hair, and change clothes. Now she wore a wine-colored blouse, leather britches, and riding boots — and she carried a bare blade: a nasty-looking shortsword with a serrated blade and a wickedly barbed point.

I raised my eyebrows. "Why the sword?" It definitely wasn't the

weapon you expected to find in the hands of a beautiful woman.

"Someone has to watch your back," she said in a no-nonsense voice. "If you and Dad are going after Freda, you'll need help. There don't seem to be any other *men* around" — she shot Aber a pointed look — "so I have to pitch in."

Aber said, "I'll leave the manliness up to you. You have a bigger pricker than I do, anyway." He seemed to find that amusing and snickered a bit.

"Do you know how to use that thing?" I asked Blaise.

"Try me and see."

I chuckled. "Aber's right, you know."

Her eyes narrowed. "What do you mean?"

"You aren't our sister. The real Blaise belongs in the afraid-of-breaking-fingernails camp."

"There's no reason a woman can't look good *and* defend herself."

I just shook my head. We definitely had interesting characters in our family. Every time I thought I had my siblings figured out, new twists in their personalities appeared. Blaise as protective warrior-beauty queen . . . definitely not the image I'd had of her.

Completely businesslike now, she joined our father at the bed. He had been studiously ignoring us. Dad had pulled a small pouch from some inner pocket and had emptied its contents onto the quilt — rings, bits of colored glass and stone, a few fingerbones, a large agate marble. He picked through everything and selected what looked like a small piece of charcoal.

"Do-it-yourself Trumps?" I guessed. That seemed the likeliest way into Thellops's lair.

Without a word, Dad hurried to the wall beside the door. Smooth and freshly whitewashed, it offered a clean surface ideal for drawing.

He sketched a rectangle the size of a door. Then, with a few simple lines, he added a rough representation of a workroom: a long wooden table cluttered with bottles, jars, and tubes filled with bubbling liquids; tall bookcases; and a jumble of books and papers. More than anything, it reminded me of Dad's workroom in Juniper. It just needed a few mummified cats and a selection of bizarre and complex machines to be complete.

Aber cocked his head and studied the wall critically. "That one can't possibly work," he said. "There's no representation of the Logrus underlying it."

"An ignorant comment based on foolish assumptions," Dad muttered impatiently. He added a horned skull atop one bookcase and a glowing ball of light in one corner, then smiled half to himself.

"What do you mean?" Aber demanded.

"You are an idiot, my boy. The Logrus is immaterial."

"So you're using the Pattern?"

"Of course. Not that it matters. Neither one needs to be incorporated into the drawing."

"But it's the same idea. You need a magic underpinning to the image —" he began.

"Try telling the Logrus that. Or the Pattern. Both exist with no underpinnings whatsoever. They merely *are*."

Dad returned to the bed and began gathering up his rocks,

bones, and bits of glass, all of which he put back into his pouch. He dropped the charcoal in on top.

"That's crazy." Aber shook his head.

Dad looked at Blaise and me. "Prepare yourselves."

I drew my sword and went to stand beside him. As we all faced the picture on the wall, I half wondered if Aber might be right. Dad's drawing ranked among the worst Trumps imaginable. Sketchy black lines, faintly drawn from memory . . . how could it possible work?

But then, as I studied the image, I sensed an almost tangible *power* radiating from it. As Dad stepped forward and concentrated, the picture suddenly colored with browns and grays and ruddy oranges, coming to life. Instead of a black-and-white line drawing, we suddenly gazed through a shimmering doorway into Thellops's workshop.

Without hesitation, Dad stepped through into that room. He looked around quickly.

"Empty," he announced. His voice sounded distant.

"Impossible!" Aber muttered, staring.

"Not at all." I glanced at my brother. "You need to pay attention to what Dad's doing." Some time ago, our father had mentioned offhandedly that Aber had no idea how Trumps really worked. I hadn't repeated that comment, since I'd known it would hurt Aber. But clearly my brother needed to adjust his methods of Trump-making if he intended to keep up.

"But —" Aber began, looking with bewilderment from the drawing to me and back again. "How —"

"I'll explain later. Right now, I want you to find some whitewash and cover up the Trump on the wall. Summon it using the Logrus if you have to. I don't care — just get it. I don't want anyone following us through the picture on the wall."

"Come quickly!" Dad called, voice flat and far away. He held out his right hand to Blaise. She took it and he helped her step through.

"What if you need rescuing?" Aber asked. "I can't help if I can't get there."

I said, "We won't. If we fail, we'll be dead."

He sighed. "Okay. I'll do it as soon as you're gone. Anything else?"

"I can't think of anything."

Dad called, "Hurry up, my boy!" The doorway to the workshop suddenly rippled like a lake touched by morning breezes.

I hefted my sword. Hopefully Dad's plan would work.

In fast. Rescue Freda. Run away.

Simple, at least in theory.

Lowering my head, I walked through the drawing on the wall. Aber vanished behind me. *Down* and *up* flip-flopped several times. Strange colors and smells hit my senses in pulsating waves — reds that smelled of cheese, yellows that stank of wet skunk, browns and grays like rotting horseflesh. Gagging, I tried not to retch.

Voices reached me, but oddly garbled. Suddenly Dad's face pressed close to mine. I looked up into his brown eyes and gasped. His pupils flickered with reds and yellows, as though fires burned behind his face. His skin might have been the paper of some paper lantern.

He said something, but I couldn't quite make out the words. He might just as well have been speaking some barbarian tongue. Since he seemed to expect an answer, I gave a curt nod and forced myself upright. I couldn't hold up Freda's rescue.

That seemed to satisfy him. Turning, he headed for the door.

Taking a shuddering breath, I glanced around the room. Light came from a dim ball hovering in the corner, just below the ceiling. Much like Dad's workshop in Juniper, this appeared to be a private retreat for study and magical research. If we'd had more time, I would have liked to go through it carefully. There was no telling what useful notes or devices we might find in here.

Suddenly the room tilted to the left. I staggered into the table and caught myself against it. Everything swam drunkenly, and gravity flip-flopped several times.

Blaise gripped my shoulder. Gulping frantically, I looked into her face.

I couldn't make out the words, but I read her lips: "Are you all right?"

"Dizzy . . ." I muttered.

Something in my ears made a little popping sound, and the next time she spoke, I actually heard words:

"Want me to slap you?"

"Hah!" I said. Maybe my "Chaos legs," as Aber had called them, were returning. "Just try it."

"If you think it will help . . ."

I released the table. "Only if I get to break your arm!"

"He's all right," she said to Dad.

"Are you sure?" Dad asked, hesitating. "He looks sick."

"I'm fine," I growled. I had no intention of sitting out Freda's rescue.

"Don't worry," Blaise said, patting my cheek. "If you can't keep up, I'll carry you." She glanced at our father. "Can you locate Freda? I sense her presence, but not clearly. Is she close?"

"Yes," Dad said. "This way, I think." Pushing open the door, he hurried out into a hallway.

Blaise motioned me forward, so I went next. She brought up the rear.

Dimly glowing balls of light hovered overhead at regular internals. Light puddled on the ceiling above them, casting a dim yellow glow across the stone floors and wood-paneled walls.

Dad headed right, and I followed two paces behind. He seemed to have a clear idea where he was going. We passed doors with faces, each exactly the same as the last. They had all been carved from slabs of ebon-colored wood, with an identical face in each one's exact center: horned forehead, deep-set eyes, broad nose and cheekbones, cleft chin. Each face had its eyes closed, as though sleeping.

If these doors acted anything like the ones in Dad's house in the Beyond, they might wake up at any moment, spot us, and raise an alarm. I made certain not to touch any of them.

I was about to suggest we return to Thellops's workshop and search for keys to the doors when the floor began trying to slide out from under my feet. Stumbling, I had to lean against the wall every few paces to keep my balance.

Blaise caught up and grabbed my arm to steady me. "Do you

need to go back?" she asked in a hushed voice, her tone no longer kidding.

"I'll make it," I said.

She hesitated. "If it comes to fighting," she said, "stay behind me. I'll protect you as much as I can."

"Thanks, but I fight my own battles!"

"A lot of good it does us if you end up dead!"

I shook my head stubbornly. "Then we'll just have to be careful. I'm not hiding behind you, Blaise. Don't ask me to."

She frowned, but didn't press the point. Which was fine with me, since I had no intention of giving in. Besides, I had a feeling I'd be back to normal soon . . . my Chaos-legs were definitely returning.

Dad navigated a twisting course through hallway after hallway. The passages seemed to curve back on themselves like serpents devouring their own tails. Hadn't we come in a full circle? Were we back where we had started? I couldn't tell. Still we passed door after identical door — the count must have run into the dozens by now. Several times I had the impression of descending on a slight incline, though the floor always appeared level. More tricks of Chaos. . . .

Dad stopped in front of a door like so many others we had passed. It had no markings or numbers to identify it.

"Prepare yourselves," he said. "This is the one."

"I'm ready." Swallowing hard, I tightened my grip on my sword. Nothing to do now but storm in, letting heads fall where they may.

"Wait, Dad," Blaise said. "Are you sure?"

"I know Freda's voice," he said, eyes distant. "She is calling from inside. I am certain of it."

"I don't hear anything," I said.

Dad made a dismissive gesture. "You are deaf to the Logrus, my boy. Her spirit is crying out in agony. You are not attuned to it, so you cannot hear it. Blaise and I can."

I glanced at Blaise, who nodded. "Yes. I hear her, too." Then, to our father, she added: "I know Freda is in pain. I feel it. But I'm not certain she's inside this room."

"I am."

"If you make a mistake . . ."

He nodded. "I know. But the only way to find out — is so!"

Before Blaise or I could stop him, Dad rapped sharply on the carved wooden face on the door, right in the center of its forehead.

The face twitched. Its eyelids flew open, and it glared at us with blood-red eyes.

"How dare you touch me!" it snarled.

I gulped. If this guardian was anything like the doors in Dad's home in the Beyond, it would take the magical equivalent of a battering ram to get through now that Dad had pissed it off.

"I am your master," Dad said.

It blinked. "You are not Lord Thellops!"

"No," Dad agreed.

"Who are you," it said in haughty tones, "and what do you want? Speak fast, or I shall summon guards and have you executed for this outrage!"

Dad said, "You know who I am."

"You . . ." The face stared blankly at him. "Are you are the one? The maker?"

"Your name!" Dad commanded. "Obey me!"

"I am Oberon," said the face.

I gaped. "Did you say *Oberon?*" Maybe I hadn't heard correctly. Chaos might still be playing tricks on my senses.

"Yes," said the door, looking at me, "I did say Oberon. What of it?"

"Uh . . . I wasn't sure I heard you correctly." I shot a puzzled glance at Dad. "That's my name, too. Funny coincidence."

"You are Oberon?" Dad said to the door, ignoring me. "Yes, I thought so. Do you remember *me?*"

"I think . . . I think I know you," it said, staring at his face.

I stared at Dad unbelievingly. How was he doing it? Hypnotism?

Calmly, Dad nodded. "I am Lord Dworkin. I made you for Thellops many years ago. I carved you with these two hands. I painted the light into your eyes and into your heart. Do you remember me now?"

"Yes . . . Lord . . . *Dworkin* . . . yes. You are the one. I will obey . . . master."

Ah, so Dad had made Thellops's doors! Sometimes it paid to be an inventor. His confidence about getting through to Freda suddenly made sense.

Now, though, I had a question or two of my own. Had he named me after a door, or named the door after me? After we rescued Freda, I intended to find out.

Dad smiled kindly, like a proud father at his son. "I have returned, as promised. Now open for me."

The face blinked several times. "None may enter, by Lord Thellops's command."

"*I* may enter," Dad said firmly. "I made you. Your first instructions came from me. Recall them."

"You . . . you may pass through me at any time, day or night, without question. I must obey you in all things."

Dad leaned forward. "What else?"

"Now and forever . . . you are my one true master."

"Good. Now, let us pass."

"Yes . . . master."

The lock clicked several times. The door swung open.

Dad drew himself up, sword ready. I looked at him with new respect. He must have made these doors for Thellops many years ago . . . and made sure they would always open for him. The crafty devil. Had he planned a career as a burglar?

"Faster!" Dad commanded. "Be quick and be silent!"

The door swung completely open, revealing darkness. From inside came a strange snuffling, snorting sound, almost like a pig rooting for food in its trough. A monster? A guard of some kind? I raised my sword, prepared to defend myself, but nothing charged from the darkness. What was it waiting for?

Without hesitation, Dad strode forward. He disappeared into the room.

The snuffling noise grew louder.

"Come on!" I said to Blaise. Then I charged after him.

TWELVE

 found myself in warm, humid darkness, unable to see anything. From somewhere ahead, I heard a faint tap-tap sound of footsteps, and more snorting noises. My heart pounded. My every nerve jangled in alarm. I did not like feeling blind and helpless.

"Dad!" I called. "Can you see anything?"

"Light!" Dad commanded.

Brilliant white flared all around us. We were not in a room any more — and yet neither were we outside. A strange foglike grayness surrounded us. I could see Dad and Blaise, but nothing else. It reminded me of the fog through which I had fallen after Dad created the new Pattern. Could they be related, somehow?

The snuffling grew louder, but I saw nothing that could have made such a sound. When I glanced over my shoulder, I saw the door we had just entered. It made a hole in the grayness. Slowly, as I watched, it began to shut.

I leaped to hold it open — how else could we get out once we rescued Freda? — but didn't reach it in time. As the latch clicked, the inside of the door faded, leaving nothing but grayness where it had been.

Great. Now we were trapped in here.

Or were we?

Closing my eyes, I felt for the door. I already knew I couldn't trust my senses in the Courts of Chaos. Perhaps this gray fog was nothing but an illusion designed to befuddle our eyes.

My fingers encountered nothing but air. I walked right through the place the door had been. We *were* trapped here.

"Oberon!" Dad said.

"Me or the door?" I asked.

"Pay attention, my boy." His voice echoed oddly. "Stop fooling around and get over here."

I turned back to him. He walked swiftly to the right, with Blaise at his side. I jogged to catch up.

The snuffling grew louder.

"Where are we?" I asked.

"Inside."

"Inside what?"

"Freda."

I stopped short. *"What?"*

"He is using her. I can feel it clearly now. He is searching the Shadows for us."

"How?" I demanded. "Like Lord Zon did?"

Zon had drawn my brothers' blood from their bodies with magic, then used their blood to scry on the rest of us. One by one he had murdered my brothers and sisters.

"Zon is an amateur compared to Thellops."

Still we walked for what seemed miles, though in the grayness I had no way of telling. Finally Dad halted. Slowly he inched to the left. Then he inched back to the right. Then he took a few steps forward, stopped, and went back.

Listening to the snuffling sounds, I tried to figure out what he was doing. Suddenly I realized we had reached a central place in the grayness, where the snuffling noises could be heard the loudest. Every time we moved away from this spot, the cries lessened.

Nodding to himself, Dad turned to me. "Give me a Trump. Quickly!"

"Whose? Freda's?"

"Yes."

I pulled my Trumps out, found my sister's, and handed it to him. Holding it up, he gazed at it, concentrating.

Suddenly the card turned black. I had never seen anything like that before. As I leaned closer to see, it burst into flames. I had to leap back, slapping at my singed beard and eyebrows.

Dad dropped the Trump with a yelp. By the time it reached the ground — if ground existed beneath the grayness — nothing but ashes remained.

"Damn him!" Dad said, nursing blistered fingers. "I should have known!"

"So . . . you can't contact her from here?"

"No. The Logrus is preventing it."

"Give me your charcoal," I said suddenly. An idea had occurred to me — why not use the Pattern? No one in Chaos had a defense against it yet, so maybe a Pattern-based Trump would work here.

Dad fumbled out his pouch and passed it to me, leaving bloodstains all over it. I fished out his piece of charcoal. Then I summoned a mental image of the Pattern. It seemed to hang in the air before me — brighter than ever, lit with a bright blue glow.

Unfortunately, I had nothing to draw on. Frantically I looked around. What could I use?

"Blaise —" My gaze settled on her. "Would you mind showing your back? I need your skin for a minute."

"You're not thinking of using *me* as your chalkboard —" she began, clearly horrified by the idea.

"Charcoalboard, actually. Unless you have a better idea?"

"Will this work?" she asked Dad.

"I cannot be sure," he admitted. "In theory, it should. But if Thellops has a counter to the Pattern, you might burst into flames like her Trump just did."

"It better work." She sighed, turned around, and pulled up her blouse in the back, revealing smooth white skin. "Do it quickly. And if you kill me, I'll never forgive you, Oberon."

I kept the Pattern in my mind, visualizing it as I sketched a large rectangle, then a line drawing of Freda. I was no artist — far worse than Dad — but it came out reasonably well. I recognized Freda's face, from her hair and upturned chin to the slight dimples in her cheeks.

The power of my Trump hit me in a wave. It *glowed*. I could see lines of blue energy radiating from it.

"It's burning!" Blaise whispered.

I gulped in panic. But she neither turned black nor burst into flames.

"Get Freda," Dad told me urgently. "Hurry —"

I leaned forward, concentrating on the picture I had drawn. Slowly it came to life, becoming a window through Blaise's back. There, surrounded by more gray, I saw Freda huddled with her head in her hands, sobbing softly. Her cries matching the snuffling noises we still heard echoing around us.

"Freda!" I called. Was she injured? Could she hear me? "Freda! Over here!"

I reached farther into Blaise's back and chest. My wrist and elbow went through. Blaise moaned. I reached up to my bicep, them to my shoulder. Distantly, I noted Dad gripping my sister's arms, holding her upright and steady.

"Freda!"

Finally she looked up. "Oberon? Is that you?"

"Take my hand. Quickly!"

She reached for me. As our fingers touched, a spark leaped between us. Blaise gave another plaintive cry and started to sag. Despite the burning in my fingertips, I seized Freda's wrist and pulled hard.

She came out through Blaise's back smoothly, straight into my arms. I went over backward with her elbows and knees digging into my soft parts. But I didn't care — we had done it! She was free!

Then lights flared around us. I pressed my eyes shut. Another trap? Or —

My stomach knotted in sudden fear. Blaise! Had she just burned up, like the Trump?

I opened my eyes, blinking frantically at the colored spots swimming before my eyes. Slowly my vision returned to normal.

The fog had disappeared. We were in an unfurnished room —

bare panel walls, plank flooring, a high beamed ceiling.

And Blaise — still there, still alive, with her blouse down over her back. The magic had ended. We were all safe.

Dad helped Blaise up; I helped Freda. She hugged me desperately, tears streaming down her cheeks, and then she hugged Dad and Blaise. She smiled at us through her tears.

"I knew you would come!" she said. She clung to my arm. Her whole body shook uncontrollably.

"Of course we came," I said. "How could we not?"

"I never gave up hope."

I smiled and brushed a stray lock of hair off her face. "Let's go. Aber is waiting for us at an inn."

When I pulled out Aber's Trump, Dad thrust his hand over the card, blocking it.

"No," he said. "Thellops will destroy it. Save it for use in Shadow."

"Then how do we get out?" I asked. "Should I draw another Pattern-Trump? Or will you?"

"Too late, too late!" he cried, looking toward the door, an expression of sudden horror on his face. "Listen! *Thellops is coming!*"

THIRTEEN

n uncontrollable shiver went through me. From somewhere outside, I heard a low **thump . . . thump . . . thump** sound. Its force vibrated through the floor and into the soles of my boots. Something was coming. Something *big*. And it seemed to be getting close.

I swallowed hard and glanced at Dad. "What do we do?" I asked.

He smiled almost philosophically. "We die."

"You made it out alive last time."

Thump . . . thump . . . thump . . .

"We met at the Edge, where shadows of Chaos and the Pattern meet."

"Neutral territory," I said.

He nodded. "Terrible things are happening in Chaos. He has finally taken sides. When I told him I wanted Freda back, he . . . tried to destroy me. I barely escaped. Here, in his home, with the Logrus close at hand . . ." He swallowed. "His powers will be ten times greater."

"A cornered rat is the most dangerous," I said. "He would be wise to let us go."

Thump . . . thump . . . thump . . .

"Oberon the door!" Dad called.

The face appeared on the inside of the door. "Yes, master?"

"Do not open for Thellops!"

It frowned, but said, "I will obey, though it costs me my life . . ."

Thump . . . thump . . . thump!

And abruptly the noise stopped. Thellops had reached the door. The door moaned and shook as terrible blows rained down on its other side. The wood began to splinter.

Blaise had dropped her sword. I snatched it up and ran straight toward the door.

"No!" Dad called. "You must not!"

They expected me to fling the door open and face Thellops in some last heroic gesture. But that was the last thing I had in mind. I knew I would lose any fight with Thellops. Tired, still disoriented and off-balance — how could I possibly face a master-sorcerer of Chaos?

I summoned an image of the Pattern to my mind. I wrapped myself in it. I coiled it around Blaise's sword. The air around me sang with power.

The door began to scream as its wood splintered. Throwing all my weight behind the blow, I drove Blaise's sword into the wooden face, through its gaping mouth. The Pattern hummed with power. The face screamed. Three feet of tempered steel penetrated the wood — and kept going through it and out the other side.

I felt a rough jolt as my Pattern-wrapped blade hit something on the other side. Thellops? I hoped so. The blade kept going another foot. Not even a Lord of Chaos could live through a foot of steel in his heart.

Releasing the hilt, I stepped back. Slowly I let the Pattern fade away.

The door was dead now, its wooden face frozen in a scream of pain and horror. A dreadful silence came from the other side. Time seemed to stand still. When I glanced back at Dad, Freda, and Blaise, I found all three staring with horrorstruck expressions.

Then I turned, grasped the sword, and pulled. The steel almost sang as it slid free. Its hilt tingled in my hand, and I realized it had somehow been changed — though whether the Pattern, the door, or Thellops had done it remained a mystery.

As I raised the sword, I heard the soft thud of a body falling on the other side. A gush of dark blood suddenly flooded under the door. I danced back, just managing to keep my boots dry.

I wiped the blade clean on my shirt's tail, then handed it back to Blaise. Dad was staring at me with an unbelieving expression on his face.

"How . . ." he whispered.

"I'm not as weak as you think, Dad." I left it at that.

Pulling out my Trumps, I found Aber's, raised it, and concentrated. A moment later, he answered. He was sitting in a huge round bathtub, surrounded by mountains of bubbles and three of the most beautiful women I had ever seen before. Clearly, he had wasted no time in abandoning the inn where we'd left him.

"That didn't take long!" he said cheerfully. He stepped out of the tub and put on a robe. "I assume, since I see Freda behind you, that you met with success?"

I grinned. "Bring us back," I said. "And prepare for the celebration of a lifetime!"

*   *   *

An hour later, after a long hot bath of my own (Aber seemed to have made off with all the available women, unfortunately), I shaved, brushed my hair, and put on the odd-looking clothes that my brother provided: a high-collared white shirt, loose black pants with what looked like a snakeskin belt, and low-cut black leather shoes — surprisingly comfortable. After a lifetime of military boots, my feet felt strangely light.

Suitably cleaned up, I left my weapons on the table by the bed, then went downstairs to join my family. I found them seated at a large round table in the inn's cavernous dining hall. The room must have had two hundred tables of various sizes, with a large dance floor at the center. Half the diners were out on the floor, swaying to the odd atonal sounds coming from a band composed of what looked like variations on flutes, guitars, violas, and drums.

"You cleaned up nicely," Aber said, smiling. "Though you forgot your necktie."

I stared at the intricately tied piece of black cloth at his collar and frowned. "Is that what the scrap of cloth was for? I didn't know. I polished my shoes with it."

"Here." Freda reached under the table for a second, then pulled one out — surreptitiously using the Logrus, I assumed. Leaning across to me, she looped it around the back of my neck, then quickly knotted an intricate bow in front. "Much better."

"Thanks." It felt too tight and binding, though, and I couldn't help but pull at it with one finger.

Freda slapped my hand. "None of that."

"Yes, Mom."

She shook her head. "If you hadn't just rescued me . . ."

I chuckled. "I guess that buys me a lot of good will."

"A lifetime of it."

"Have some wine!" Aber said. He filled my glass from a tall-necked green bottle. "It's a little sweet, but quite good. Locally made, too." He leaned back and squinted at the label. "It says so right here — Product of Selonika. Royal Charter of Prince Marib."

Dad cleared his throat and raised his glass. "To Oberon! Our man of the hour!"

I raised my glass. "To all of us! Everyone here contributed to Freda's rescue. Dad got us safely in . . . Blaise provided a ready sword!" I gave her a wink. "And of course Aber got us safely out. We're not just a family, we're a crack squad of commandos!"

"Hear, hear!" everyone agreed. We drank.

After that came huge slabs of steak, baked potatoes, strange bulbous green and red vegetables, and more wine than I knew what to do with . . . and as the evening wore on and the music grew loud and wild, dancing spread between the tables, and everywhere laughing men and women danced, drank, and celebrated. Dinner became a pleasant, warm blur. I couldn't remember having such a grand time in months, if not years.

Late that night, very late, I left the dining hall in search of an outhouse. I found it, relieved myself, and headed back to rejoin the others. As I strolled along a white pebble path toward the dining room, I listened to cicadas *brr* and crickets chirp. A cool, pleasant breeze blew steadily, keeping away pesky insects, while high overhead a moon grown golden and huge limned the trees and bushes around me with silver highlights. I had a pleasant buzz from all the alcohol, and I felt really good. All told, a perfect evening.

When footsteps suddenly crunched on the pebbles behind me, I felt a jolt of alarm. Enough had gone wrong in the last few months that I expected to be attacked at any given moment.

Without hesitation, I threw myself to the side, tucked into a roll, and came up with a knife in each hand. I never should have left my sword in my bedroom.

A ball of light flared over the path, illuminating it like noon on a cloudless summer day. Magic! I blinked and shaded my eyes. This was no mere holdup. A manlike creature dressed in red robes and carrying a tall wooden staff stood before me. A pair of short horns curled back over a slightly pointed skull. I guessed his age somewhere between forty-five and fifty — though considering how long-lived the denizens of Chaos were, I could have been off by a hundred years — or a thousand.

"You won't take me without a fight!" I snarled.

"Ah! You *must* be Oberon, then." He nodded pleasantly, leaning on his staff. I glanced around, but he seemed to be alone. "Your talent for survival is becoming legend in certain circles."

"Who are you?" I watched him warily, but he made no move toward weapons. "I don't believe we've met."

"The name is Suhuy." He said it like it meant something, but it didn't — at least, not to me.

"Lord Suhuy?" I guessed. "Of Chaos?"

"If you wish." He shrugged. "Such titles are meaningless. It is a man's deeds that matter. Those speak for him long after he is dust."

"True." I lowered my knives. Clearly Suhuy wasn't scared of me. "I assume you're here to kill me," I said.

"Whatever gave you that idea?" He continued to lean heavily on his staff, as though he needed it to walk. "An old man like me doesn't go around attacking people. It would be . . . unseemly."

"Then what do you want?"

"Merely to look upon the face of the man who killed Lord Thellops. I thought you would be taller."

"Why seek me out if not revenge?"

"I have no need for revenge." He smiled again. "Thellops was neither well liked nor well understood in Chaos. Many are secretly relieved that he is gone."

I folded my arms. "All right, then. You've looked upon my face. Return to the Courts of Chaos and seek me no more."

"So quickly to the point." He tsk-tsked, shaking his head. "All the niceties of conversation are lost on the young . . ."

"Too many people from Chaos have tried to kill me over the last year. I find my patience at an end."

"Is it my appearance that disturbs you?" He took a step forward. His body seemed to melt and reflow, and a moment later he stood there as a young human boy in a white tunic, with olive skin and wide innocent eyes. "I will change, if it makes you more comfortable."

I shook my head. "Go home, Suhuy."

He took another step, becoming a beautiful woman in a sweeping green gown, with long black hair, an ample bosom, and the delicate face of an angel. Against my will, I let out a horrified gasp. I knew her: this was Helda, my poor dead love from Ilerium. Hell-creatures had killed her before trying to kill me.

"See?" Suhuy said in Helda's voice, soft and sensuous. "Those born of Chaos need not appear threatening to you . . ."

"Enough games!" I threw a knife at his head.

Helda/Suhuy caught the blade between thumb and forefinger, an inch from her left eye. She flowed, becoming a horned old man again. He leaned heavily on his staff. The knife was gone.

"Very well," he said. "I will speak plainly, since that is what you want."

I tensed. Here it came — the attack I had been expecting.

But Suhuy merely said, "There is an elaborate game being played out in Chaos and in Shadow. You must know this by now. We are all pawns to larger powers. In killing Master Thellops, you upset the gameboard . . . and elevated me to a new rank."

"Not intentionally," I said.

"Nevertheless, I find myself in your debt." He inclined his head slightly. "All in Chaos are not your enemies, Oberon. Remember that in years to come."

"What do you *really* want?" I asked. If he had a point, I wished he would get to it. This whole conversation made me distinctly uneasy.

"Right now . . . I want nothing. In fact, I have a gift for *you*. Lo!"

He pointed with his staff. The air between us crackled with lightning. It formed a sphere, which bulged like a pregnant calf. With a sound like thunder and a blast of hot wind, it broke open. From inside tumbled a gaunt, half-naked man. He struggled to rise from the pebble path, then fell back. I stared at his long matted hair and his torn and filthy pants. He stank like an open sewer.

"What sort of trick is this?" I cried, half gagging from the odor.

Suhuy covered his mouth with a delicate lace handkerchief. "Thank me another time," he said. When he raised his staff, the ball of light over his head winked out. He was gone.

"Oberon?" a weak voice called.

I hurried forward and knelt beside the man.

"I'm here," I said softly. "Who are you?"

"It's me," he said in a weak voice. "Conner . . ."

FOURTEEN

onner!" I rolled him over, but couldn't see his features clearly in the darkness. And that stench!

"Help me . . ." he whispered. "Water . . ."

I hesitated, knowing I couldn't carry him inside in this condition. Too many people would ask too many questions. Where could I get him cleaned up the fastest? Another Shadow?

No — even better. This inn had a series of fountains in the middle of the flower gardens. I had noticed a series of interlocking pools from my suite earlier. If I could clean Conner up there, he wouldn't smell so bad when I brought him back up to my room.

I threw his arm over my shoulder, but he was too weak to stand and walk, even with help. Finally I picked him up and carried him. He couldn't have weighed more than ninety pounds — he had been reduced to little more than skin and bones. King Uthor or Thellops or Lord Zon had been starving him for months.

As I trotted down the pebble path with my burden, I passed men and women seated on secluded benches among the roses, kissing gently and groping not-so-gently, but I paid them little heed. They were too wrapped up in their own business to notice us.

When I reached the first pool, pale shapes of fish drifted ghost-like beneath the surface, passing among the dark silhouettes of lilypads. In the center, a marble statue of a nymph on a pedestal poured an endless stream of water from an amphora.

I sat Conner on the low wall around the fountain, and he leaned down to the water and drank greedily for a long time. Then he sat back, gasping. After a minute, he drank again. I waited patiently. He needed time to gather his strength.

At last he sat up and looked at me.

"Where are we?" he asked in a rough voice.

"It's just a Shadow," I said. "I don't know its name. Dad, Blaise, Freda, and Aber are all inside the inn — that big building over there." I pointed. "I'll take you in as soon as you're cleaned up a bit."

He licked his lips. "You wouldn't happen to have any food, would you? Maybe some bread or cheese —"

"Sorry, afraid not. I didn't want to leave you here while I went back to the kitchens. If you want, though, I can run back —"

He didn't wait for me to finish, but reached out and pulled what looked like half a leg of lamb from mid-air. Of course he had used the Logrus. The meat steamed, obviously fresh from someone's dinner table. From the smell, it had been basted with mint jelly, too.

He bit into it eagerly, chewing and swallowing in great gulps. I didn't blame him for not waiting; I would have done the same thing in his place.

I sat beside him and watched him eat. When he finally finished, he drank again, more slowly this time, then washed his hands and face.

"Better?" I asked. His strength seemed to be returning. Along with his table manners.

"Yes, thanks. Who else did you say was here?"

I told him.

"That's it?" He stared at me incredulously.

I nodded. "And now you."

"All the others? What about Titus?"

"Are you strong enough to walk?" I asked, changing the subject. I didn't want to tell him the bad news about Titus yet. He had been very close to his twin.

"I . . . almost." He sighed then shook his head. After another short rest, he managed to stand and wade waist-deep into the pool, where he kicked off his rags, dunked his whole body under the water, and began splashing and scrubbing his body. When he finally emerged five minutes later, he didn't stink nearly as badly. Then he used the Logrus to find clean clothes and put them on, heedless of the occasional passers-by who gave us strange looks and a wide berth.

"What happened to you after Dad, Aber, and I left the Beyond?" I asked him.

He pulled on his pants slowly. "Uthor's men . . . it was a long time ago." He gave a shudder. "Titus and I went to stay with our uncle, but they arrested us anyway. That was the last I saw of my brother. In the dungeons under the palace, King Uthor had me tortured for a while, but I didn't know anything about you or the Pattern. Not really. Finally, I couldn't take it. I confessed to everything they asked. I remembered saying I helped cause the storms and plotted with Dad to overthrow the king. That made them happy. I signed a lot of papers, admitting my guilt, and after that they threw me into a cell and forgot about me. I lived off rats and mice, mostly."

"Horrible!" I murmured. "What about the Logrus? Couldn't you use it to call someone?"

"Spells block it in the dungeons."

"Oh." That made sense, since prisoners would certainly try to use it to escape. "And then . . . ?" I prompted.

"Then an old man came for me —"

"Suhuy?" I asked.

"I didn't know his name." Shrugging on his shirt, he tried to button it with shaking hands. I stepped forward and helped. "He said he was bringing me to you. He pointed his staff at me. The next thing I knew, I was lying face down on the ground at your feet."

"Interesting," I said thoughtfully. As much as I appreciated the safe return of my brother, I needed to know more about this mysterious Suhuy and his motives. Why did he want to meet me and make a good impression? How could rescuing Conner possibly be of benefit to him . . . unless he knew of our coming fight with Uthor and expected Uthor to lose. My thoughts about the powers of the Pattern being greater than those of the Logrus returned. Might I have hit on the truth by accident? I would have to talk to Dad about it. Maybe, between us, we could figure it out.

"Do you know if any other family members are still being held by Uthor?" I asked.

"Mattus, I think."

"Mattus and Titus were both executed, according to Aber."

"No! Are you sure?"

"He saw their heads stuck on the palace gates."

Conner sat alongside the pool and began struggling to pull on his boots. Twice he almost fell backward into the water. In other circumstances it might have been comical. In other circumstances I would have laughed.

He said, "Someone told me King Uthor had arrested Freda — but that can't be true. You said she's here."

"We rescued her from Thellops. He was using her to spy on us."

Conner rose. He produced a swordbelt using the Logrus and buckled it on. Then he faced the inn and took a deep breath.

"Ready," he announced.

"For what?"

"Dinner!" He grinned feebly.

The others were still seated at our round table. When Conner and I walked in, I found the lights had been turned down; more dancers swayed on the floor now, and the band played a fast if discordant tune.

It took everyone a moment to realize I hadn't returned alone. Then another moment to realize the unkempt stranger was actually the long-lost Conner.

"I found him outside, looking for us," I said. "He escaped from Uthor's dungeon . . . with a little help from a friend."

After much back-slapping and hugging and not a little crying from Freda, we dragged over another chair and ordered more food. While Conner tucked into a couple of thick steaks, I pulled Dad to one side and told him about what had really happened.

"Suhuy . . ." he murmured. "I know him. He was Thellops's apprentice. He would have become Keeper of the Logrus a thousand

years or more from now, when Thellops died . . . he must consider
that sudden promotion a favor and be seeking to pay you back for it.
He would not want to be indebted to any of us."

"He was talking about a game . . ."

"Oh?"

I repeated Suhuy's comments about upsetting the gameboard.
Dad chuckled, then shrugged.

"There is a philosophy, based on the earliest writings of our
people, which claims all of Chaos is a game for greater beings. Those
who follow it call themselves Kindred. Perhaps he is one . . . a harmless enough faith, as faiths go. The Kindred seek to grow more powerful and, through their increased importance to the game and its
outcome, grow closer to those who roll the cosmic dice. If he is one
of the Kindred, you have done him a great favor by eliminating
Thellops. Elevating Suhuy to a new position of power and rank
would be important to him."

"That must be it," I murmured. And yet I still had a feeling,
vague though it was, that something did not quite make sense.

"Our family is much reduced," I said. "Conner may well be the
last to join us."

"There is at least one more. . . ." He chuckled, but did not elaborate even when I gave him a questioning look.

I let it go for now. I would pry the truth out of him when I had
more time.

As for Conner . . . he was still gorging himself at the dinner
table. If he wasn't careful, he would make himself sick. Still, with
Freda and Blaise doting over him like over-protective aunts, I knew

he would be fine.

"We can't stay here," I said suddenly. "If Suhuy can find us, so can King Uthor."

"Blame the Logrus," Dad said. "It may be tracking us for them. Every time we use it, we are be telling them where we are and what we are doing."

"Aber told me the Logrus didn't work that way!"

He chuckled. "Have I ever mentioned that Aber is a fool?"

"Too often," I said.

He snorted. "You cannot rely on gossip for a true understanding of how the Logrus and its powers work. It is tied to the King of Chaos and the Keeper of the Logrus. My researches have proved this conclusively. If the king and Thellops did not know what every single person was using it for — including us — it is only because there are millions of people using the Logrus at any given time. Yes, Chaos and its Shadows are that big. But if either one of them focused his attention on one man or his family . . . yes, he would know what we were doing, and where."

"Then you must all stop using the Logrus. It's convenient, I know . . . but surely the Pattern can be made to work just as well. And Pattern-based Trumps seem immune to the Logrus and its influence."

"I agree," Dad said. My surprise must have shown because he quickly continued: "I made a mistake in Juniper. I underestimated our enemies. I had no idea Uthor and Thellops were involved. Of all the people in Chaos, only they had the power to spy on us through the Logrus. I will not see that same mistake repeated. Once we leave here, we are through with the Logrus. Forever. Any who disagree will be cast out for the common good."

I nodded. "Very well." I felt exactly the same way. We had to take every precaution against Chaos.

"Where shall we go?" Dad said. "We need a new home — a world we can shape to our own liking. I have a vague impression of a likely Shadow close to the Pattern . . ."

"I took you there from the Pattern. It's a promising land, well laid out, but it's empty — no people at all. We will have to bring in everything and everyone we need."

"Then we will do this thing. We will build there at once." He clasped me on the shoulder. "And this time, Oberon, we will not repeat our mistakes!"

FIFTEEN

espite our ambitions, we did not manage to leave the inn the next day, or even the next week. Conner must have been running on pure nerve the night before. When he awakened in the morning, his months of imprisonment had caught up with him. Too weak to do much, he lingered in bed, with Freda and Blaise playing nursemaids. They plied him with light soups and delicate pastries from the inn's more-than-capable kitchens, to Conner's delight. He seemed to enjoy the attention.

Since the Logrus had already shown Suhuy and (I assumed) everyone else in King Uthor's camp where we were staying, I figured it wouldn't matter if my family continued to use it here. Everyone to his or her own talent . . .

I put Aber and Blaise on gold-gathering duty. The two of them spent an afternoon pulling in several tons of gold through the Logrus. Gold bricks, gold nuggets, gold plates and silverware — they found it all and brought it into our suite. When the floors groaned from the load, I hired several wagons and carted it all down to the Imperial Bank of Selonika, where its deposit caused quite a stir.

The bank manager dispatched runners to the palace every few minutes with updated totals as clerks weighed and carefully logged in our wealth, and they quickly returned with a line of credit marked "unlimited." No less a personage than Prince Marib himself signed the letter.

It also came with an invitation to luncheon at the palace. I sent my brother. While he and the prince dined and became fast friends, I took Blaise on a shopping spree. We bought dozens of horses, mules, goats, sheep, cows, pigs, chickens, and other domestic animals. And then we bought several dozen large heavy-canvas tents, lanterns and oil, picks and shovels, seed and grain, and enough foodstuffs to last us at least six months. Beds and furniture . . . tables . . . silverware . . . we would need everything ahead of time, especially since no one would be able to use the Logrus to bring in last-minute items. Blaise hired maids, butlers, cooks, and other servants.

We needed a warehouse to hold all these purchases, so I bought one of those, too — and hired an accountant and a dozen burly workers to manage everything. Money flowed like water. A steady stream of deliveries began to arrive almost immediately.

With my permission, Aber revealed to Prince Marib some of the truth about our family. We intended to export supplies from his Shadow to ours until we established our own economy. Envisioning a huge profit, Prince Marib seemed delighted at the prospect, according to Aber, and quickly sent us lists of his city's best chartered architects, stonemasons, hostlers, and various other tradesmen who could help. Aber, Blaise, and I spent the rest of the day visiting them, hiring their services at higher-than-normal cost, and generally arranging things. They would hire whatever construction workers were needed to commence construction of a castle and town immediately.

Foundations needed to be dug first, and that could begin even before the blueprints were finalized.

In the meantime, our father spent the day in his room, drawing new Pattern-based Trumps. He made a set for me first, one showing each of the surviving members of our family — and with some amusement I noticed his drawing of Aber showed a court jester complete with pointy green hat and curly-toed shoes with bells on their tips. Tit for tat; that's how Aber portrayed Dad on his Trumps. At my request, Dad also created a Trump showing my bedroom at the inn. This way I could return as needed. Since I had already paid in full for everyone's suites at the inn for the next fifty years, this room would always be held empty for me, for use whenever I needed it.

When he finished the Trumps — clearly not his best work, sloppy but serviceable — we Shadow-walked back to the empty world I had selected for our new home. He wanted to see it for himself.

We spent the last daylight hours on a quiet ramble through the hills and small mountains ("Ideal for a castle," he commented), down through the ancient oak forests ("enough wood for a half-dozen towns"), then onto the white sandy beach ("a good natural harbor"). The weather remained mild, the sun bright, and game plentiful, from birds and fish to rabbits and deer. The only thing missing was a stone-quarry, but we both agreed a site for one could easily be found in the west.

Using my new Trump, we returned to the inn for a late dinner. The pessimist in me half expected to find the place ablaze and the guests slaughtered as Uthor's hell-creatures overran the city, but everything appeared calm and peaceful.

Almost too peaceful.

On the second day after Conner's return, Aber and I breakfasted with Prince Marib at the palace. His Majesty's invitation had been extended to me through Aber, and although I suspected it originally might have included our father, by the time Aber delivered it, it only included me. I was delighted to accept, however. It wasn't every day I got to dine in a palace, and I planned to pick up ideas for our own castle's construction.

The prince sent a covered carriage for us at eight o'clock in the morning. Aber and I stepped up into the cab, the driver whipped up the matched team of white geldings, and off we raced up the streets of the city.

"Is there anything I should know about the prince before we meet?" I asked Aber in a quiet voice.

"He's quite a lot like you."

"Short, bald, and middle-aged?" I said, raising my eyebrows. "I've seen his statues . . ."

Aber laughed. "Idiot . . . not physically alike. But he did remind me of you. You both have an annoyingly noble streak. You're always thinking of everyone else, rather than just yourselves . . . the greater good, I guess you'd call it." He shrugged. "In his case, he's thinking of his whole principality. Trade with us will make everyone here rich, if they handle it right, and he knows it. He doesn't want to screw that up."

"That's the mark of a good ruler," I said. I looked out the

window at the passing buildings. Merchants were already opening their shops, rolling down bright canopies and rolling out barrels of fruits, vegetables, and other items. Children laughed and darted here and there, playing games. A few old women scrubbed the sidewalks on their hands and knees. They all seemed happy and well-fed.

Aber said, "Everyone seems to like him, both personally and as a ruler. You have that talent, too."

"I think you overestimate me," I said. "Mostly I just want us all to survive."

"And thrive," he said.

"Well, yes."

He smiled. "If we get to pick our king, you've got my vote."

I raised my eyebrows. "Dad's first in line. He's the king."

"Uh-uh." He shook his head. "He's a creature of the Logrus, like the rest of us. The Pattern is yours alone. Besides, he doesn't have the skills of a leader — or the interest. He'd rather putter around his workshop, inventing things and playing with his magical toys. He can't organize a whole new world. You've been doing all the work. You deserve the title."

"Maybe . . ." I frowned. I had always assumed Dad would be our leader. And yet, what Aber said made a lot of sense. Dad had made more than his share of bad decisions over the years, and he didn't exactly inspire loyalty.

"And," Aber continued, "you have the military experience to protect us. That has to be more important than anything else right now. I don't want to get slaughtered in my sleep. Dad —"

"We'll talk more about it later," I promised, as the carriage rolled through the high marble gates of the palace. "Right now, we have a prince to impress."

Prince Marib, looking splendid in a brilliantly feathered crown and robes of deep purple trimmed in gold, greeted us in a garden located at the center of his palace. Tame monkeys laughed and chattered from the intricately trimmed trees around us as his steward ushered us to cushioned seats around a small glass table.

I bowed graciously, and Aber did the same.

"Please, be at ease," he said, smiling cordially and motioning for us to sit. "While we acknowledge the formalities of the past in Selonika, we don't cling to them. Your brother has told me you come from the far-off land of Chaos. Please observe whatever customs are usual to your people. I am eager to learn more of them."

"You are very kind."

I sat to his right, and Aber sat to his left. At his gesture, beautiful women began wheeling in trays of delicate pastries and sweetmeats. They served us on glass trays, then withdrew.

Marib began to eat at once, but lightly. We followed his example.

"I understand you are pioneers," he said. "I will do whatever I can to assist you. However, doubtless due to my own shortcomings in education, I do not quite understand the magics Aber mentioned, and neither do my ministers. Can you tell me more of this place called Shadow, where you will dwell?"

"Of course," I said. I explained quickly about all the worlds — the Shadows — and how they existed side by side. No need to go into the Pattern with him. Then I told him how my family had the ability to travel between these worlds, and after a conflict with a world called Chaos, we set off to live on our own.

"And who will rule there?" asked Prince Marib.

"Oberon will," said Aber.

I shot him a warning glance. "That has not yet been decided," I said.

Marib leaned back in his cushioned seat. "Oh, I think it has, my friend. If half of what Aber has told me is true, I see in you the seeds of a great and noble ruler."

I pretended modesty. But I could not help but feel flattered. And I wondered: maybe I *should* be king.

Prince Marib extended his offer to assist us in whatever way he could, and we left soon after breakfast ended by exchanging vows of friendship between our peoples.

On our way back to the inn, I said to Aber: "You were right. I like him."

On the third day after his return, Conner was up and about, with new color in his cheeks and new flesh on his bones. Now he looked merely thin rather than emaciated. Still Freda and Blaise plied him with food at every turn.

"At this rate I'll weigh four hundred pounds by the end of the month!" he complained to me.

I laughed. "You need to distract them with something else. Right now, all of their maternal instincts are focused on getting you well."

"You keep telling me about this new Shadow," he said. "How about taking me there? I'd like to see it. I assume you and Dad are going back today."

"Yes. I think so. But keep in mind that it may affect you. Blaise did not react well to it."

"I'll take that chance. And if not, I can always return here. Dad gave me a Trump of my room."

I nodded. "Very well. We'll make a day of it, then. I know Freda wants to see it, too."

Quickly I called down to the kitchens, and they set about making a picnic lunch for us. Nor was the manager content to pack us off with a simple basket. He insisted on a full complement of waiters and chefs, a portable grill, ice chests for the selection of wines, plus tables and chairs and sufficient linens. Our simple meal rapidly became a vast and complicated endeavor.

I sighed. At least I wouldn't be organizing it. Cold roast beef sandwiches and beer summoned through the Logrus would have been much simpler.

SIXTEEN

t was nearly noon by the time our vast entourage got underway. Sixteen wagons strong — with horses for Aber and me — left the city. Our company had swelled to eighty-six. Twenty of them were early surveyors sent by the architects, who would begin making all of the preliminary measurements and sketches. The others included various servants who would set up tents and an advance camp, cooks, waiters, a wine steward, and a dozen others whose purposes remained a mystery to me.

Only Dad elected not to join us, saying he had errands of his own to run. Mysterious and secretive to the last. Well, we didn't need him right now, and I had a new Trump of him courtesy of Dad, so I could reach him whenever I had to.

It took an hour to reach our future home. The wagons slowed us down considerably. But as the familiar hills and forests came into sight, I felt a quickening of my blood and spurred my horse. Aber hurried to keep up, and side by side we ascended a mountain and gazed down at a pristine beach below.

"This is it!" I said.

"Beautiful." He twisted in his saddle, looking in all directions. "I want a room with a southern view. And lots of windows."

I chuckled. "Then it will do?"

"More than do! It's perfect, as long as it lasts!"

I studied him. "How do you feel? Tired? Sick?"

"Huh? Fine, of course."

"No ill effects?"

"No-o-o . . . should I have some?"

I smiled with relief. "I was half afraid everyone else would get sick here, like Blaise did."

He pointed down the mountain, where the wagons had just drawn to a stop. "She looks fine now, as far as I can see."

I shaded my eyes and studied her, plus Conner and Freda. None of them lay down suddenly and went to sleep, which had to count for something.

Aber stood up in his saddle, waved, and shouted a "Halloo!"

Freda waved back. Everyone climbed down from the wagons and hiked toward us. Servants, meanwhile, began to unload everything and set up tables for lunch.

Ten minutes later, my sisters and brother joined us. Blaise looked pale and faintly sick, but not as bad as before. Conner and Freda were winded, but well.

"You look good," Freda said to me. "Almost glowing. This world agrees with you."

I laughed. "This place . . . it's in my blood. I feel strong here, more powerful and alive than I've ever been before."

"It is the Pattern. Its nearness . . ." She turned slowly, studying the land. "It is . . . different here. Not like Chaos. Nor quite like Juniper. There is something powerful about it . . . an energy I can *feel.*"

"It's better," I said.

"Different," she repeated.

"Enjoy it while it lasts," Aber said with a sigh.

I glanced over at him. "What do you mean?"

"Do you really think King Uthor will let us build here? He will march against us immediately."

"You forget," I said, "that this is *my* world, not his. It's built from the Pattern within *me*. I feel like a god here. So let him come — I'll kill him and hang his head from my castle gates!"

"Castle? Gates?" Aber turned slowly, staring at the emptiness. "He isn't going to wait for us to build. I bet he's gathering his forces now."

"It doesn't matter," I said. My imagination soared. Towers — walls — ramparts — a whole city will rise here, on the side of this mountain! "We will bring as many workers as it takes. We can rebuild Juniper in a year."

"Not Juniper," Freda said sharply. "That was Father's. Make this *your* city, Oberon. Put *your* stamp upon it."

My own city . . . yes. I could see it in my mind's eye. Tall towers with minarets, proud pennants flying. High stone walls, shining white in the rising sun, surrounded by a beautiful town with red-tiled roofs and well-cobbled streets. Down to the sea, where the sun shone like amber on the waves . . .

"Amber," I whispered. It fit this world. It resonated nicely with Juniper's name, too . . . a proud and unashamed continuation of our father's legacy.

"*Amber?* Is that the best you can come up with?" Aber asked.

"Kind of boring. How about Aberton? Now *that's* a name with personality!"

"No," Freda said flatly.

"Or just Aber. It's shorter."

"Only by one letter," I said.

Freda said, "Absolutely not!"

"Or maybe Oberonia?" he went on, grinning at me. "What do you say, brother?"

I had to laugh. "Actually, I kind of like Oberonia!"

"No," Freda said firmly, turning to me and folding her arms stubbornly. "Do not encourage him, Oberon. He becomes very silly if you let him."

"How about Fredania?" Aber suggested with a knowing smirk.

She glared. "No! This world will be called *Amber*. That is the end of the discussion."

"I like Amber," Conner said.

"So do I," said Blaise.

"Then it's settled," I said. "We'll call it Amber. The name fits, and I like it."

"No sense of fun . . ." Aber muttered.

"It is settled." Freda sighed and looked to the distance. "Now comes the hard part."

"We all know an attack will come," I said. "The only question is — when?"

"Maybe building here isn't such a great idea," Aber said. "Dad had a hundred years to prepare Juniper, and he still couldn't hold it."

"We must build Amber to withstand greater forces," Freda said. "We know what we will face. This time, we will be ready."

Aber shook his head. "Easier said than done!"

"Higher ramparts and stronger walls will only do so much," I said. "I've seen what primal chaos can do. If Uthor unleashes it here, nothing will save this Shadow."

"We cannot hide like animals," Freda said.

"I didn't say we should." I swallowed, eyes turning to the distance. "We need a home. A place to plan and gather our forces. If war is inevitable, I'm not going to wait for it to come to me. We'll attack first."

Aber gasped. "Attack the Courts of Chaos? Are you mad?"

I looked at him levelly. "I've never been more serious. If I have to fight, it's going to be on *my* terms. If Uthor has spies in Amber, we'll have spies in Chaos. If he gathers an army to attack us here, we will attack him first. I'm not like our father — I'm going to fight, and I'm going to win. No matter what it takes."

Freda looked at me strangely. "I see our father in you," she said. "But there is something else, something more."

"I have a mother, too," I reminded her, thinking to the unicorn I had seen three times now. I half believed my father's claim that she had birthed me. "If any of what I suspect is true, she is quite remarkable."

"Your mother, yes, that must be it," she murmured. "For the first time . . . I believe you will succeed."

I chuckled. "Let's not get maudlin. We have work ahead of us. Hard work, and a lot of it."

"I don't like the sound of that!" Aber said with mock alarm.

"Think bigger, beyond yourself." I gestured grandly, taking in the mountain before us. "Look at this world as a blank slate. We have architects — stonemasons — carpenters, all at our call. We can buy food in great supply. We will hire all the help we need from Selonika and other nearby Shadows. Amber itself will provide the rest. A quarry for granite and marble. Lumber by the ton. Enough land for farming, fish from the sea and meat from the forests . . ."

"Whoa!" Aber said. "We haven't even had lunch yet!"

"Can Amber really be built so quickly?" Freda asked.

"Yes. We'll do it the old-fashioned way . . . with greed." I grinned. "And, for anyone who doesn't want gold, there's plenty of land available. We need farms and wineries. For anyone really valuable to us, we can hand out minor titles —"

"You would set up a peerage among the Shadow-people?" Blaise asked, looking aghast.

"Why not?" I grinned at her. "I've lived in Shadows my whole life. There were more people of honor and integrity in Ilerium than I found in all of Chaos."

"But none of them can control Shadow or Chaos," Conner said. "They have no real power."

"Oh, a few generations of interbreeding with the likes of us, and I think they'll share our powers, too. I certainly intend to take a wife. Every king needs his queen."

"Then you *will* be king?" Aber asked, sounding hopeful. "Not Dad?"

"Oberon must be King," Freda said. "The Pattern has chosen him."

"Great!" Aber grinned. "It was my idea, you know. As a reward, I expect a few extra titles, at the very least."

"As the king's brother, you will be a prince," Freda said. "That is sufficient."

"How about Arch-Duke of Aberton?" I asked. "And — uh — Lord of All the Marshlands?"

"Much better!" He laughed. "Do we have marshlands?"

Freda frowned. "You are both being frivolous."

"We also have to figure out where Aberton is," I said, ignoring her.

Aber turned and looked to the south. "Isn't it over there? I want to see it from my rooms in the castle."

"Could be." I shaded my eyes. "I bet it's just beyond that forest."

"Insane, both of you!" Freda threw up her hands and stomped off.

Aber and I both broke up laughing.

SEVENTEEN

No, no, no!" I shouted. I pounded my fist on the table inside the tent, where dozens of sketches and blueprints lay in disarray. "I don't care whether the mules are sick, only half the workmen are here, or it's raining flaming toads! Work begins today!"

The two construction supervisors cringed before my wrath. "Yes, King Oberon!" one of them squeaked. They bowed their way out of my tent.

Three weeks had passed since our picnic atop Mount Amber, as we now called the mountain where the castle was to be built. Nothing but delays, delays, and more delays had plagued the beginning of construction. Like a rusted wheel, the machine of our builders needed to be unstuck to turn . . . my anger provided the solvent.

I rose and paced. Aber, with his feet up on the table, just chuckled.

"It's not funny!" I roared. I'd had it with the lot of them.

"Did I say it was?" Aber asked. "The sooner I have a real roof over my head, the happier I'll be. I hate rain, I hate sun, and I hate living in a tent. If you didn't need my help with the blueprints, I'd be back in Selonika right now, living the good life." He sighed.

"Oh, go ahead back," I said. I waved him away. "There's not much more to do today, anyway. Tomorrow, after you've slept off your hangover, come on back and we'll see what more needs to be done."

"You don't have to tell me twice!" He leaped up and ran out through the tent's open flaps.

Sighing, I sprawled back in my chair and began looking through the architect's sketches again. Something about the west wing bothered me, but I just couldn't figure out *what*, exactly.

"Oberon?" I heard Freda say as she swept in. "I wish a word with you."

"Of course. Join me." I indicated the seat Aber had just vacated. "Wine?"

"Thank you."

I poured a cup of red wine for her.

"What's wrong?" I asked.

"The problem," she said, "is a lack of supervision. Conner and you make sure work gets done well and quickly, but you cannot be everywhere at once. As soon as you leave, the workmen grow slack. I have seen it time and again at the sawmill, the quarry, or here as they dig the foundation . . . these men move at their own pace."

"I know." I let out a long sign. "Everything is behind schedule. And yet . . . we have all the available men working in shifts night and day. What more can we do?"

"We need more help," she said.

"All right. Hire more workers. As many as it takes, from Selokina or any other Shadow."

"No . . . I mean more help from our family."

That puzzled me. "I know Aber doesn't work as hard as he might, but —"

"No, you do not understand. I am not asking *Aber* to do more. He has done a wonderful job so far. I need more family members. I want to invite several of my aunts and uncles to join us. And I want permission to search for the rest of our missing brothers and sisters."

"Will your relatives come?" I asked. "They must know how difficult life here will be, at least in the beginning. We can only offer tents . . . and a lot of hard work."

"It is still preferable to their present lives in the Courts."

I paused. "You already spoke to them about it, didn't you?"

She raised her head. "Yes. They are being persecuted by Lord Uthor for daring to help me. He has made it . . . *unpleasant* for them. They seek asylum. I know they will work hard —"

"Enough!" I raised my hands and smiled. "Of course they may come. If you vouch for them, I will gladly offer whatever protection I can."

"Thank you, Oberon!" She beamed. "I knew we could depend on you!"

"How could I not help them? Any who seek freedom from Uthor's tyranny should be welcome in Amber." I cleared my throat. "You also said something about finding missing family members?"

"Yes. We have had no news of so many of them . . . and I miss Pella. I cannot believe Uthor killed or captured them all. If Blaise and Aber were smart enough to remain free . . . why not a few more?"

"I suppose it's possible," I said slowly. I saw what she meant. We had plenty of other brothers and sisters who were just as clever and resourceful. Maybe more so.

"And . . ." she hesitated.

"What is it?"

"The last time we were in Selonika, I went through all my Trumps. I tried every one of them, for the living and the dead."

"Yes?"

She leaned forward urgently. "I thought I sensed something from Isadora, Fenn, and Davin. A flicker of contact, quickly blocked."

"Davin!" I exclaimed. He had fallen, along with our brother Locke, while defending Juniper against attacking hell-creatures. "Impossible! He'd dead!"

"I am not sure. Remember, we never did see his body."

"True." Taking a deep breath, I looked away. Davin had earned my grudging respect on the battlefield. If he had been captured instead of killed . . .

"All right, I'll grant you that much. Davin may be alive. What of Isadora? And Fenn?"

"I want Father to make a complete set of Trumps for me — one card for every one of his children, living and dead."

"Dead?" I asked. "Why?"

"There are . . . certain ways to raise the dead in Chaos," she said grimly. "Uthor may have done it with Davin. We cannot be certain. It would take a fresh body to fully restore him. Later, he could be brought back as a zombi . . . an animated corpse which can do simple tasks for its master."

I did not like the sound of that. Rising, I paced. She had given me a lot to think about.

Three more of us possibly alive . . . having Fenn and Davin here would make an enormous difference in the coming battle. But first we had to get them back. Finding them had to be a top priority.

"A complete set of Trumps sounds like a reasonable request. Go ahead and ask Dad."

"I did, but he refused."

"What! Why?"

"He did not believe I sensed them. He said he did not have time to indulge my whims. Whims!"

"He has not been quite right since he made the new Pattern," I said, remembering some of his outbursts.

"But this is important — so important, it must not be delayed."

"I agree. I'll speak to him tomorrow morning." I patted her hand, and she smiled in relief. "In the meantime, Aber just went back to Selonica. Why don't you go, too, and try your old Trumps again? Perhaps this time . . ."

"Very well." Freda said. She rose. "Come with me?"

I hesitated. The day was not yet half over. Plenty of work remained here.

"Please?" she said. "I want you with me when I try Davin, Fenn, and Isadora. If you sense them, too, Father cannot deny it."

"All right. I'll go — but I can't stay long."

She nodded, then pulled out her deck of Trumps. The one Dad had made, which showed her room at the inn, sat on top. She concentrated on it and took us through when it came to life.

She must have been planning to bring me back with her. A table with two chairs sat to one side as if waiting for us. She sat and motioned me opposite her.

Then she handed me her deck of Trumps, face down. Without being asked, I shuffled them and handed them back. I had seen her read the future through them before. Was that what she had in mind?

She set the deck down, then turned over the first card. It showed our brother Locke, who had died a hero's death defending Juniper. For a second Freda traced the smooth bonelike surface of the Trump lightly with her fingertips, but then she moved it to the bottom of the deck.

"Why don't you try him?" I said.

"But he is dead. We cremated his body."

"Humor me. I have been lied to so many times lately, I'm having a hard time believing anyone or anything. For all I know, he was replaced by a double in Juniper. Right now, he might be locked in a tower somewhere waiting to be rescued."

She pulled Locke's Trump out again. Raising it, she concentrated for a minute on his image, then shrugged.

"Nothing."

She set it face-down on the table beside her, and moved on to the next card, which showed a beautiful long-legged woman with reddish-blond hair — Syara. I had barely exchanged two words with her in Juniper.

"Nothing," she repeated.

Then she drew the next card. Fenn.

She raised it, hesitated. "There . . . almost!"

I hurried around to stand behind her, leaning forward to see. As we both concentrated, I felt a faint conscious stirring from the card. Was it him? I could not be certain.

Finally, we had to give up. We had not been able to exchange any words with him, but *something* conscious was connected to his card.

"See?" Freda cried. "I was not mistaken! You felt it, too."

I agreed. "Why couldn't we reach him, though?"

"It could be anything," she said. "Distance. The Logrus. He may be unconscious or consciously blocking contact. Father must make me that new set of Trumps based on the Pattern!"

"I will tell him as soon as I see him. Now, what about the others?"

She picked up the next card. *Pella*. Her full sister.

"Nothing . . ." she said.

We finished her deck with no more successes.

EIGHTEEN

ven though we hadn't managed to contact Fenn, I returned to Amber buoyed with optimism. Suddenly I had hope of seeing more of my brothers and sisters again.

I set to work with a new enthusiasm and spent the rest of the afternoon reviewing the castle's foundations with the architect, one Yalsef Igar, a frail-looking old man whom Prince Marib had recommended highly. Indeed, I had found his plans to be a nearly flawless interpretation of my vision of the castle.

My earlier threats and screaming had done wonders in motivating the construction supervisors . . . they now had their team of a hundred and fifty men hard at work shoveling dirt into barrows, rolling boulders down the mountainside, and cutting away trees, bushes, and underbrush. After stripping off the tree branches, mule-teams hauled the logs toward the new sawmill, half a mile away on the river.

"Bring in more men," I said to Igar. "You have a year to finish. Cut the time in half and I'll triple your pay."

"*Triple?*" he gasped.

"In gold."

"I will do my best, Your Majesty!"

I nodded. "Good."

After ten minutes of watching the men at work, I returned to my tent. A new set of floor plans lay open on the table for my inspection. I had just begun reviewing them when I felt a sense of contact.

I looked up, opening my mind, and found Dad waiting impatiently.

"Here." He threw a Trump at me, and I caught it instinctively. "Hurry!"

"Dad —" I began.

"Join me later."

He broke contact before I could say another word. Typical. He never let anyone get a word in if it didn't suit his purposes.

He had tossed a newly drawn Trump to me — and it showed the Pattern, glowing blue against the rock, with trees and bushes in the background. The paint still felt a bit sticky under my fingers. It hadn't quite dried yet.

A coldness swept through me. He'd said to hurry. Had Uthor reached the Pattern, somehow?

I tore my sword from its scabbard, then concentrated on the Trump's picture. The scene came to life quickly. I leaped forward.

On the edge of the Pattern, I paused. A stillness hung over everything; colors seemed more vibrant and every edge and line as sharp as a knife, from the leaves on the trees to each blade of grass.

I was not alone here. A tall, gaunt-faced stranger with skin the color of sun-bleached bones stood on the far side of the Pattern, studying it intently. If he noticed me, he made no sign of it.

He wore all black, from his broad, flat cap to his shirt and pants to his knee-high boots. As far as I could tell, he carried no weapons.

As he slowly circled the Pattern, his gait struck me as odd, and I suddenly realized he had an extra joint in his arms and his legs. It bent backward, giving him a curious hop at the end of each step. Clearly he wasn't human. But neither was he anything like the King Uthor's hell-creatures, or any of the other creatures of Chaos I had seen.

"Hey!" I shouted. I took a step in his direction. "Hey there!"

He glanced across at me and nodded politely, as though he were an honored guest and I his host. Then he resumed his careful examination of the Pattern.

Since he didn't seem to be doing anything overtly threatening, I lowered my sword. Why had my father sent me here? To chase him off . . . or to help him in some way?

I hesitated, looking around again, but saw no one else. Since I had a few minutes before he reached my position, I pulled out my Trumps. When in doubt — ask. It was a good rule for interpreting orders.

Raising Dad's Trump, I stared at it and concentrated. *Nothing.* Not so much as a flicker. Dead? Unconscious? Somewhere I couldn't reach? I had no way of knowing. He hadn't seemed in any immediate danger, just rushed.

I would have to figure it out for myself. Nothing like a quick question-and-answer session to sort things out.

Cautiously I walked around the Pattern and joined the stranger in black. He barely acknowledged my presence. Up close, I realized for the first time how big he was . . . he towered over me by at least a foot. And he was completely hairless. Smooth white skin like parchment stretched tight over sinewy flesh. He had not a scrap of fat anywhere on his body, which gave him a curiously skeletal appearance.

Everything about him struck me as *wrong*, somehow. There was no reason for it, but I took an instant dislike to him.

"Are Oberon?" he said.

"Yes. Who are you?" I demanded.

"True name meaning. You may call Ish." He smiled, showing long, pointed white teeth. It could have been an expression of friendliness or even reassurance, but I found it unnerving.

"Ish," I said. I swallowed hard. "What are you doing here?"

"That which emerged calls now."

"The Pattern?"

"I not born Chaos, if you fear," he said. Then he calmly stepped around me and continued walking his circuit of the Pattern, taking long hopping steps.

Not born Chaos? What did that mean? Could he be a creature of the Pattern, like me?

"You shouldn't be here," I said, giving chase. "My father — Dworkin — sent me. I think he wants you to leave."

"New. In place." He turned and bowed from the waist. "Apologies. Dworkin work time. This better."

He paused expectantly as I tried to puzzle through his jumble of words. Could he mean he liked this Pattern better than the last one? Had he seen them both?

"You saw the other Pattern?" I asked. "The first one my father drew?"

"Many." His head bobbed twice. "Gift. Son-of-Dworkin?"

He held something small toward me. Without thinking, I stuck out my hand, and he dropped a small, cold, hard object onto my palm.

It was a man's ring. Gold, with what looked like a small ruby set into the top, it caught the light and glinted faintly.

"Uh . . . thanks," I said. I held it up, examining it.

"Spikard," he said firmly. "Old."

"Gold?"

"*Old,*" he repeated. "A power. Yours. *Spikard.*"

He motioned for me to put it on. After a second's hesitation, I slipped it onto the index finger of my right hand.

At first it seemed much too loose, but then it suddenly tightened. Panicked, I tried to yank it off — but it clung to me like a leech.

"What have you done to me?" I cried.

"*Spikard,*" he repeated. "Good."

The ring grew warm. The warmth spread up my arm . . . but instead of burning, it left me with a sense of great well-being. Full and warm and safe . . . life was good . . . the spikard would protect me. I *knew.*

Shivering, I took a step back. This spikard alarmed and frightened me. I was *not* well and safe. I had a strange ring on my finger trying to put reassuring thoughts in my head!

"Stop it!" I cried.

The ring pulsed once, and my unnatural sense of well-being left. I was myself again, or so I hoped.

Ish tilted his head, then pointed at the Pattern. "Walk?"

"What is this thing?"

"Spikard. Good."

It pulsed once as if in reply.

I glanced down at it. "Can you understand me?"

It pulsed again.

"Are you a friend?"

It pulsed four times . . . an emphatic yes, I assumed.

"Should I walk the Pattern?"

Another pulse.

All right . . . an intelligent ring. This might lead somewhere in-teresting.

"I want you off my finger. *Now.*"

The ring pulsed, then grew loose. I slipped it off, then fought my sudden impulse to heave it as far away from me as I could. In-stead, I slipped it into the pouch at my belt, the one with my collection of Trumps. This spikard might prove valuable or useful once I understood it better. I'd ask Dad and Freda about it.

Ish pointed at the Pattern again. "Walk?"

"I already walked it twice."

"Dworkin walk," he insisted. "Oberon walk."

I stared. "My father walked it?"

"Walk."

"Not this time. I don't know who you are or what you're doing here, but I'm not taking any orders from you." I pointed the sword at him. "Leave. *Now.*"

He tilted his head to the side, clearly confused. Then his body flattened and folded into itself almost like a piece of paper. In a second, he had vanished.

I let out the breath I had been holding. I had never seen anything like that before . . . and I was pretty sure he hadn't used the Logrus or the Pattern.

Stepping forward, I swung my sword through the place he had been standing just to make sure he hadn't turned invisible. He really *had* gone. Hopefully he wouldn't find his way back again. We couldn't have strangers poking around the Pattern . . . even unarmed, hairless white giants.

Sheathing my sword, I took a deep breath. What now?

The Pattern shimmered.

The sky overhead almost glowed, the deepest, most perfect azure I had ever seen.

I pulled out Dad's Trump and tried it again, but got no response. Then I tried Freda. She answered immediately, and her image was as clear and sharp as if she stood next to me.

Quickly I told her what had happened.

"Do not touch the spikard again," she told me. "It is dangerous."

"How?"

"It is tied to the Keye —"

"The what?"

"The Keye . . ." She hesitated. "It is ancient, like the Logrus, and very powerful. There is no time to explain. Father must not ask the Feynim for help or protectio —"

"Whoa! The Feynim? Who are they?"

She knotted her hands. "They are ancients. Older than Chaos.

You must stop him! He must not deal with them — it is forbidden!"

"I'll try to find him. Do you have any idea where he is?"

"He may be with them . . . beyond the edge of Chaos." She looked me in the eye. "Walk the Pattern, Oberon. It has great powers. Use it to find him. Hurry!"

NINETEEN

y the time I reached the center of the Pattern, I felt drained physically and mentally. It seemed no easier on this, my third try. But I knew it could be done, and I pushed through the pain and all the barriers, and finally I emerged, gasping and soaked with sweat.

I staggered forward. Without a second's hesitation, I visualized my father. "I want to join Dworkin," I said aloud. "Send me to him."

Everything lurched a bit as I stepped forward. Disconnection followed.

Blackness.

I felt a spectral wind through my hair. The smells of dust and decay filled my nostrils.

Cold.

Shivering, I blinked and found myself in a cavernous hall carved from stone. Glowing circles on the walls and floor, in clusters of thirteen, provided a wan light. A cool, moist breeze moaned unceasingly from the left.

A brighter light shone ahead. I peered at it and saw what looked like a table surrounded by high-backed chairs. My father stood there, surrounded by thirteen tall, gaunt, hairless old men. They were clearly of Ish's race.

I approached, clearing my throat gently to make my presence known.

Fast — so fast their movements seemed to blur — the thirteen around the table moved. Swords out, they surrounded me.

Slowly I raised my hands.

"Who?" one of them demanded. His words were spoken in a strange, ringing language I had never heard before, and yet I understood it.

"My name is Oberon," I said. It sounded too simple, too plain, so I quickly added a title for myself: "Lord of the Pattern. King of Amber."

"My son," Dworkin said.

They murmured to themselves, staring at me with unblinking eyes. Slowly they resumed their seats. I went to stand beside my father.

"Go," said one of them. The leader?

Dad shook his head. "I want an answer first."

"*Go.*"

He raised his hand and made a gesture of dismissal. All around us, the air around sparkled. Everything around us bent and seemed to fold, and then they were gone and we were back at the Pattern.

It all happened too fast. I stared at my father.

"What just happened?" I demanded. "Who were they?"

"The Feynim?" My father shook his head unhappily. "Allies, I hoped, but they refuse to get involved."

"*What* were they?" I demanded. "They weren't like us — or the hell-creatures."

"True. They are not of Chaos or Pattern, but older. Much, much older. And powerful. I am not sure they have a name as we understand it."

I remembered Ish's odd comment about his true name having no meaning.

"One of them was here," I said. "Looking at the Pattern."

"They have some interest in us and our doings. They thrive on other people's discord, I think. I sent you here to make sure they did not destroy the Pattern . . . or change it subtly to our disadvantage."

"Can they do that?"

"Possibly. Yes. I suspect they changed the last Pattern, but subtly, trying to fix it. They did not succeed, however."

I stared at the Pattern. What powers they must possess, if they could do as much as Dad said. Changing the Pattern seemed impossible.

Then I remembered the spikard and pulled it from my pouch. It grew warm in my hand, and I fought a sudden impulse to put it on. It *wanted* me to wear it.

"Not now," I said. "Settle down."

The urge passed.

"Where did you get that?" Dad asked, eyes widening.

"Ish gave it to me. He was the one here."

"Give it to me." Dad stuck out his hand.

I started to hand it over, but hesitated. The ring had grown warm in my hand. I had to fight an impulse to put it on again. It *really* didn't want to go to Dad.

"It's not meant for you," I said. "They gave it to me for a

reason."

Happy now? I mentally asked it. I put it back with my Trumps.

Dad sighed, but nodded. "Of course. I understand. Take care of it, my boy. A spikard is a precious gift. Perhaps even . . ."

"What?"

"Perhaps invaluable against Chaos. I half remember something about them. Something I read or heard a long, long time ago . . . something about the Feynim and their war against Chaos . . ."

"They fought Chaos?" I gasped.

"It was a very long time ago. So long that no direct written records of the war survive."

"What happened?"

"I am not sure. All I know is that Chaos lost. The Feynim drove King Ythoc and his army from their lands, never to return. I think they used spikards for . . . something in the battle. A barrier?" He shook his head. "I cannot remember."

"Perhaps Freda will know," I suggested. If my spikard could help defeat King Uthor, I would do whatever was necessary to master its powers.

"What do you know about spikards? What can they do?"

"Oh, I know a little of them. They have many uses. And many forms. I have handled two spikards over the years, one in the shape of a sword, one in the shape of a woman's necklace. They are centers of power . . . an older power than those born of Chaos know and use. I have heard they can keep you young, make you stronger, and help make spells more powerful. Their owners may draw on them for strength when they need it most."

"Then it's a good thing."

"Generally, yes."

"Is it like the Logrus? Or the Pattern?"

"Not really." He pulled out a Trump of his own. It showed the mountain where Amber Castle was being built. "Come, we must get back. The castle will not build itself."

"Don't change the subject. Is it intelligent?" I had to know more. "Can it control me? It seemed to be trying to communicate with me —"

"Did you put it on?"

"Yes. But only for a minute."

"Hmm. Sometimes it's safer not to know."

He raised his Trump again, but I caught his arm.

"That's not an answer. Stop hiding things from me! This is *my* world, Dad. *My* universe. *My* Pattern. It's all part of *me*, and I'm part of it. You may have drawn the Pattern, but you don't have the same connection to it. If I'm going to protect it, I need to know what's going on. I want the truth . . . about everything. Let's start with spikards."

"The truth . . ." He chuckled. "You would not believe me if I told you."

"Try it!"

"Suhuy was right. All this —" A sweep of the arm took in the Pattern and all the Shadows it created. "This is but a game, and we are all pawns. Sometimes players make moves that we cannot see and cannot comprehend. Giving you a spikard . . ." He shrugged. "It changes the powers on the board. Just a slight shift of power toward us . . . toward *you*. Now it is another's turn to play."

I snorted. "Let me guess — you're one of the Kindred, like Suhuy."

He threw back his head and laughed. "No. I recognize truth when I see it, though, as should you. If I choose not to play, if I choose to leave the board and escape my destiny, it is *my* decision — for good or ill!"

"You make the game sound inevitable."

He spread his hands. "A pawn may still aspire to greatness."

I shook my head. I felt like a pawn, all right — but *his* pawn, not some greater power's. He had lied to me so often now, I couldn't separate facts from his flights of fantasy. For all I knew, Ish and his kind might be cousins on my mother's side. Maybe *they* were unicorns, too. How would I know?

After a moment's thought, I said, "I don't mind playing. I want to win. I *will* win. But it helps to know what the rules are, Dad. Help me understand."

"Well said."

"Go on, then." I folded my arms stubbornly.

Smiling, he shook his head. "No one tells us the rules. We must discover them as we go."

Of course, another evasion. Why wasn't I surprised?

I decided to try another tack. I said, "So . . . if we are the pawns . . . who are the players? The Feynim?"

"If we are pawns, they are knights."

"And Chaos?"

He chuckled. "The gameboard, perhaps. Or perhaps one small

square . . ."

"You *know* I'm not happy with that answer."

"It is the only one I have."

TWENTY

hen we returned to camp, I just stood and stared in amazement. The changes were nothing short of miraculous. An army of stonemasons, carpenters, and other workmen must have descended on Amber during our brief absence — scaffolding had been built along the outer walls, and derricks had already begun moving huge blocks of stone into place. Inside the walls, one wing of the castle had gone up. Dozens of workers on the roof installed red slate shingles.

"The king! The king!" a voice cried.

Work halted as hundreds of workmen turned and craned to see me. They cheered. I gave an uneasy wave.

A moment later, Aber and Freda came running through the opening where the front gates would go. They raced down the winding dirt road to us. Freda gave me a huge hug. She had begun to cry. Grinning, Aber pounded me on the back.

"About time!" he cried. "Where have you been?"

"All this —" I waved at the castle. "How did you do it?"

"Hard work." He shook his head. "More of it than I've ever done before."

Freda let go of me and stood back. "Welcome back," she said. "Where did you find him, Father?"

I looked at the two of them. "Why are you making such a fuss? I've only been gone an hour!"

"An hour!" Aber laughed. "Oberon — you've been gone for *four months!*"

"Impossible!"

"The Feynim," Dad murmured. "I had no idea . . ."

Freda shuddered. "You did not make a bargain with those *creatures —*" she began.

"No. They refused to help us," I said.

"Good. We want nothing to do with them."

"Tell me — what has happened here?" I stared again at the castle. "All of this, and so fast!"

"Believe it or not," Aber said proudly, "we are actually three days *ahead* of schedule. Now that you are back, things should go more smoothly."

I didn't like the sound of that. "What do you mean?"

"There have been some problems," he admitted. "Come inside. I'll show you around and tell you all about it."

Freda nodded. "Go on, Oberon. I have a few matters to discuss with Father."

"Very well." I looked at Aber. "Lead on. I want to see and hear about everything I've missed."

As soon as we were out of earshot, my brother's voice dropped to a conspiratorial whisper. "Blaise is gone."

"What! Where?"

"I don't know. She disappeared one night. Just up and vanished. She took all of her possessions with her . . . I'm not sure if she went back to Chaos or is hiding in one of the Shadows."

I sighed. "I can't believe it."

"And," he went on gravely, "Uthor knows where we are. There have been problems . . . sabotage in the construction. All our mules and horses were poisoned one night. And dozens of workmen have been killed. It hasn't been pleasant."

"Where is Conner?"

"In the forest with the army. There have been a few skirmishes with Uthor's forces. Scouts, he thinks. Uthor is spying on us." He swallowed. "Dad and Conner have been trying to keep on top of things, but —"

"What do you mean about Dad?" I asked, puzzled. "He's been with me."

"You're crazy. I had breakfast with him twenty minutes ago!"

"What!" I stopped dead in my tracks.

"He went to his room to work, and a few minutes later he showed up outside with you. Didn't he go get you, then return with a Trump?"

"No. He was with the Feynim. I went and got *him*."

Aber swallowed. "One of them is an imposter."

I drew my sword. "Show me his room. Maybe he's still there."

"This way!"

Turning, he raced between stacks of lumber, piles of stone, and stacks of red roofing tiles. I followed him through a doorless entryway where carpenters were busily laying a plank floor, then up a partly finished staircase. He turned right at the top and entered a wide corridor. Plasterers on ladders were at work on the walls and ceiling. They gave us curious glances as we dashed past.

"Here," Aber said, stopping in front of a high closed door.

I tried the handle, but it had been locked from the inside. Taking a step back, I gave it a savage kick. It flew open with a loud crash, and I sprang in with my sword held high.

With a single glance, I took in the canopied bed, the long table littered with scrolls, blueprints, and other papers, and the wardrobe in the corner. The imposter was nowhere in sight. I stalked over to the wardrobe and threw its doors open, but aside from a few neatly folded shirts, pants, and undergarments, it lay empty.

Where could he have gone? I crossed to the window, in case he had jumped out, but saw no one below except workmen carrying stacks of lumber.

"Any idea where else he might be?" I asked.

"No. He did have a stack of Trumps, though . . . I saw him carrying them."

I nodded. "He must have heard the watchman shouting when Dad and I arrived. Probably grabbed whatever he needed, used his Trump, and fled back to Chaos."

"I can't believe he fooled Freda and me!" Aber muttered, shaking his head. Then he gave a snort. "I don't suppose mine was the real one and yours is the imposter?"

"No. Mine is the real Dworkin. I know it."

We regarded each other soberly for a moment. Then I remembered the Feynim, my spikard-ring, and all the questions Dad hadn't been willing or able to answer. Maybe my brother could help.

"Can you tell me anything about the Feynim?" I asked him.

"Not much." He frowned. "Nobody has heard from them in generations, not since they mopped the floor with King Ythoc. They're mostly legends now . . . bogeymen to scare little children. How did Dad get in touch with them, anyway?"

"I don't know. They seemed interested in the Pattern."

He nodded slowly. "That makes sense. They would be interested in a new primal power."

"Do you mean the Pattern?"

"Yes. They were interested in the Logrus . . . that's what led to the fight with King Ythoc. They wanted to see it. He refused and invaded their lands. Ten years of fighting followed."

"Dad let them see the Pattern."

"Probably a wise move." He frowned. "I wonder if they ever did see the Logrus . . ."

"Why would they be interested?"

"Who knows. It's not like they need it — they have their Keye, of course."

"Keye?"

"You know — like the old nursery rhyme. 'What turns no lock but opens all doors? The Feynim Keye of course . . .'" His voice trailed off.

"I've never heard that before," I said.

"It's just nonsense for kids." He shrugged. "A grain of truth wrapped in sugar and rhyme."

We spent an hour searching the castle and its surrounding lands, but found no trace of the fake Dworkin. I wasn't surprised; he must have returned to Chaos and made his report to King Uthor by now. Every plan and word and deed made in the castle over the last four months would now be known in Chaos.

Angry and sick at heart, I called Conner through his Trump and brought him back immediately. Four months had changed him enormously. No longer thin and weak from starvation, he had filled out with new muscle and sported a short brown beard, shoulder-length hair, and a sun-bronzed face. He had assumed command of the army and begun setting up our defenses — which included hourly patrols along all the natural borders surrounding Amber, a line of guardposts, and cutting several roads for supplying troops. All in all, a good start.

"It's nice to have you back," he said, sipping the wine I poured for him. "I don't want to be king."

"King?"

"Dad — the imposter, I mean — kept telling me that you weren't coming back. That I had to take the crown for myself."

I chuckled. "I'm glad you didn't! It's only been a few hours for me since I left. The changes everywhere . . ." I shook my head. "I'm impressed. Everyone seems to have pitched in."

"Except Blaise. She never liked it here." He made a face. "We're better off without her."

"Am I the only one who likes her?" I said with a laugh.

"I think so!"

I shook my head, remembering the trouble she had in getting used to this Shadow. Wherever she was, I wished her well.

After a few more pleasantries had been exchanged, Conner continued telling Dad and me about our new army. It numbered just over ten thousand so far, with most of them stationed along the forest.

"I don't think we will have much longer to wait before Uthor acts," Conner said. "My men have run across his scouts half a dozen times so far."

"Did you question them?" I asked.

"They fought to the death."

"I am surprised Uthor has waited this long," Dad said. "It is not like him."

"There must be a reason." I chewed my lower lip thoughtfully. "Will it be an open attack? Like the one in Juniper?"

"A thousand time worse," Dad said. "That one was designed to look like a minor personal vendetta, carried out against me personally by a single Lord of Chaos. This time we will face an attack from the throne, with the full force of Chaos behind it."

"Then we will need fighters," I said.

"A lot more of them," Conner agreed. "A hundred thousand couldn't hold Juniper. Must we have a million? Ten million?"

"We will raise as many as we need," I said grimly. "In that, we have an advantage over Chaos. We can recruit from all the Shadows we want, and quickly."

Dad said, "True . . ."

I turned to Conner. "Is there someone you can leave in charge of the army for a few days? I need you off in Shadow recruiting more soldiers, too."

He nodded. "I have several lieutenants I trust."

"Good. Assign one to the castle and one to the borders."

"I will go, too," Dad said. "And I will take Freda with me."

"Freda?"

"She can be quite persuasive."

"All right. We need all the help we can get."

"What about Aber?" Conner asked.

I frowned. "Someone must stay here to supervise the workers. Fighting isn't to his taste or talents, anyway. He wouldn't know what to look for in an army."

Half an hour later, I walked alone toward the forest, away from the castle, letting my imagination soar. A hint of mauve in the leaves, a twist of the trail, and the world began to flow and change around me. Taller trees. Oaks giving way to pines. A rocky ground. And people . . . most especially people.

Each new element I introduced to the landscape brought me closer to my goal. I kept my destination firmly in mind . . . a land of beautiful fields, clear skies, and matchless warrior-priests, who worshipped me as a god. If such a place existed in Shadow, I would find it.

The forest trail opened onto a road made of jet-black stone. As I walked over a hill, fields of wheat and rye spread out before me as far as I could see, worked by thousands of slaves from conquered nations. Overhead, an eagle soared, its voice raucous.

A pair of golden chariots pulled by high-stepping black horses sped toward me. Two men stood inside each chariot, their long moustaches and golden hair whipping behind them.

I paused in the middle of the road, hands on my hips, waiting patiently. The large yellow sun warmed my back. Scents of thyme and wild lavender rode the breeze. This was a pleasant Shadow; I wouldn't have minded living here.

The two carriages skidded to a halt ten paces from where I stood. Four men — one old, three young, all dressed in beautiful golden armor — leaped to the ground and knelt before me.

They had to be King Olam and his three sons. I knew all their names, just as I knew the history of their world. It had come into my mind, and I had sought it out, following a path through Shadows until everything matched my vision.

Thus had I come to the Kingdom of Ceyoldar . . . where millions worshipped a warrior-god named Oberon who happened to look just like me.

"Rise, Aslom," I said, trying to sound godlike. My voice hung in the air, low and powerful. "I am Oberon, returned to lead my chosen people to glory!"

Aslom stood slowly, scarcely daring to gaze upon my face. He looked every day of his fifty-five years. Although decades spent outdoors on military campaign had creased and weathered his face, his eyes spoke of a pleasant temper and a keen intellect. The broken nose and long white scars on his hands and along his left cheek and jawline spoke of battles fought through the years. He was the greatest king and warrior his people had ever known.

"Most exalted Oberon, Lord of Light, Shaper of Dreams!" King Aslom cried, trembling slightly with awe and fear. "Our lives are yours! Command us, I beg you! We live to serve you!"

I gazed beyond him to the three younger men still kneeling in the road with their eyes respectfully downcast. Only the youngest dared to cast wondering glances at me when he thought my attention lay elsewhere. They shared his sharp-hewn features, but few of his battle-scars. Give them time . . .

"You brought your sons," I said, smiling.

"All is as the prophecy said, Lord Oberon!"

"All?" I asked. This would be the test. "Where is your fourth son, King Aslom?"

"You must tell me, Lord!"

The sharp twang of a bowstring sounded behind me. I had known it was coming, but it still surprised me. All gods needed to be tested now and again to prove their divinity. An arrow in the back would be my test.

I whirled, arms a blur, turning faster than any mere man could ever move. Time seemed to be slowing down as I focused on the arrow heading straight for me. It whistled faintly as it flew, a black shaft with black fletching, its barbed arrowhead tipped in gold. How fitting for a god.

I snatched it from the air before it could strike me and continued my pirouette. I wound up facing King Aslom again. He gaped, eyes wide, hardly able to believe what he had just seen. A miracle to them . . . a trick of speed and coordination for me, as easy as catching a ball.

Then fear began to replace joy in his expression. I *was* the god, and on his order, his son had just tried to kill me. What would I do? What punishment fit this crime?

"A fair shot, but it will take far more than an arrow to kill me," I said easily, letting a note of amusement creep into my voice. Better to treat it as a joke and let him off the hook. Tightening my fist, I snapped the arrow in half, then tossed it casually at his feet. "Bring forth your first-born son," I continued. "I want to look upon him."

"Iankos!" cried King Aslom. "Join us!"

Still pale, Aslom knelt again and bowed his head. He dared not look at my face — I couldn't blame him for his shame. Things were going even better than I had hoped.

Iankos — a lanky version of his father — trotted out from the bushes behind me and joined his brother, kneeling with eyes turned down.

"Command us, Lord Oberon!" King Aslom cried. "How may we serve you?"

His sons looked startled when I called each by name: "Iankos. Eitheon. Lymnos. Haetor. Stand and let me look upon your faces."

They rose slowly, the three eldest daring now to gaze upon me with awe and wonder. The youngest, Haetor, had a curious expression somewhere between suspicion and disbelief. There had to be an unbeliever in every family, after all. Despite my trick with the arrow, he still had doubts. If I could convince him, they would all be won to my cause.

"You do not believe the prophecies about me," I said to Haetor, smiling. "It is good to be skeptical."

"Lord Oberon!" he protested. "I do believe!"

"You want to test me," I said. I drew my sword in a smooth motion. "Do not protest. I see it in your heart."

"Most exalted one —" he began uncertainly.

"Draw your blade, Haetor," I said in a kindly voice. "You will not be satisfied until you have tried your steel against mine. This I know."

King Aslom threw himself at my feet. "Spare him, Most Revered Oberon!" he gasped, eyes desperate. "He is young and rash!"

Aslom's other sons shifted unhappily. I glanced at them and smiled. Had their father commanded, I knew they would have drawn their swords to protect Haetor from me . . . even at the cost of their own lives. Such loyalty would serve me well against Chaos.

"Be at ease, good King Aslom," I said softly, so only he could hear. Haetor must be his favorite, I decided. I would play to his emotions. "Your son is not destined to die this day, but he must learn his place if he is to serve me. I have important plans for his sword. In years to come, he will become my strong right hand. As will you. I have need of you all."

"Thank you!" Aslom whispered. "Thank you!"

I looked at Haetor and motioned him forward. The boy swallowed audibly. Clearly he was having second thoughts about facing a man who might be a god.

"Draw your sword," I told him. "Would you slay me this day?"

Haetor knelt suddenly, blushing furiously. "Forgive me, Most Exalted Oberon!" he cried.

"Rise!" I said sharply. "Draw, Haetor! Show me what a warrior-prince can do! Or are you a coward, ashamed of your meager talents?"

He climbed to his feet. Then, in a single fluid movement, he drew his sword and attacked.

I had wanted a race of warriors. I had deliberately sought out a Shadow where the strongest, fastest, bravest swordsmen lived . . . where they worshipped me as a god. But I never imagined how fast Haetor would move — or how brilliant a natural swordsman he might be. With the supple grace of a dancer, he launched a blistering attack that would have overwhelmed lesser men. I fought defensively, slowly giving ground before him, watching the darting tip of his blade for an opening. It moved like a hummingbird, left and right, up and down, testing my defenses and my speed. Other than my father, I had never seen a finer fighter. His enthusiasm, finesse, and technique could not be faulted.

But neither could mine. For every move he made, I had a counter. If his sword hummed with speed, mine sang. If his footwork dazzled, mine shone brighter than the sun. We fought differently, but the match was still uneven.

Finally, I saw the faintest of hesitations. His sword turned slightly out of position following my riposte, and his recovery had a second's hesitation. I knew, then, that his arm had grown tired.

I leaped at him. Sparks flew as steel rang on steel. I advanced, falling into a deadly rhythm — thrust, thrust, lunge — thrust, thrust, lunge. He fell back, and his face showed sudden alarm.

Then, with a twist of my wrist, I ripped the sword from his hand through sheer strength of muscle. It went sailing through the air and landed point-down in the field to our left. Slowly, it rocked back and forth.

Haetor gazed dumbly after it, clutching his right hand to his chest. Then he faced me bravely, standing tall as he waited unflinchingly for my death-blow.

Swifter than he could follow, I dropped my own sword and closed with him. My left hand seized his throat while my right hand grabbed his armored stomach. Like a child lifting a doll, I raised him over my head.

"Listen well, princeling," I said softly, so only he could hear. "I can crush the life from your throat, or pluck your heart from your chest as easily as you can pick an apple from a tree. Your life is mine to give or take. Do you understand what that means?"

"Y-yes, Lord Oberon!" he whispered. His face had gone pale.

"Gods," I continued, voice low, eyes narrowing, "are quite hard to kill. Remember that."

He began to shake with fear. I saw belief in his eyes . . . and sheer terror as he realized suddenly life and death lay solely in my hands. I had but to close my fist and his throat would be crushed. I had but to press my fingers another few inch into his chest and his heart would fail.

I tossed him twenty feet, into his brothers' arms. They staggered, but caught him and set him down. As he reeled dizzily, I threw back my head and laughed.

"You will do well, young Haetor!" I said. That sounded like something a god would say to a loyal subject. "I have seen your future, and it is glorious!" I wished it were true. What *did* his future hold?

Haetor fell to his knees before me. "I swear to serve you for the rest of my life, Lord Oberon. Command me. I am yours!"

"Retrieve your sword," I said. "We must all return to the city.

Aslom?" I faced his father again.

"Yes, Lord Oberon?" He still looked greatly relieved that I had spared his youngest son.

"Tonight we will celebrate my arrival. Tomorrow you will begin gathering in your armies."

"You will lead us into battle?" he cried eagerly.

"Yes!"

"Against what foe?"

"The hell-creatures of Chaos!"

"Against the hell-creatures!" he shouted. His sons drew their swords and raised them, taking up the cry: *"Against the hell-creatures! Against the hell-creatures of Chaos!"*

TWENTY-ONE

*-ber-on, O-ber-on, O-ber-on!"* chanted the tens of thousands of men, women, and children jamming the streets of Ceyoldar. People had been streaming into the city day and night as word spread of my arrival. They had been calling my name for hours once it became known I was staying in the palace.

When I finally made my appearance with the dawning sun, a deafening cheer went up. They must have recognized me from the thousands of statues decorating the city — excellent likenesses for the most part, if I did say so myself. Today I wore magnificent gold-plated armor, beautiful but impractical, which the priests had provided for this day's ceremonies. A beaming King Aslom, dressed in shining silver armor and wearing his crown instead of a helmet, escorted me to the main courtyard. His four sons and a bevy of white-robed Priests of Oberon trailed after us.

The king and I stepped up into a waiting pair of golden chariots pulled by white horses, taking our places behind drivers in simple white tunics. At a signal from the king, the palace gates opened, the drivers clicked to their horses, and we rolled out slowly and majestically into the cobbled streets of Ceyoldar.

Footmen with staffs ranged ahead, calling warnings, making

sure the crowds gave way. They needn't have bothered; everyone fell back before me, awe and wonder in their faces. It disconcerted me a bit, but I made sure not to show it. After all, these would be my troops when we faced Uthor's army.

"*O-ber-on, O-ber-on, O-ber-on!*"

As we passed, the crowds dropped to their knees, bowing their heads. Still they called my name.

Slowly and majestically, side by side, our chariots steered through the packed streets. We headed straight for the center of the city. There, half a mile ahead, rose the towering Temple of Oberon — a gigantic pyramid covered in gleaming white marble. Its outside walls consisted of a series of steps gradually ascending toward a flat top. I had never seen anything so large or imposing.

"*O-ber-on, O-ber-on, O-ber-on!*"

Trying my best to look godlike, I neither waved nor smiled. I did, however, nod approvingly now and again. That seemed to meet everyone's expectations.

When we rolled to a stop before the pyramid, I stepped down. Children began to scatter white rose petals before me. A choir began a solemn hymn in my honor.

Silently, I began to climb the steplike white marble sides of the pyramid, flanked by King Aslom and his sons, followed by the high priests. The sun warmed my back; a cool breeze swept in from the south. A few birds soared overhead, their cries lost in the almost deafening roar from behind and below me.

"*O-ber-on, O-ber-on, O-ber-on!*" the crowds continued to chant. "*O-ber-on, O-ber-on, O-ber-on!*"

It seemed to take forever, but I finally reached the top of the pyr-amid — a square area perhaps thirty feet on each side. A golden throne sat waiting for me at the edge, allowing everyone below to see me. At least it had a cushioned seat, I saw with a twinge of good humor — someone had given at least a little thought to his god's holy posterior.

Turning, I raised my arms. Instantly the crowd hushed. From this height, I gazed across the whole of the city, from the distant riverfront wharves to my left to the sprawling palace behind its whitewashed walls straight ahead to the crowded tenements on the right.

Though I knew many thousands of men, women, and children had assembled to see me, I was unprepared for the sheer numbers of them. People jammed every street as far as I could see, and they packed rooftops, windows, and balconies. I had never seen so many at one time before . . . there had to be hundreds of thousands of them.

I cleared my throat, suddenly nervous. It was one thing to ad-dress troops before a battle. It was quite another to talk to so many strangers, all of whom believed I was their god.

"Good people of Ceyoldar!" I called.

Criers took up my words, spreading them quickly across the whole of the city.

"I am Oberon!" I told them. "I am here to lead you into battle on a great cause! . . . We must defeat the foul hell-creatures of Chaos, who even now are preparing to march against Ceyoldar! . . . If they prevail, all who live in this city and in these lands will be slaughtered! . . . From the youngest babe to the oldest crone, none will be spared the sword! I say to you now . . . to all able-bodied men . . . go home and get your weapons! . . . We march at dawn tomorrow! . . . *We will fight the hell-creatures, and we will prevail!"*

Hundreds of thousands of voices began to cheer. The sound struck me like a physical blow. I raised my arms triumphantly, then sat back in my throne.

Girls in white robes appeared from somewhere within the pyramid, and they began to fan me with the broad green leaves of some native plant. Others approached with trays of delicately spiced meats and succulent fruits.

I waved them away. Stretching out my legs, I half closed my eyes, basking in the morning sun. This was the good life, indeed. The cushion felt just right.

That night, in the palatial suite King Aslom gave up for my use, I lay back panting and spent for the moment. A dozen beautiful naked women reached out to caress and massage me. Ah, the powers of a god! If only I had the time to properly enjoy this world! If not for the coming fight with Uthor's forces, it would have been easy to dally here, taking my pleasures and reveling in my new-found position. People didn't worship me nearly enough back home. Especially beautiful and willing women like these. . . .

Still, duty called. It had been far too long since I had talked with Freda and Dad. Best to check in with them in case something important had happened.

"Leave me now," I said with a reluctant sigh.

"Great Oberon . . ." purred Kelionasha, whose nymphlike plea- sures I had enjoyed twice already that night. She seemed to sense my approval. Her small, delicate breasts brushed gently across my chest as she trailed kisses up my neck, sending a new shiver of delight through me. "Have we displeased you?"

"Not at all." I smiled and traced the line of her jaw with one finger. "The business of a god calls me now. I must tend to it."

"Can it not wait?" Her tongue traced a light pattern through the hairs of my chest, around my nipples, and then strayed lower. Her hands began to caress and stroke gently. As I shuddered with pleasure more of these beautiful women reached out, a dozen hands mas- saging scented oils into my shoulders, neck, and legs.

As Kelionasha swung around and straddled me, I pushed all thoughts of Amber from my mind. Another hour wouldn't matter one way or another.

"For you," I whispered, pulling her mouth down to mine, her long black hair falling in a cascade across my face, "even the gods will wait."

Hours later, completely drained, I managed to persuade the still more-than-eager women that I needed them to leave. It was a struggle. They didn't want to go, and somewhere deep inside, I very much wanted them to stay.

Finally, half pouting, they rose and began to file from the room, taking an assortment of veils, incense sticks, aphrodisiacs, perfumes, and bottles of scented oils. Kelionasha lingered at the door, her lovely eyes lingering on my face.

"Shall we return later?" she asked in that sultry voice.

I laughed. "Even gods need to rest. But maybe, just you, in an hour . . ."

She smiled and darted off.

Alone now, I pulled out my deck of Trumps, flipped through it quickly, and pulled out Aber's card. I raised it and concentrated on the image, and almost instantly I reached him.

"Oberon!" he said, sounding altogether too cheerful for his own good. He had been sitting at a worktable painting a new Trump. "You look exhausted. How are things going with the army?"

"I *am* tired. But things are going well here." Briefly I told him of the progress I had made in raising an army in Ceyoldar. "It looks like I'll be bringing back tens of thousands of warriors. What's happening there?"

"The weirdest thing," he said, shaking his head. "Dad came back without any troops and without Freda. He wouldn't tell me what happened, except that he ran into problems. He retired to his workshop."

"Without Freda?" Mental alarms went off. This definitely sounded like trouble. "Where is she? Did you contact her?"

He shrugged helplessly. "I tried, but couldn't reach her. I don't know if she's busy, or . . ."

Uneasy now, I began to pace. "What else did Dad do?" I asked. "Could he have been a spy from Chaos? A shape-shifter, perhaps?"

Aber hesitated. "No . . . I'm fairly certain it was Dad."

"How?"

"He, er, went out of his way to insult me. Called me a layabout and a worthless piece of horseflesh. Among other things."

I chuckled and relaxed a bit. That did sound like our father.

Aber continued, "But then he asked where you were — he didn't seem to remember you all left yesterday. Like I said, it was strange. He seemed confused, but he wouldn't admit it. I thought his concussion might be bothering him again, or . . ."

I nodded thoughtfully. "Hmm. But with an imposter running around, we must be careful. Is he still there?"

"I left him in his workshop fifteen minutes ago."

"What was he doing?"

"Damned if I know. I didn't feel like hanging around and getting insulted, so I left."

I frowned as another possibility occurred to me. "Maybe you should get Doc Hand again . . ."

He shrugged. "If you ask me, Dad could use a few *more* blows to the head. Maybe it would knock some manners into him."

"Okay. Keep an eye on him. I'm going to try to reach Freda. Maybe she knows what happened to him."

"All right. For all we know, his mind started to go again, so she sent him home."

I nodded. "Do me a favor — post a guard on his workshop. Watch him. Let me know if he tries to leave Amber."

"Okay."

I covered his card with my hand, breaking our connection. Then I took out Freda's card and concentrated on it. It took her a moment to answer. She was somewhere in near darkness; I had to squint to make out her tired-looking face.

"What is it, Oberon?" She sounded half asleep. "It's past midnight here."

"What happened to Dad?" I asked. "Did you send him home?"

"What are you talking about?" She blinked and yawned. "I didn't send him anywhere."

"I just talked to Aber. He says Dad just got back to Amber, and he's acting strangely. He can't remember anything."

"Impossible. Wait a moment." She rose, turned up an oil lamp, and went into the hall in her dressing gown, carrying the Trump. "We are both staying in a comfortable inn. Dad should still be in the next room."

I waited impatiently while she pounded on his door. Then Dad whipped it open, bare sword in hand. He had a wild look in his eye. Leaning out, he glanced up and down the hallway.

"What's wrong?" he demanded.

"Oberon says you just returned to Amber," she told him. "Have you left your room tonight?"

"Certainly not!"

To Freda, I said, "Get back to Amber, both of you. See if you can find that imposter and hold him. I'll return tomorrow morning with troops . . . a lot of them."

She nodded curtly. "I will let you know if we catch him," she said. Then she broke the connection.

I put her Trump down and began to pace again. It seemed Uthor and his spies knew a lot about us . . . enough to fool Aber, anyway. Showing up and heaping abuse on him appeared to have been exactly the right thing to do.

Well, it wouldn't work for long. Never mind Kelionasha — I had to get ready to leave Ceyoldar.

At dawn, I planned to be on the road to Amber.

TWENTY-TWO

hen Freda called me again an hour later, I was on the road leading King Aslom's forces down out of the city. I spurred my horse and rode twenty feet ahead so I could talk to her privately.

"We have him!" she announced. "Father caught him in his room. He is bound now, magically and physically."

I felt a rush of excitement. "Can you hold him there until I get back?"

"I think so. He can do no harm where he is."

"Good. I have a hundred thousand warriors with me, give or take a few thousand. Tell Aber to start laying in supplies. Since Uthor knows where we are anyway, he might as well use the Logrus to save time."

"Excellent. I will let him know."

I took me two days to lead King Aslom's forces back to Amber. It was neither terribly far nor a hard march; but the sheer logistics of getting so many people up and moving at the same time took far longer than I would have expected. My own experiences in Ilerium, as one of King Elnar's lieutenants, proved less than adequate to the task. Elnar's army had numbered in the low thousands, and I had commanded scarcely a hundred and fifty men. Here I commanded nearly a thousand times as many.

Finally, though, the horses and wagons and war-chariots and miles-long lines of infantrymen all came within sight of the forest. A road had been cut straight through to the castle — visible from here only as a faint smudge on a distant mountainside — and we were quickly challenged by a squad of armed men.

I rode forward to greet them.

"It's the king!" one, then another, began to mutter. Quickly they knelt, heads bowed.

"Rise," I said, reigning in my stallion. "You must be vigilant. We caught an imposter at the castle pretending to be my father, Lord Dworkin, two days ago. Challenge everyone who passes, whether you know them or not."

"Yes, Your Highness!"

"You —" I pointed at a sergeant. "What's your name?"

"M-Mevill, Sire!"

"I must go ahead. You will take my horse and escort King Aslom and his men to Castle Amber."

"Y-yes, Sire!"

I rode back to King Aslom and his sons, who had drawn to a halt in their golden war-chariots, and apprised them of my plans. They nodded agreeably. After all, who were they to question the great Oberon?

Dismounting, I turned my horse over to Sergeant Mevill, pulled out a Trump of the caste's courtyard, and stepped through. It must have been quite a sight for Aslom and his sons — more proof, if any were needed, that I was a god.

I found Freda and Dad in the main hall. They hurried over to greet me.

"Is that imposter still here?" I asked.

"Yes," Dad said. "He is trapped in my room. We have been waiting for you before questioning him."

"Good. Let's have a look at him."

They led me upstairs, back to the room whose door I had kicked open three days before. The door hadn't been repaired yet and still hung open.

Inside, someone who looked just like my father sat on the edge of the canopied bed. He had bitten his thumb and was dribbling a thin line of blood slowly onto the floorboards . . . trying to draw a Trump, by the looks of things. Only it wasn't working. I felt no power coming from the spattered red lines.

He looked up, saw me, and said: "By the pricking of my thumbs, something wicked this way comes."

"Very funny," I said. I turned to Freda. "Do you recognize that picture?"

She stared at it, tilting her head slightly. "Yes. It is the Third Tower. It lies well beyond the Courts of Chaos."

"What is it?"

"A place of ancient power and prophecy."

"Prophecy?" That sounded interesting.

She nodded. "Visions sometimes come to those who meditate there. There are thousands of them recorded in the Great Record. Perhaps he knows of a prophecy concerning us, or Amber, and wishes to return and consult it."

The fake Dworkin rose and crossed to the doorway, gazing out at us. Raising one hand, he touched the space where the door would have been, but seemed to run into an invisible barrier.

"He cannot get out," Dad said. "Spells have sealed the room."

"Release me," the imposter said.

"Why? So you can report back to King Uthor?"

"I do not serve Uthor."

"Who, then? Lord Zon?"

"No."

"Or . . . Suhuy?"

He did not reply this time. I raised my eyebrows.

"So it's Suhuy, then."

"Release me, brother."

"And it's 'brother' now?"

Freda gasped then and clutched my arm. "No . . . Oberon! They have done something to him — this is Fenn!"

I stared at him. Stared hard. "Fenn?

"Yes, brother. You must let me go. Please."

Swallowing, I looked at Dad, who shook his head faintly. I motioned with my head to one side, and we retreated up the hall to where he couldn't hear us.

"Fenn . . ." Freda whispered. "How horrible."

"I think he looks rather handsome," Dad said with a hint of a smile. "Never better, in fact."

She glared. "This is not a time for jests!"

"At least we know how he managed to fool you and Aber," I said to her. "Fenn would know what to say and exactly how to say it convincingly. Now comes the big question . . . what do we do with him?"

"He must have his old appearance restored, of course," I said. "Dad . . . is that something you can do?"

"I am not sure."

"Why is Suhuy sending spies?" Freda asked. "As Keeper of the Logrus, he should not be involving himself in politics."

"Tell *him* that," I said. "If returning Conner to us doesn't count as playing politics, what does? Unless he wants to play on both sides . . . by secretly helping us *and* King Uthor, wouldn't he keep everyone's favor?"

"Possibly," Dad said.

"What matters with Fenn is his motivation," I said. "If he came unwillingly, forced by Suhuy to do his bidding, perhaps he can be freed of whatever compulsion is upon him. If he's a willing spy, though . . ."

They both nodded. Having decided, we returned to Fenn and peered in at him. He had returned to his seat on the bed.

"Well?" he demanded.

"We don't know what to do with you," I said.

"Let me go. I must return to my master."

"Or . . . ?"

"Or I will die." He said it in such a matter-of-fact voice that I knew he believed it.

I swallowed. "How?"

"He gave me a slow poison. I must return each week to make my report and take a dose of the antidote. If I miss one week, I become weak. If I miss two weeks, I become violently ill. If I miss three weeks . . ." He shrugged. "So, you can see I have no choice."

"How long has it been?" I asked.

"Four days."

Grimly, I turned to our father. If anyone could help Fenn, he could.

I said, "You have two weeks to find a cure. Don't let him out until he's well or dead."

He nodded gravely. "Yes, Oberon."

Without another word to Fenn, I went to find Aber. We still had to prepare for a hundred thousand visitors.

TWENTY-THREE

ate that night, as I lay in bed unable to sleep, I held the spikard and stared at it. The ruby glinted in the dimness. Somehow it reminded me of the jewel around the unicorn's neck.

Dad didn't seem to think it was dangerous. And yet . . . somehow, it made me uneasy.

As sleep stole upon me, I set it on the table beside the bed and shut my eyes. I would try to find out more about it in the morning.

I slept.

Sometime later, I felt a sharp pain on my finger and came awake. It was the ring, I realized. It had tightened painfully for a second, then released me. How had it gotten on my finger?

It tightened again. *A warning –*

I kept my breathing low and even, but strained every sense. A rustle near the door made the hair on the back of my neck bristle. Someone had entered my room.

Slowly I eased my hand under my pillow, careful to make no sound, and curled my fingers around the hilt of a long-bladed knife. Then, in one quick movement, I sat up and threw it.

A satisfyingly loud *thunk* reached my ears as it struck something meaty near the door, then came a louder *thump* as a body hit the floor.

Folding my hands together, I concentrated on light, shaping a ball with my thoughts while holding the Pattern in my mind. When I opened them, a brightly glowing sphere drifted toward the ceiling.

A creature dressed all in black lay on the floor by my door, the hilt of my knife jutting from one eye. I rose, dressed calmly, and pulled on my boots. Then I went over to investigate.

Clearly it was a creature of Chaos. Horns, scaled skin, pointed yellow teeth, red eyes, and thick gray-green blood . . . akin to the hell-creatures that had plagued my life for so long.

The blades of its knives had been painted with a greenish substance. Poison? Undoubtedly. Someone wanted me dead. Someone in my very own house. No creature like this one could have gotten past the sentries at the castle doors or on patrol atop the walls. Which meant someone with the ability to use the Pattern or the Logrus had brought it here.

I searched its clothes, felt something hard and cold, and drew out a pair of Trumps. The first showed the Courts of Chaos as seen from an open square. Buildings leaned at odd angles and strange colors filled the sky. I didn't look at it long; I didn't want the scene to come alive. The second Trump showed the hallway outside my door.

So . . . he had come prepared. Trumps would have provided his way into Castle Amber and then his escape back home once he killed me.

It confirmed my worst suspicions.

Someone in my own family had sent him.

I studied the Trump of the hallway with greater attention. The details had been crudely done, and the brush strokes showed signs of haste, but I still sensed the raw power it contained. Whose work, though? I had seen Trumps drawn by both Aber and our father, but those had been polished works of art in comparison. Could either of them deliberately disguised his work? Or did another family member have the talents needed to make Trumps?

Fenn? It seemed possible. He had been trying to draw a Trump from his own blood. And yet . . . why would he want me dead? His master, Suhuy, seemed to want me alive and well.

Blaise? I'd never heard of her drawing Trumps. Conner? Freda? Aber? I frowned.

I had drawn a Trump myself, I remembered. Crudely drawn on a wall, it had nevertheless worked. Maybe anyone born of Chaos or the Pattern could make one, given sufficient time and motivation. I would have to ask Aber about it.

Maybe a spy from Chaos had infiltrated Amber by posing as a workman? That seemed the possible answer. He had looked around, worked on the hallway outside my room, and made the Trump at his leisure.

After dragging the body into the hallway, I shouted for the new valet Aber had gotten me. Denis came running, barefoot and dressed in his night clothes.

"Sire?" he said, staring down with horror at the body.

"Take care of this," I said, nudging it with my foot. "Be careful with the knives. They're poisoned."

"Of course. Um, Sire . . . Lady Freda asked to be informed of anything odd that happens. Should I let her know?"

"Why not? Assassins are fairly common around here." I smiled with grim amusement. Of course Freda had already begun setting up a network of spies and informants. With all the plotting in our midst, I couldn't blame her.

Without another word, I went back to bed. I didn't bother to undress or extinguish the floating ball of light; I just flopped down on top of the covers. Somehow, I had the feeling this night's events weren't quite over.

Idly, I rubbed my ring. The spikard had saved my life. How had it gotten onto my finger?

Five minutes later, a light tap sounded at my door.

"Enter!" I called, sitting up. Freda didn't waste much time.

It was Aber, though, who opened the door and stuck in his head. "You'd better come with me," he said grimly. "Freda has something to show you."

"All right." I joined him in the hall. He'd thrown on a dressing gown and from his tousled hair it looked like he'd been roused prematurely from his sleep.

"Freda, you said? Where is she?"

"Working downstairs."

He led the way to the grand hall. Torches burned in their sconces in the hallways; guards on duty by the doors to the courtyard snapped to attention, raising their pikes. I gave them a brief wave and they relaxed a bit.

Aber headed for the left wing — empty, as far as I knew. Like most of Castle Amber, the corridors here still had rough stone walls and floors made of broad wooden planks. It would be months yet before everything could be properly finished. The outside walls and fortifications took priority. Niceties like polished floorboards and paneling could wait for now.

"In here." Aber opened a small door to the right and lead the way inside.

It was a small, square room. A small lantern sat in the corner. By its flickering, uncertain light, I saw the assassin's body lying in the exact center of a large circle.

Freda, on her knees, completed the circle with a black paint-brush as I watched. Then she began writing a series of runes around the outside of the circle.

"What are you doing?" I asked with interest. I had never seen anything like this before. I studied the runes, but could not puzzle out their meaning. Something magical, I assumed.

"We must trap his spirit," she said matter-of-factly, "if we are to question him."

I raised my eyebrows. "Do you mean a ghost? The last thing I want is an assassin haunting the castle!"

"You *are* a silly boy. Stand over there until I'm ready for you. Don't smudge the circle; the line is still wet."

"Is this safe?" I asked Aber.

"Got me," he said, looking uneasily at Freda's work. "I've never seen anything like it before."

Our sister said, "We only have a few minutes left. These things must be done quickly, before the spirit departs. Pay attention and follow my instructions exactly. Everything will go as planned."

"Best listen," said Aber, hooking my arm and pulling me back.

"All right, all right."

Together we retreated to the corner with the lantern. I couldn't take offense at Freda's brusqueness; I knew she meant well. And if we really could question the assassin, so much the better.

She worked quickly. I felt a mounting suspense. If the ghost revealed who had betrayed us, it might go a long way toward turning the events in our favor.

Freda finished the last of the runes and stood. Taking a deep breath, she raised both arms toward the middle circle and the assassin's body.

"Come forth!" she cried. She clapped her hands three times. "Come forth!" she cried again. "You are bound to this place! Show yourself, spirit!"

I leaned forward expectantly. A strange glowing mist rose slowly from the assassin's body. It took shape . . . head . . . torso . . . limbs. It rushed from side to side, trying to flee, but the runes and circle formed a barrier it could not pass.

"Speak!" Freda intoned. She clapped her hands three times again. It drifted around to face her. "You are bound here! Obey me!"

The ghost bared its spectral teeth in a snarl. "Let me go . . ." it cried in a hollow voice that sent chills through me. "The darkness calls . . ."

Aber gave me a nudge. "Go on. Question it."

Freda looked pointedly in my direction. I swallowed hard and stepped forward.

"Who sent you here?" I demanded in a voice stronger than I felt.

"Abomination . . ." it wailed. Then it hurled itself in my direction, but came up short at the edge of the circle.

I stood unflinching. Freda's magic better hold; if this ghost got free, it clearly meant to do me whatever harm it still could.

"Who sent you?" I demanded again.

Hissing, it drew back.

"How do I know it will speak the truth?" I asked Freda.

"The circle holds it trapped," she said. "It cannot leave until released . . . whether that takes five minutes or five hundred years. Be persuasive."

Quite a bargaining chip. I took a deep breath and stepped closer to the edge of the circle. The ghost threw itself toward me again, and when it failed to reach me, drew back once more.

"Who sent you?" I demanded.

"Fiend!" it shouted. "Abomination!" then it began to curse me and my family for a thousand generations. Once more it flew at the boundaries of the circle, trying to escape. But Freda's magic held; it could not get away.

"Answer me!" I said.

"Let me go. . ." it wailed. *"Let me go. . ."*

"Tell me what I want to know, and I will consider it."

"No. . . I cannot. . ."

"Do you want to spend eternity here, trapped in this circle?"

It gnashed ghostly teeth but made no reply.

"Come," I said to Freda and Aber. "It won't cooperate. We'll have the room walled up in the morning." I turned toward the door.

"No!" it called. *"Wait . . ."*

I glanced over my shoulder. "Will you answer my questions?"

"Yes . . ."

"Very well." I folded my arms. "Who sent you?"

"Uthor . . . King of Chaos . . ."

I nodded slowly. I had known it would be either King Uthor or Lord Zon.

Now to find out who had betrayed us.

I said, "Who drew the Trump that brought you here?"

"I do not know . . ."

"Where did you get it?"

"From the king's own hand . . ."

Unfortunate, if true. Maybe it didn't know who had betrayed us.

I frowned. What other information might prove useful?

"Where is Uthor's army now?" I asked.

It hissed and dashed at the far edge of the circle, trying to escape. Clearly it did not want to say any more; it still held that much loyalty to its old liege.

I said sharply: "Speak! If you ever want to leave this place, tell me what I want to know!"

"I cannot . . ."

"You will! You *must!*"

It gnashed spectral teeth. Again it hurled itself against the walls of its prison, all to no avail.

"Speak!" I commanded. "This is your last chance! Where is

Uthor? Where are his men? I want to know the location of his camp!"

For a moment I thought it would refuse to answer, but finally it spoke in a low voice.

"The king is close. . . . He will be here soon. . . . He will kill you all and free me. . . ."

Aber gasped. "King Uthor left the Courts of Chaos? Is that what you're telling us?"

"Yes . . ."

I glanced at my brother. "Is that important?"

"Of course it is!" Aber said. "If the ghost is telling the truth —"

Freda said, "It *is* the truth. I feel it."

"I don't understand." I looked from one to the other. "Uthor should lead his men into battle. It's what kings do."

"You really don't understand," Aber said, his voice low and urgent. "King Uthor hasn't left the Courts in six hundred years!"

"What!" I blinked in surprise. "Why not?"

"It is the custom," Freda said. "His sons or his generals fight his battles. Only a dire emergency could possibly bring him forth."

An emergency . . . like the now-corrected Pattern casting a new set of Shadows? Like the creator of those Shadows building a new castle and fortifying it against attack?

Grimly, I smiled. This could easily turn to our advantage.

I said, "Then he's just made his first mistake."

TWENTY-FOUR

*et me go. . . !"* the ghost cried.

"One more question," I said, turning to face it again. "Where can I find Uthor's camp?"

"Far from here . . ."

"He cannot know, truly," Freda said in a quiet voice. "He is not born of the Logrus or the Pattern. He can neither walk through Shadows nor visualize Uthor's camp in relation to Amber."

"A pity." It had been worth a try, though.

"Very well," I said, giving Freda a nod. I was satisfied; I didn't think we could learn much more from it. "Set the ghost free."

"Are you sure?" Aber said softly. "Maybe we should keep it here a little while longer, just in case. You might think of another question or two. If we let it go, we won't have this chance again."

The ghost hissed angrily. *"Liars . . . !"* it cried. *"I knew you would not let me go . . . !"*

"Be silent!" I snapped. To Aber, I said, "It kept its word. I must keep mine. Freda?"

"I agree," she said.

Reaching out with the toe of her right shoe, she carefully rubbed at the edge of the circle. It took a few seconds, but when the line broke, the ghost rushed past her with a cry of joy.

Outside the circle, it hesitated and looked back at me. Slowly it turned.

"You kept your word . . ." it said.

"Yes." I folded my arms. "I always keep my word."

"I did not believe you would. . . ."

"A bargain is a bargain. Be on your way. Do not return, spirit."

Still it lingered. *"I will answer the one question you failed to ask . . ."*

Curious, I leaned closer. "What is that?"

"Your true enemy is not Uthor. . . . He spoke of you with something akin to admiration. . . ."

"Huh!" Aber said. "Murder is an odd way of showing admiration!"

I said to the ghost, "Then why did he order you to kill me?"

"Because he fears what will happen if he does not . . ."

Then, with a sigh, it faded away, gone to whatever afterlife remained.

I puzzled over those parting words. What could possibly happen to Uthor if he failed to order my death? He was the king — his wishes should have been paramount. A real threat must hang over him, something that forced him to take immediate action.

What might he fear? A rival for the throne, perhaps? Someone powerful enough to lead a revolt against him if he appeared weak or indecisive?

Lord Zon, perhaps?

I sighed. If only they saw fit to leave me alone. I had no interest in Chaos or the Logrus. I only wanted to live in peace. Everything I had done so far had been to protect myself . . . *They* kept attacking *me*, after all.

Was the Pattern really that powerful? Had it truly weakened Chaos so much that Uthor needed to move decisively against me to keep lands safe and his subjects satisfied?

We already knew Uthor had time on his side . . . months to pre-pare versus days for us in Amber. We would have to move quickly or be caught unprepared.

Freda said, "You understand the threat."

I nodded. "Yes. He will attack soon."

"You must be ready."

She held out her right hand. In it I saw a stack of Trumps, face down.

"More of your future-telling?" I asked with a laugh.

"Humor me, Oberon."

I shrugged, took the deck, shuffled it twice, and handed it back. Turning, she headed for her room . . . probably to read them in pri-vate. She knew how little I believed in predictions.

"Let me know if there's any good news!" I called after her. "I could use some about now!"

Aber said, "You shouldn't make light of her talents. She *is* a pow-erful sorceress."

"Anyone can foretell the future. The trick is getting it right."

"Futures can change, you know. That's why so many predictions don't come true. Oh! I have something for you!"

"What?"

He reached into the pouch at his belt and drew out a new Trump. The colors were bright, almost glassy. I accepted it.

"Nice. New paints?"

"I spent the morning yesterday hunting up pigments. These are nothing like the ones I used to have, but they will do."

It showed the main courtyard of the castle. Quite a nice likeness, too.

"You may have to get back here in a hurry," he explained. "This is in case Freda and I aren't around."

I grinned. "Thank you!"

"Oh, it's nothing much." He made a deprecating gesture, but seemed delighted by the praise. "My small contribution."

I added it to the stack of Trumps in my pouch, hesitated, then pulled out Dad's. Aber said nothing, but his eyes begged: *Please don't!*

"I have to," I said. "He must be told what's going on. He might be able to help in some way. Why don't you come along?"

"You know Dad can't stand me!"

"Oh, he can stand you. He just doesn't like you!"

"And that makes it worse." Sighing, Aber looked away.

I'd spoken half in jest, but I saw that it had touched a nerve. I hadn't meant to hurt him. I really needed to curb my tongue.

Quickly I added, "I really didn't mean it quite the way it sounded. I —"

"I know what you meant, Oberon!" he said. "Don't worry about it. The truth is painful sometimes, but I'll get over it. I always do. Besides, I'll have the last laugh. I plan to outlive him. Longevity is the best revenge."

I chuckled. "At least you have a plan."

Raising Dad's Trump, I concentrated on the picture. The jester slowly changed, becoming a dwarfish man dressed all in brown. He had been puttering about in the basement, in the large meeting room.

"What is it?" he demanded.

"I need to talk to you," I said. "I killed an assassin in the castle. He had a Trump."

"What!" Dworkin cried. "Are you hurt?"

"I'm fine."

He reached out for me, and I took his hand. With a quick step, I was standing in his library. The shelves were a maddening jumble of books and scrolls.

"Where did you get these?" I asked, staring.

"The Logrus."

I shook my head. Only a few weeks here, and he had already amassed a lifetime's supply of reading matter, true packrat that he was.

He chuckled. "Do not fear the Logrus, my boy. It's the arms of the thing . . ."

I gave him a puzzled look. "Arms?" Had his dementia returned?

He laughed. "Those who serve its cause. Uthor's men. Thellops. Others."

I opened my mouth, but before I could reply, someone outside began to ring a loud bell. We exchanged quick glances, then ran for the door. *What now?*

Conner burst in on us, grinning from ear to ear.

"What is it?" I demanded

"We've found Uthor's camp!"

TWENTY-FIVE

t took half an hour to mount our scouting expedition. Ten men strong, the party consisted of Conner and me, two of Conner's lieutenants, and six men from Ceyoldar — two of King Aslom's sons, Haetor and Iankos, plus four of Ceyoldar's best cavalry officers. Aslom and his two other sons were busy organizing their camp on the beach below the castle. A hundred thousand warriors needed ample space.

We headed out as soon as fresh horses could be saddled and supplies could be packed. At my brother's suggestion, we brought heavy wool cloaks, hats, and gloves.

"I found a place to observe them from the mountains," he said. "It's cold and a little treacherous, but I don't think they will spot us."

"Good." That sounded like an ideal plan.

Finally, as late afternoon sunlight slanted down through the treetops, we entered the forest. Connor shifted through Shadows immediately, and the land grew rocky. As the temperature began to drop, the sky turned gray and sullen with the promise of snow. Oaks gave way to pines, then the pines gave way to scraggly, gnarled underbrush.

I noticed how the men from Ceyoldar stared at everything around them with wonder. They knew this was the way we had entered Amber, but nothing looked the same. Ah, the powers of a god. . . . Smiling to myself, I caught up with my brother.

Now the road grew rocky and narrow; forced into a single-file line, we climbed a steep path, moving into rugged snow-draped mountains. A cold, crisp wind gusted into my face, stinging with occasional flakes of snow. I blinked hard and squinted into the wind. We would need capes soon. I started to look for a place to stop.

"How many men would you say Uthor has?" I called ahead.

"I estimated between forty and fifty thousand — though not all were fighters," Conner replied. "From the look of things, he brought half the court sycophants with him."

That didn't surprise me; King Elnar had sometimes allowed Ilerium's court to watch battles in which victory was certain. If nothing else, it impressed the ladies . . . and kept intrigue to a minimum. You didn't plot against a monarch with a powerful army at his back.

"Uthor is too confident," I said, half to myself. Another mistake.

"He always is." Conner chuckled. "You aren't Dad, and this isn't Juniper. He's going to be in for quite a surprise on the battlefield this time."

"You sound pretty certain."

"Oh, I have a some surprises in mind . . . I've been talking to a few powerful Shadow-beings, and I can guarantee reinforcements when the battle starts."

"Care to elaborate?"

"Not just yet. When the time is right . . ."

I grinned. "Let's hope we aren't disappointed. We still haven't seen Dad and Freda's troops yet, either."

Hard-packed snow rose high to either side of the path, and the air grew thin as we ascended. Still we rode. Two thousand feet up, we came to a small plateau.

"Cold-weather gear!" I called over my shoulder, breath pluming in the air. I swung down from my saddle and pulled cloak and gloves from my pack. Made of heavy white wool, they shielded me from the cut of the wind as soon as I put them on.

I noticed the men from Ceyoldar all shivering as they gratefully threw on their cloaks. I motioned Haetor and Iankos to my side. They hurried forward, bowing.

"I don't feel cold the way you do," I told them. "You should have said something. We would have stopped sooner."

"Yes, Oberon," Iankos said. "Next time . . ."

Conner joined me. "We go on foot from here," he said.

"Is it much farther?"

"A couple hundred yards."

"We will make a camp here," I said to Haetor. "You're in charge. Iankos? Come with us." I turned to my brother. "Lead on!"

Conner crossed the plateau to where the trail continued. Hugging the side of the mountain, it curved to the left and out of sight. An outcropping of stone shielded it from the ice and snow above.

Without hesitation, Conner strode forward. I came next, letting one hand touch the mountainside for balance, and Iankos brought up the rear. The wind picked up, giving a low moan of sound, and the air grew colder still. I pulled my hat lower, covering the tops of my ears. This was not the sort of weather I liked.

At last the trail leveled, then started down. Becoming wider, it ended abruptly at a little shelf.

Conner dropped to his hands and knees. Creeping forward slowly, he peeked over the edge. I joined him, and Iankos did the same.

"There they are," Connor said unnecessarily, pointing.

Far below, in a lush green valley split by a meandering river, Uthor had made his camp. Tents by the score lined the water's edge. Huge pens held horses and lizardlike animals I had never seen before. Smoke from a thousand campfires cast a haze across everything.

To the north, at the far end of the valley, squads drilled and practiced with swords, axes, pikes, and strange long-bladed weapons. Everywhere I looked, I saw the bustle of movement. The sheer numbers astounded me.

"So many . . ." Iankos murmured. I knew how he felt. At my most conservative estimate, there had to be two hundred thousand warriors camped below us — and maybe a lot more.

"He has brought in reinforcements since yesterday," Conner said. I glanced over at him. He was frowning faintly. "He must be gathering in everyone that he can. He must plan to attack soon."

"How can we hope to stand against *that?*" Iankos murmured, almost to himself.

"We will," I said sharply, "because we must."

He bowed his head. "A thousand pardons, Oberon. I did not mean to doubt you. Of course, with you leading us, victory is certain!"

"It is not certain . . . but I think it likely!"

"It's like Juniper all over again," Conner said, voice low. "They will use magic and try to block our access to the Logrus."

"You're forgetting one important detail," I said.

He glanced over at me. "What?"

"We aren't in Chaos anymore," I said slowly. "Here, *we're* the masters. *We* control the Pattern and the Shadows. He's at our mercy."

I crawled back and stood. When I let my vision slip into that magical sight I had found in Lord Zon's keep, everything around me took on a strange bluish glow . . . lines of force connecting everyone and everything around us.

There had to be a way to use the Pattern to keep Uthor at bay. I just had to find it. We needed something big to take care of Uthor's army . . . a tidal wave . . . an earthquake . . . *something* of that size and power.

Or . . . maybe an avalanche? I smiled. Tons of falling rock, ice, and snow could bury most of their camp, if it hit the valley. But how?

I had called on the Pattern several times while in Chaos to strike at Lord Zon, so I knew it could be used to manipulate elements of the physical world. But could it affect a whole mountain? Could it cause an avalanch of sufficient power to bury a whole valley?

Unfortunately, we didn't have time to experiment. It might take weeks or months to learn to use the Pattern like that.

Another idea struck me. Why shouldn't we use the Logrus, too? Everyone else in my family could call on its power at will. If the Pattern couldn't cause an avalanche, maybe the Logrus could . . . I'd have to talk to Dad. He might be able to make it happen.

"I've seen enough," I said to Conner.

He rose. "Back to Amber?"

"Yes. We'll use a Trump this time. Speed is going to be important."

We headed back to rejoin the others, maneuvering along the mountain's curving ledge as quickly as possible. When we got there, we found them gathered around their horses.

"Let's go!" I called. "Everyone together now! Lead your horses, hands on the flank of the animal in front of you so we don't get separated!"

I pulled out my deck of Trumps and found the new card Aber had given me lying on top. I picked it up, concentrated on the castle's central courtyard, and the scene leaped to life.

Without a backward glance, I led my horse through. Mentally, I held the passage open for the others to follow, though they shouldn't have needed it, since they maintained physical contact the whole time.

When we were all safely returned, I passed my horse's reins to one of the half-dozen stableboys who came running. I threw off my cloak and gloves.

Then I heard running footsteps and a frantic wheezing. What now? I turned, curious.

"Your Highness!" An elderly steward came running up, breathless, hands fluttering frantically. "Your Highness! A word, Sire!"

"What is it?" I asked wearily. Couldn't the routine matters of state wait until morning?

He dropped to one knee. "Visitors are here from Chaos — waiting in the main hall —"

"What!" I cried. Conner and I exchanged a startled glance "Who is attending them?"

"Lord Dworkin. He said — to bring you — at once!"

I frowned. "Who are they? Relatives?"

"I do not think so — Sire! They are — soldiers — come under a flag — of truce —"

"When did they arrive?" I demanded.

"Right after you left! They asked for Lord Dworkin. They have been behind closed doors ever since!"

"Where are Freda and Aber?" I asked.

He wrung his hands. "Gone! Fled!"

"What! Why?"

"Your father told them to, Sire!"

I didn't know what to think. Should I be alarmed? Afraid? If Aber and Freda fled . . .

"Any ideas?" I asked Conner, who was staring thoughtfully off into space.

"None." He looked as puzzled as I felt.

"All right," I said to the steward. "Take us to them. Quickly!"

"This way, Sire!"

Turning, he hurried inside, down several corridors, to the closed double-doors to one of a private meeting room. He fretted there until, with a sigh, I stepped past, threw open the doors, and entered. Conner followed me in.

I found Dad seated at a long table with his back to me, facing three men I did not recognize. All wore silvered chain mail. The one in the middle had a thin circlet of gold around his head; the other two had horns and vaguely reptilian scales. Wine and half a dozen banquet dishes lay before them; clearly they had eaten while awaiting my arrival.

For a second I wished I'd had time to order a crown for myself. A true king needs all the fixtures when entertaining.

Conner stopped beside me. I whispered, "Is that Uthor?"

"Yes." He sounded stunned. "I can't believe he's here!"

"Watch my back."

He nodded gravely, one hand dropping to rest lightly on the hilt of his sword.

Advancing, I took a position next to our father. There I crossed my arms and set my feet.

"Good evening," I said, giving all three a polite nod — but no more acknowledgment than that. "News of your arrival just reached me. I am Oberon."

The three men rose with languid grace. The one in the middle gave a dismissive wave of his hand.

"We were not expected," he said. His voice sounded deeper and more melodic than I had expected. "We are pleased to find you here. Your father has been kind enough to entertain us while we waited for your return. He has . . . a most refreshing *wit*."

All three chuckled at that. I left my own expression carefully blank, but surreptitiously studied Uthor. When he smiled, I saw that his teeth had been filed to needlelike points. It wasn't pleasant. I could easily believe he had killed my brothers — and so many others.

Despite their beautiful armor, neither he nor his men bore any weapons. They had probably left them behind under the flag of truce. Still, I knew well that they could summon their swords using the Logrus faster than I could draw my own.

"May I present my son," Dad said without bothering to look behind himself. "Oberon, this is King Uthor of Chaos."

I felt my hackles rising. This was the man who had destroyed Juniper. This was the man who had helped kill so many of my friends and family. More than anything else, I wanted his head on a pole over the castle gates.

Somehow, I managed to control my temper.

"An honor," I said, forcing myself to be polite.

"Of course it is," Uthor said. He gave a formal bow. When I returned it, he sat back down heavily.

"May we offer you the hospitality of Amber?" I asked. That seemed the most appropriate thing to say.

"Thank you. Dworkin has made us quite comfortable. You may leave us."

"I am king here," I said, putting an edge in my voice and leaning forward. "You will talk to me or not at all."

"*King?*" Uthor said, smirking. "How . . . charmingly presumptuous." He raked his gaze up and down my travel-stained clothes. "You wear your title well, sir."

"At least I have the manners to accompany it." I folded my arms and gave him an icy stare.

"Of course you do." He actually smirked.

"May I remind you, Uthor, that you are a guest in my home?"

He sighed. "We are not here to challenge titles, no matter how trivial." I bristled at that. Uthor leaned back in his seat. "Your father has told us something of your making, after all."

"Oh?" I glanced at Dad. My "making"? That struck me as a curious turn of phrase, but I did not comment on it. Perhaps it was some sort of Chaos formality when talking about new kings; I had little schooling in court etiquette. I'd ask questions about it later, in private.

"Uthor," I said, deliberately leaving off his title, "I am a man of plain words. All that has happened — here and in Chaos — has given me little cause to like or trust you. Either get to the point or leave."

"Your honesty is most refreshing," Uthor said. He toyed with the stem of his goblet. "An excellent wine, by the way. Worthy of a king."

"I am not here to discuss the merits of table wines."

My father cleared his throat. "Patience, my boy. King Uthor is visiting under a flag of truce, after all. Hear him out."

"Very well." Easily I slid into the seat next to my father. Conner continued to stand behind us. To Uthor, I said, "I'm listening."

"We have much in common . . ." Uthor murmured, giving a vague wave of his hand.

"Indeed. Several common acquaintances." Slowly I reached into the pouch at my belt, found the Trump his assassin had been carrying, and placed it on the table before me. Uthor's eyes flickered down to it, but if he recognized it, he showed no reaction.

Uthor continued, "I am here . . . to discuss . . . an alliance." The words seemed almost painful to him.

I raised my eyebrows. "An alliance? Between Amber and Chaos?"

"Between brother kings." His lips twisted back almost involuntarily as he spoke; he tried to hide it by taking a sip of his wine. I could tell he did not like calling me a brother of any sort; he clearly considered me his inferior.

I leaned back, studying him. An alliance . . . this *was* an unexpected development. He had to be desperate to make such an offer.

"We may have some common interests," I said. I had to find out more before agreeing to anything. It sounded too good, too easy, to be true.

"A few, at least." Uthor refused to meet my gaze. "And certainly one common enemy."

Leaning back, I studied him. A common enemy? I thought him responsible for all the murders and assassination attempts on family members.

"Who might this enemy be?" I asked at last.

"Zon Swayvil, of course."

Zon . . . *Lord* Zon. But hadn't Uthor set Lord Zon against us? Why would those two be at odds now, when they both seemed to want Amber destroyed and my whole family dead?

Dad said, "Zon Swayvil has seized the throne and proclaimed himself King of Chaos. Assisted by the Logrus, of course."

"And he will die for it!" Uthor snarled, leaping to his feet.

TWENTY-SIX

h." I leaned back in my chair, mind racing.

Suddenly it all made sense. Lord Zon had been using the fight between Chaos and my family to weaken King Uthor's position. We had all been nothing more than pawns in his game of thrones . . . moved, then forgotten when he made his play for a larger prize . . . all of Chaos!

I realized how desperate Uthor must be to come to us here.

"Why should I help you?" I asked calmly.

I picked up the assassin's Trump and turned it over in my hands pointedly. "Clearly you have no great affection for my family, the Pattern, or its Shadows."

Uthor looked me in the eye. "I will not pretend otherwise. I do not like you. I do not like your father or your family. I gladly would have seen you all dead, your bloodline destroyed, and the Shadows erased forever."

"But . . ." I prompted.

He swallowed. "I am prepared to live with them, if necessary."

"Perhaps we should wait to see what Zon offers us," I countered. "He holds Chaos. His position is better than yours."

Uthor leaned forward. His face grew hard, and I could tell it pained him to speak these words. "I have never shirked from my duties," he said slowly. "This is a time of hard choices. You and your family are enemies of Chaos. You turned your backs on the Logrus and its power. I had no choice but to set myself against you."

"Much as Lord Zon has," I said.

"Swayvil wants power," Uthor said sharply. "He used you to distract me. Instead, I should have been watching him — and now I have been betrayed by the Logrus." He waved me to silence when I opened my mouth to ask what he meant. How could the Logrus betray him? "Listen well, son of Dworkin. You will only get one chance to join me."

"When must I decide?"

"Now."

"Wait here. We must confer."

He nodded.

"Dad?" I said.

He rose, and together with Conner, the three of us went into the hall. I shut the door behind us.

"Zon," I said, "seems to be the more dangerous enemy. But if we join with Uthor, can we trust him to keep his word?"

"I trust him," Dad said simply. "He has not been a great king as kings of Chaos go. But he has always acted out of a sense of duty. And I have never known him to break his word."

"Conner?" I asked.

"I agree. And if it means peace . . . if it means we can return home to Chaos . . ."

I nodded. I had pretty much decided the same way. Their opinions confirmed it.

I opened the doors and went back inside. Uthor rose.

"Very well," I said. "I accept your offer. Let there be peace be-tween us. Together — together, we will defeat Zon and reclaim Chaos for you!"

TWENTY-SEVEN

here were papers to be drawn and signed, sacred vows to be made, and oaths of mutual defense to be sworn. The three of us — Dad, Uthor, and I — worked throughout the night on the details, haggling, negotiating, compromising.

Finally, just before dawn, we had our agreement.

Simply put, in exchange for military and tactical support of King Uthor, our whole family would receive an official pardon from the king. Our family's confiscated lands in the Beyond and all former titles would be restored. Any family members still alive in the king's dungeons would be freed.

And, most important of all, Amber — and all its Shadows — would continue to exist under my sole rule — provided no more Shadow-storms struck Chaos.

Chaos and Amber would be separate . . . and equal.

It seemed too good to be true. And as I regarded King Uthor across the table, preparing to sign the last of the documents, I stroked my spikard ring and wondered that it did not pulse in warning.

Perhaps, as Dad said, Uthor really was a man of his word. I certainly hoped so.

He finished signing the paper with a flourish, then passed the pen to me. It still had sufficient ink in the nib, so I signed next to him. Then I used a signet Dad had provided, showing a unicorn, and Uthor did the same with his, which showed a griffin.

We both rose. He did not offer to shake hands. Neither did I.

"I will bring my army to your camp at noon," I told him. "And together we will march on Chaos."

"Until then." He nodded to me. "Iart! Snell!" he called to his men. Turning, the three of them strode from the room.

I leaned back in my seat, feeling exhausted but triumphant. We had done it. Amber would be safe.

Dad leaned forward. "Do not rest easily," he said. "Zon Swayvil holds the throne now. It will be difficult to dislodge him."

"One enemy at a time," I said, grinning. Nothing could dampen my enthusiasm today. "With Uthor on our side . . . and our combined forces . . . of course we will restore the rightful King of Chaos! How can we fail?"

"I hope not . . ." His eyes grew distant.

It took most of the next morning for King Aslom's forces to break camp. Fortunately they were seasoned veterans and well organized. They broke their camp quickly, loading their pack-animals and wagons, then with Aslom and his sons in their battle chariots, the cavalry mounted, and the footmen in ranks, we marched.

Conner and I took the lead again, and he moved us through Shadow. This time, though, we would come around to the other side of Uthor's valley, making camp in whatever fields we could find.

It was a long, hot, dusty trip, broken twice for meals and rest. But as evening approached, the Shadows grew true, and I knew we were close.

Three of Uthor's scouts rode out on black warhorses to meet us. All three were hell-creatures . . . the *lai she'one* . . . with glowing red eyes beneath their steel helms. Their armor jingled faintly as they moved.

"King Oberon," said the one in the lead, who wore a lieutenant's insignia at his collar. "I am Nox. I will be your liaison to the king's staff." His words were polite, though his tone showed scorn. "Your warriors are to camp north of here. My men will show them the way. I am to escort you to the king immediately."

"Very well." Again, I wished I had thought to bring a crown of my own. Too many details to remember . . . I would have to find a secretary at some point to manage such things.

"I'll take the men and get them settled in," Conner quickly offered.

"Thanks. Aslom! Haetor!" I called. A king could not enter another's camp unescorted. "You will come with me."

"Yes, Oberon!" they both cried. They steered their chariots forward, bumping across the rough ground.

"Lead on," I said to Nox.

Without a word, he wheeled his black stallion and headed for the valley where Uthor's forces were camped. As we followed, I heard Conner shouting orders to our men.

As we entered the long rows of tents, which seethed with movement as Uthor's men hurried through their duties, I heard a familiar voice calling my name from somewhere behind us. I craned around in the saddle and spotted Aber riding quickly toward me. He wore no armor and carried no sword; clearly duty hadn't called him here.

"My brother," I said to Nox.

He grunted and shrugged. Clearly he didn't care one way or another if Aber joined us.

My brother was out of breath when he finally caught up, bent over and gasping for air.

"What is it?" I asked him.

"I have a message from Freda," he said in a low voice. "A prophecy. King Uthor's life is in grave danger."

I shook my head in bewilderment. "We're about to ride into battle against Lord Zon — of course his life is in danger. So is mine!"

"No! You don't understand!" He shook his head. "Uthor won't live to see the battle. You must let me talk to him. I have something for him — a ring. It will help protect him."

A ring? A spikard, maybe? I remembered how mine had warned me against the assassin in Amber. It couldn't hurt, and it might further cement our alliance.

"All right," I said. "I'll present you to him when we get there."

"Good. Freda said you'd help," Aber went on. "She saw it in the cards."

"Not that again." I rolled my eyes. "I'm half minded to say no, just to prove to you once and for all that nothing is shown in her cards but what we make of it."

"She knew you'd say that. And she knew you'd let me through anyway, because you're playing with the King of Chaos's life. Uthor *won't* be happy if he finds you're keeping things back from him. Especially information that might save his life."

I sighed. He had a point.

"I already said I'd present you."

We were almost at the center of the camp. Here the press of Uthor's forces kept our pace slow and deliberate; several times we had to wait while wagons full of supplies trundled past.

Finally, though, we reached a series of huge pavilions. Aber and I dismounted and gave our horses' reins to waiting attendants. Flanked by Aslom and Haetor, we followed Nox past lines of guards standing rigidly at attention and into the central area, which had a throne and lines of supplicants waiting to consult with Uthor.

As soon as he spotted us, though, he motioned us forward. He looked old and tired suddenly. Clearly the strain of his struggle against Lord Zon had begun to tell on him.

"Your arrival is most timely," he said. "Good. The dispatches from home are not promising. We must move swiftly."

"How soon?" I asked.

"Tomorrow."

I nodded slowly. "Very well. We are ready and will await your command."

Aber cleared his throat.

"Ah . . . my brother has a warning for you from my sister," I said. "She has some talent in future-telling."

"The Lady Freda?" He leaned forward, looking at Aber with interest. "Speak. She has a true gift, I know. Any warning she sends will be given proper weight."

Aber stepped forward and dropped to one knee before King Uthor. "Highness."

"Rise," said Uthor. He looked faintly pleased at Aber's obeisance.

"This is for you."

He pulled something from a pouch at his belt and held it out. I craned to see. It looked like an ancient gold ring, inscribed with characters I could not make out.

"What is this?"

"The Sign of Chaos."

It seemed to mean something to Uthor and the others around us. Uthor gasped. Everyone else shifted and muttered to themselves. Clearly they had heard of it. And clearly it meant something good.

"What is it?" I asked Nox in a quiet voice.

"An ancient signet," he said in a hushed, almost reverential voice. "It was lost centuries ago — stolen by the Feynim. To have it back, most especially at this troubled time . . . it is a great omen!"

Grinning, Uthor stood and held the ring aloft for all to see. Then he turned the ring slowly, studying the characters engraved on side.

With a triumphant grin, he slipped it onto the index finger of his right hand. As he did, his face took on first a puzzled expression, then one of horror.

Suddenly his ring-finger turned black. The blackness spread rapidly up his arm and to his shoulder. When he opened his mouth to scream, no sound came out. His face, frozen in a horrible grimace, turned black as well.

I rushed forward to see if I could help, along with Nox and all the others. But nothing remained to be done. Uthor's whole body had turned to stone.

Off balance, like a statue shoved from its pedestal, King Uthor toppled forward. When he hit the hard-packed ground, his arms and head snapped off. The head rolled over and stopped at my feet, eyes staring blindly up at my face, as if accusing me of treason.

I swallowed hard and took a step back. The soldiers around me began to moan and cry out.

"He did it!" someone shouted, pointed at Aber.

"Me?" My brother folded his arms stubbornly. "You're crazy! The ring did it!"

"That's right," another soldier shouted. "He brought the ring!"

I stepped forward. "There's no proof my brother knew anything about it!" I said. "The ring might have been poisoned long ago, or magics laid on it —"

"Murderer!" shouted Nox. He drew his sword, face livid.

I dropped my hand to the hilt of my own sword and gave a warning growl. "We are all friends here. We are bound by a treaty."

"Traitor!" another called. More swords left their sheaths. A shiver ran through me.

"You're wrong!" I said desperately. My brother might be a lot of things, but I couldn't believe he would kill King Uthor and me.

Aber stepped forward. "Let me speak!" he shouted. "Please, let me speak!"

The muttering around us died. I took a deep breath. This situation could still be saved. I just hoped Aber could convince Uthor's men of our innocense.

Already my thoughts turned through the possibilities. If they could be rallied under my flag . . . if I could lead them all against Lord Zon . . .

"I didn't know the ring would kill him," Aber said in a loud voice. "I'm just a messenger!"

"You have a message?" I asked, puzzled.

"That's right." He swallowed hard then looked me in the eye. "Lord Zon sends his greetings. Ta, brother."

With an apologetic shrug, he stepped back and disappeared in a sudden flash of light.

TWENTY-EIGHT

 could only stand there, mouth open, stunned at what he'd just said and done. He had betrayed us. Betrayed *me*. I couldn't believe it — and yet everything started to fall into place.

How long had he been working for Lord Zon?

A long time, a little voice inside me said.

He must have been the one who let the assassin into my room in Juniper. And he must have been the one who betrayed the location of the first Pattern to King Uthor . . . All along, he had been working with both sets of our enemies.

A low upswell of voices began around me.

"Quiet!" I shouted. "We must —"

The muttering grew louder. Steel glinted and flashed as Uthor's men drew their weapons. I realized with a certainty I'd never felt before that they intended to have my head — along with my brother's. Only he'd had the sense to flee.

Trumpets sounded . . . not low, mournful notes as befitted a king's passing, but the sharp *tat-tat, tat-tat* of an alarm. Men began to shout and run for weapons. Uthor's men paused, looking around with mounting concern.

"Attack! Attack!" came the cries of sentries. *"To arms!"*

Someone screamed, "Watch for arrows!" as missiles started to rain down in our midst.

I seized the nearest shield from beside King Uthor's throne and raised it against the attack. A heartbeat later, two arrows pierced its thick hide with sounds like the savage thump-thump of a war-drum, their cruelly barbed tips coming to a halt less than an finger's width from my nose and right eye. Two of Uthor's lieutenants weren't so lucky — one caught an arrow in the eye, the other to his neck and chest. Both died instantly.

A distant voice shouted, *"It's Swayvil! He's attacking! Swayvil is — !"* and a brief scream followed.

Forgetting me for the moment, Uthor's lieutenants ran to mount their defenses. They called orders, trying to rally their camp's defense. More arrows fell.

I glanced at Haetor and Aslom, who watched the skies warily and stayed as close to me as possible. They had their swords drawn and looked ready to defend themselves.

We had to get out of here fast. No matter who won the coming battle, I knew my men and I would not be welcome here.

"Find shields and follow me," I said to them in a quiet voice.

As I jogged I pulled out my Trumps and found Conner's. I tried to contact him, but couldn't — either the magic had been blocked or, more likely, he was too busy fighting for his life to chat right now.

Turning, I headed north. I'd try to make it to our camp before Uthor's men organized and came after us.

The initial volleys of shots ended, and I heard the sound of war-cries and steel ringing on steel from somewhere behind us. The battle had started.

I cast my shield aside. Fortunately, everyone around us seemed to be rushing toward the fighting. Word of King Uthor's death had not yet spread through camp, and no one seemed the least bit interested in stopping us or asking questions.

I glanced over my shoulder. Haetor and Aslom were having no trouble keeping up. We headed as rapidly as possible down the rows of tents. Horned men, men with tails, and things that could never have been men ran and scurried and flapped and flew this way and that, shouting questions and conflicting orders, trying to marshal troops and mount a defense. No one seemed to be in charge.

"Where to, Oberon?" Aslom asked, pacing beside me.

"To rejoin our army," I said grimly. "Hopefully they will still be there."

A second volley of arrows rained from the sky, and several of Uthor's officers fell. I recognized Nox among the wounded. I hesitated a moment. He might prove useful later. I'd need a liaison to Uthor's troops, if any of them lived through the coming battle . . . perhaps some could be persuaded to join our forces.

"Get Nox!" I said suddenly.

Haetor looked started. "Oberon —"

"I have plans for him."

"Yes, sir."

Shaking his head, keeping his shield up with his left arm, he and Aslom ran over to Nox, grabbed his arms, and lifted him. Between them, they supported him enough to get him moving again.

Picking up another shield, I led the way through the camp. Men and hell-creatures ran pell-mell through the mazes of tents. More arrows fell. My shield caught another, and one more grazed by thigh. Uthor's troops continued to run around in a panic, throwing on armor and grabbing weapons. Uthor's sentries had failed . . . we had all been caught by surprise. Damn Aber!

I made it through the rear line of tents and scrambled up the side of the valley. Uthor's men had made plenty of trails, so the going was easy. At the top, I saw an open stretch of land, and then the place where my own men had been sent to make camp. The forces from Ceyoldar had formed battle lines with shields raised, but were holding ranks. Conner, with the cavalry, ranged behind them shouting orders. I saw a few arrows lodged in shields, but apparently they had not yet come under direct attack.

"Run across as fast as you can," I said to them. "Keep low. Get Nox to a company doctor, and post guards over him. Then report back to me."

"Are we joining the battle?" Aslom asked.

"Not yet."

He nodded, then motioning to his son, together they lifted Nox and bore him off toward the lines.

I took a deep breath and raced past them, legs pounding, moving as fast as I could.

"Open ranks!" sentries shouted.

A few arrows whizzed past me, but none hit. Several footmen with shields moved back, and I made it into their protective ranks. Aslom and Haetor followed a moment later.

Conner came racing up. "What happened?" he demanded,

swinging down from his horse.

"It was Aber — he showed up and murdered King Uthor," I said grimly.

"What!" He stared at me. "Impossible!"

I shook my head. "No. It was him. He did it. He's working for Lord Zon.

"Take my horse," he said. "I'll get another."

Quickly I swung up into the saddle and took the reins.

"What orders?" he asked. "Do we stay? Do we fight?"

"No," I said. "Uthor's forces are finished. They won't follow me now — Aber has seen to that."

"So it's back to Amber," he said.

"Yes."

Turning, he shouted, "Sound ranks!" to the bugler.

Instantly the ta-ta-*tat* sounded out. Men scrambled to form lines, shields up, arms at the ready.

"Withdraw!" I shouted. "Prepare to march!"

Before I could say another word, sentries shouted, *"Arrows!"*

"Watch out!" I bellowed.

I threw my shield over my head as a rain of black missiles fell among us. A few men fell with sharp cries of agony, but most had shields up in time. The barrage did little damage.

"Pikemen to the fore!" I shouted, wheeling my horse. "Cavalry — prepare to ride ahead!"

Haetor came running. "Lord Nox is dead, sir!" he announced.

"Damn the luck. We'll probably be blamed for that, too." Nothing could be done about it now, though. I hesitated a second, trying to figure the best course of action. "Take a squad of cavalry and find out where the arrows are coming from. We have to leave now or we'll be picked off one by one."

"Yes, sir!" Saluting, he ran, calling for half a dozen men to join him. Hopefully it wouldn't be a suicide mission.

"Marching lines!" I shouted again. The pikemen and spearmen began to assemble, shields still raised over their heads. "Leave the tents and anything not easily carried! Abandon camp!"

I glanced around for Conner, but he was three hundred yards away. Instead of shouting, I pulled out his Trump. This time he answered immediately.

"How about those special troops you promised me back in Amber? We aren't going to make it out of here without help."

He smiled a wicked smile. "I know just the one."

"One what? Battalion?"

"No. One who agreed. He should be all you need."

I blinked in surprise. "Is this a joke?"

"Dragons don't normally cooperate with people. We're more of a snack to them. It took a lot of persuading. And a lot of gold."

"Did you say . . . a dragon?"

"Uh-huh."

I smiled grimly. This might well turn the tide of battle in our favor.

"Where is it now?"

"I made a Trump. I can call him any time. You want him right now?"

"Yes — but do it over here!"

"Right!"

I broke the connection and looked to my men. "Clear a large area!" I shouted. "We have a change of plans — reinforcements are coming!"

Everyone cheered. They drew back a fifty feet in all directions, which I judged a safe enough distance.

Conner reached me then, riding hard, and drew up sharply. He had a Trump in one hand.

"Ready?" he asked.

"Yes!"

"Here it is!"

He handed me the Trump. It showed a face . . . huge, scaled, with eyes like black coals.

I raised it, concentrating. A *presence* seemed to overwhelm me . . . something huge . . . something *old* and dark and powerful. Something very smart and very powerful.

"Human." The voice was so low I barely heard it.

"I am King Oberon," I said. "My brother Conner said you would help us."

"For a price . . ."

"Yes. Join us."

I reached out my hand. A claw touched it, cold as ice and harder than steel. I pulled. It felt like ten thousand pounds on the other end, but slowly it came through the connection. A clawed hand, covered with black scales, an arm — immense, powerful — then chest — neck — head and tail —

With a hop and a leap, it suddenly appeared. It towered over me, forty feet at the shoulder, perhaps a hundred and twenty from tip of snout to tip of tail. As it moved, the ground trembled. Slowly it spread its wings, and then it roared.

Arrows struck its back and sides, but they bounced off. It was well armored.

"This is Ulyss," Conner said proudly.

"Yes," said the dragon. *"Manling promises gold."*

"As much as you want," I said, "for your help today."

"My weight in gold . . ."

"Agreed."

"What must I do?"

More arrows pinged down. A man behind me collapsed with a choking gurgle, the long black shaft of an arrow jutting from his throat.

"We are in the middle of a war," I said. "Can you stop the archers who are shooting at us?"

"Yes . . ."

It reared back, took three hopping steps, and began beating the air with its wings. It a second it was airborne. Rapidly it gained altitude and speed, and then it circled. More arrows struck it, doing no damage.

Suddenly it dived. Turning, I tried to see its target. There — it was after something in the bushes to the right. When its mouth opened, gouts of flame shot out. I couldn't see what it had burned, but I could guess. The rain of arrows abruptly ceased. Rising again, it circled, looking for more targets.

"What do you think of him?" Conner asked, grinning.

"Three more dragons like him, and the day would already be ours."

"We don't have that long. As soon as Swayvil sees what's happening, he'll destroy this world."

"Primal Chaos —" I guessed.

"Yes. He'll release it here, and nothing will remain. We must leave at once."

"What about the dragon?"

"What about him?"

"You promised him gold."

Conner shrugged. "He won't survive long. If he gets all the archers, I'll be surprised."

"Their arrows are useless."

"It just takes one lucky shot. And if the archers don't get him, Lord Zon will."

I chuckled. "You have a high opinion of Zon."

"Any Lord of Chaos can kill a dragon."

"Even you?" I asked. It seemed impossible.

"Yes." He shrugged modestly. "Ulyss *was* the fifth dragon I approached. I killed two who decided I'd make a better breakfast than employer." His eyes suddenly widened. "Look!"

I followed his pointing finger. Ulyss had paused in mid attack. In the air before him hung a shadow. It had no fixed shape, and its center was as dark as a raincloud. It pulsed ever so faintly.

"Pull back!" I shouted to Ulyss, but the dragon could not hear me.

Instead, it breathed gouts of fire at the shadow. That did no damage that I could see. If anything, the shadow grew larger. Then, like a panther springing onto its prey, the shadow surged forward. It completely enveloped the dragon. I saw Ulyss's wings paused in mid downstroke, but the dragon did not fall.

Instead, the dragon began to scream. The terrible soul-rending noise cut through the air like a knife. It went on and on, growing louder, tearing through my head, tearing through my heart. I covered my ears, and still it went through me. I had never heard such a horrible sound before. It made me want to curl into a ball and die.

The scream came to an abrupt stop. As I watched with growing horror, the dragon seemed to crumble to dust. In a second it simply disappeared, its few remains swept away by the wind.

The Shadow drifted through the air for a second, as though no hand guided it. Then, slowly and inexorably, it drifted toward Conner and me.

TWENTY-NINE

hat *is* that thing?" I asked uneasily, starting to back away.

"Primal Chaos, under a master adept's control." Connor also backed up. "This would be a good time to leave, I think. Use a Trump. Call Freda. She can bring us back to Amber."

"I'm not leaving without my troops." I had gone through too much to get them; I wouldn't just abandon King Aslom and his men to be slaughtered — not as long as other options remained. "What else can we do?"

"Kill the one casting the spell."

"I can't see him. And I don't think we have time to go hunting."

He hesitated. "Dad or Freda might be able to counter it. Try Freda. Just do it fast!"

Keeping one eye on the shadow — which had definitely gotten larger since destroying the dragon — I pulled out Freda's Trump and concentrated on her image.

She answered immediately.

"Is something wrong?"

"We're having trouble with Primal Chaos. Conner says a master adept is controlling it. It just killed our dragon, and now it's heading for us."

"What does it look like?"

"A cloud. It's in the sky."

"Move it to another Shadow," she said.

I blinked. "Can we do that?"

"Of course. Tell Connor to use a — oh, give me a second. I had better do it." She turned and spoke to someone over her shoulder, then reached toward me. I took her hand and pulled her through.

She took one look at the Shadow and said, "Hmm!" Then she turned and strolled away at an almost leisurely pace, her head bowed. I noted a Trump in her left hand, but I could not yet tell what it showed.

The Shadow became a seething, writing cloud. It glided toward the three of us, faster now, three hundred yards away and closing rapidly.

My uneasiness grew. Someone had to be controlling it . . . but who? And from where? He had to be watching us to send it right at us.

I glanced around camp. My men had stopped in the midst of their packing to stare up at it, awe and horror mingling on their faces. They too recognized it as something evil.

"Bring me a bow!" I called.

"Here, Oberon!" One of the archers leaped forward, offering his.

"Thanks."

Notching an arrow, I drew back as far as I could, turned quickly, and fired into the cloud. Once — twice — a third time. The arrows entered it one after another, disappearing from sight; they did not come out the other side. Like the dragon's fire, they had no effect.

I swallowed. Then I backed up a few more feet, getting behind Freda. I didn't want to be in the path when she let loose whatever magic she'd been working.

What could I do to help? I hated waiting. It made me feel powerless.

I scanned the bushes and trees surrounding our camp. Maybe I could spot the sorcerer manipulating the cloud. I figured he had to be watching us to direct it so precisely.

As I turned toward the mountain behind us, sunlight glinted off something — a silver buckle or maybe a button — among the scraggly pines. From that vantage point, whoever it was had a perfect view of us.

I caught Conner's arm. "The wizard is hiding in the woods behind us. Watch for a reflection. There! See it?"

"Yes!" he said. He drew his sword.

"Wait." I marked the spot mentally, then turned back toward the cloud. A hundred yards away, it drifted steadily toward us.

Calmly I nocked another arrow and took aim. Then, instead of firing into the shadow, I wheeled and shot at the figure hidden in the trees. He was two hundred yards distant, but I knew my own strength, and I could hit a target that far away.

I followed that first with five more in rapid succession, covering a spread perhaps four feet across.

I don't know if I hit him or not, but I'd like to think so. The arrows certainly broke his concentration. Even as I loosed my last shot,

I heard Conner suck in a quick breath.

"Oberon!" he said in a warning voice.

I glanced toward the shadow. Twenty yards away, it had stopped moving toward us. Suddenly it began to swell rapidly outward, twenty feet across, then thirty —

"Can you stop it?" I said, backing up. "Freda?"

Whatever the shadow touched turned black and crumbled to dust. The ground — our tents — stacks of weapons —

My sister remained silent, but her face had grown hard. Her lips moved; she raised both her hands, one pointed directly toward the cloud, the other angling a Trump toward her face.

That Trump showed the Courts of Chaos. Somehow, she had opened the image on the card. Like the cloud, it seethed with dark movements. The stars in its sky moved. The buildings shimmered and swayed. Lightning flickered across the landscape, occasionally striking out through the card with little flickering tongues of light.

"Like drawn to like!" she commanded. She extended the card toward the still-expanding cloud, and as its forward edge touched her palm, her whole body seemed to flicker in and out of existence. For an instant I saw blue threads stretching from her hand toward the shadowy Primal Chaos, touching it, wrapping around it, pulling it toward her. But instead of turning her to dust, the cloud flowed along her arm, to the Trump, through it, and out of sight — back to the Courts, if that's where it had come from. I really didn't care, as long as it went away.

When the last of it had disappeared, Freda sagged. I leaped forward and caught her before she hit the ground.

"Well done!" I said.

"Did it work?" she murmured, eyes half closed.

"Yes," I said. "It's gone. Thanks."

She smiled then passed out.

"Take her back to Amber!" Conner said grimly. "I'll get our men home."

"Are you sure?" I asked.

"Yes. Hurry, before anything else happens!"

Without waiting for an answer, he sprinted toward our troops, bawling orders. Everyone shouldered packs and reformed into lines four abreast for a quick march. The cavalry lined up next to them.

I shifted Freda to my left arm and fumbled out my deck of Trumps one-handed. Finding the courtyard Trump, I used it to get us back to Amber.

Servants rushed to greet me, calling welcomes. Some held basins of water and towels to clean the dust of travel from our hands and faces; others bore trays with cups and flagons of wine, and still others carried platters laden with succulent-looking sweetmeats, pastries, and other delicacies.

"Shall I get a physician?" one of the stewards asked in a quiet voice. He motioned for two others to take Freda from my arms. They carried her toward the finished wing of the castle.

"Yes," I said. "Hurry!"

"Very good, Sire." He turned and ran.

A small army of architects, stonemasons, and several army officers appeared as if on cue — apparently it didn't take long for word of my return to Amber to spread. They all clamored for answers to pressing questions.

"Later!" I promised. Pushing past them, I followed after Freda. I had to see to her first.

They carried her into the great hall. Work continued apace, I saw as I glanced around hurriedly: stonemasons were carefully laying out an intricately-patterned slate floor, full of red and blue interlocking circles.

Without a word, they carried Freda swiftly past and up the corridor toward the wing that housed our quarters. We passed a dozen rooms before coming to one with furniture: a divan, several low tables, and three comfortable-looking armchairs.

They set my sister on the divan and raised her feet, placing pillows behind her head and spreading a light blanket across her lap.

Suddenly her eyelids fluttered and opened. She glanced around, apparently confused.

"Feeling better?" I asked, kneeling beside her.

"A little." She tried to sit up. I helped, fluffing more pillows and placing them behind her back. She seemed more physically exhausted than injured — working that spell had taken a lot out of her.

More servants, trailing after us, brought in silver trays laden with silver cups and pitchers, teapots, and still more pastries and intricately arranged fruits.

"Put everything down and go." I motioned toward the tables. To the steward, I said: "Ask our father to join us. He is still in the castle, isn't he?"

"I am not sure, Sire," he said.

"Find out." If he wasn't here, I'd have to contact him by Trump.

"Yes, Sire." Bowing, he scurried off.

I investigated the trays. One pitcher held cool water. The rest held an assortment of wines. I wanted something stronger, but wine would do in a pinch. First, though, I poured Freda a cup of hot, sweet-smelling tea. She looked like she needed it.

"Thank you," she murmured.

"Sugar and cream?" I asked.

"Please."

I added both to her cup and passed her a spoon. She stirred, eyes distant.

"Aber betrayed us," I said heavily.

"What!" she focused on me, clearly alarmed. "What did he do now?"

I told her about King Uthor's death and how my brother had vanished after relaying the message from Lord Zon. She looked distinctly unsettled.

"It must be a mistake, somehow," she said. She sipped her tea gently, brow furrowing. "Use your Trump and call him. He must explain himself."

"I'm sure he will," I said. Doubts crept into my mind. "I will have to talk to him . . . yes. It can't have been him."

"There may yet be another explanation."

"Such as?"

"Someone from the Courts may have impersonated him. Chaos is full of shapeshifters, remember. You have that talent yourself."

"The possibility occurred to me," I admitted. I poured myself a glass of the red wine and drained it in a single long gulp. Aber's parting comment still echoed in my mind. "Our brother has a certain . . . *style*, let us say, all his own. He betrayed me. I have no doubt about it. I *know* him."

"Then he must have had a good cause."

"Something secret, but heroic?"

"That must be it," I said.

Freda looked at me oddly. "Do you feel well?"

"Never better. Why?"

Her eyes narrowed. "Has . . . has Aber given you anything lately? A ring or a pendant, perhaps? Something you carry with you always?"

"Just my Trumps. Why?"

"Let me see them."

I pulled out my deck. Before I could flip through them and pull out the newest ones, she took them from my hands and set them on one of the small tables. She raised her hands over them, closed her eyes, and murmured softly for a second.

"What is it?" I asked.

"A few spells," she said. "Simple charms to make you like him."

I snorted. "He doesn't need charms for that. I've always liked him."

She made a small gesture with her left hand, then picked through the Trumps, setting five of them aside. Aber had given two of them to me in Juniper, one in the Beyond, and two in Amber.

"These are the ones," she said, "that have charms laid upon them. Two make you like him. One makes you trust him. One makes you forgive him. I am unsure what the fifth does . . . perhaps it gives him the benefit of the doubt whenever his actions are questioned."

"I don't understand . . . why would he need to charm me?"

"Because," Freda said, looking me in the eye, "he betrayed you and tried to kill you."

"I'm sure he had good reasons for what he did," I said stubbornly. "Aber wouldn't do that to me. Lord Zon must have forced him to do it."

She shook her head. Then she reached out and touched my forehead with the thumb of her right hand.

"See clearly," she told me. "Be well."

The room swam dizzily. I blinked and steadied myself on the arm of the chair.

Like a veil being lifted, I saw Aber clearly for the first time . . . the petty manipulations . . . the betrayals . . . the lies. He betrayed King Uthor, then left me there to die. The truth hit me like a blow.

"Oberon?" Freda asked.

"The next time I see him, I'm going to kill him," I said grimly. "I can't believe he cast spells on me. What a fool I've been!"

"Not a fool . . ." she murmured. "You must understand Aber. He grew up in the Courts of Chaos, where betrayal is a way of life. He is very good at what he does."

I shook my head. "I can never forgive him."

"Nor should you," she said. She paused. "And yet . . . are you sure it was him?"

"What do you mean?"

"We know of at least two doubles . . . one of you and one of Father. Perhaps there is a double of Aber as well. One who is working for Lord Zon."

"No." I shook my head. "I know my brother. It was Aber, all right."

She shook her head sadly, bit her lip, looked away. She knew he had betrayed us.

"I'll leave you to discover his reasoning," I said. "If I ever see him again, I'll have to kill him. And it's not something I want to do, damn it!"

Her gaze met mine. I recognized an icy resolve in her eyes.

"I will find out," she promised. "Believe me, if he has done this thing, he will come to regret it."

Hearing loud footsteps in the hall outside, I glanced over at the door. Our father? Sure enough, he burst in, face flushed, breath ragged. He must have run all the way here. I had never seen him so upset.

"Freda!" he cried. He rushed to her side and took her hands, rubbing them. "They said you were injured!"

"Not injured, just exhausted." She patted the divan next to her. "Come, sit with me, Father. Oberon has a story to tell you. It is very important."

I poured Dad a glass of red wine as he seated himself, and once more I told what had happened after our arrival in Uthor's camp. Aber's betrayal stung every time I thought about it.

Dad frowned. "I never trusted that boy," he muttered. "Trouble from the day of his birth. Should have put him down years ago."

"It's too late for that now," I said dryly. "The question is — what now? King Uthor is dead. Zon has tightened his grip on the throne.

Aber betrayed us and escaped. What do we do next? We need a new plan. Any ideas?"

"Get drunk," Dad said. "We must celebrate."

"Celebrate! Things are in ruins."

"Nonsense, it could be far worse," Dad said.

"How?" I demanded.

"Swayvil could be attacking us right now. Instead, he will spend months — if not years — consolidating his power in Chaos."

Freda added, "Every day our defenses grow stronger, Oberon. Time is our ally now."

I shook my head. "With the time difference between Amber and Chaos, Zon has more time that we do . . . a year for him to consolidate his victory might only be a month to us. I don't want to wait for his attack. It's a mistake."

"Freda is right, my boy," Dad said. "There is balance to the universe now. The longer it lasts, the harder it is to upset. King Uthor felt it. That's why he wanted to make a deal with us. Zon will feel it too, if you give him enough time." He chuckled. "They are both, after all, mere pawns in a larger game. Entropy will keep the Pattern safe."

Balance in the universe? Entropy? Pawns? Sighing, I shook my head. More craziness. He could prattle on as long as he liked, but *I* knew the truth.

We were out of luck.

Dad said, "Carry on with the game, my boy." He stood and clasped my shoulder. Then, chuckling to himself, still carrying his goblet of wine, he teetered out into the hall and headed back for his workshop.

"He's crazy," I said to Freda. "Completely crazy!"

"Perhaps he is the only sane one," she said, arching her thin eyebrows. She held out her cup. "Pour me some more tea, like a good boy. It's going to be a long night."

THIRTY

wo days had passed since our disastrous expedition to join King Uthor's forces. Conner managed to return with most of the troops, though he fought a running battle for several miles. We had only lost four hundred of the men from Ceyoldar. In the meantime, we had heard nothing from Aber. Freda had tried to reach him a number of times through his Trump. As long as he believed me still to be charmed, we might be able to persuade him to return.

"Is there anyone you can contact in Chaos who might have news for us?" I asked Freda over breakfast. "I'd like to know more of what's happening there. I think it might prove valuable."

"Someone in Chaos . . ." She thought for a minute. "Perhaps . . ."

Raising her hands, she drew a small white chest from somewhere else using the Logrus. I had never seen it before. It had been carved from a single piece of bone or perhaps ivory, and delicate scrimshaw showing strange horned beasts covered the top and sides. Flipping back the hinged top, she drew out the contents — a stack of perhaps thirty Trumps.

I leaned forward, watching with mingled interest and revulsion as she slowly flipped through the cards. I had never seen this deck before. The portraits showed people — and things that might once have been people — in various poses. Women with fangs and yellow-green scales instead of skin . . . men with horns or wolf-heads or an insect's antennae . . . even a puke-green blob of jelly with dozens of floating eyes . . . and so many others with such strange and horrible appearances that I could only shudder helplessly. It seemed more a freak-show than a family album. And yet she smiled down at each one fondly.

"Did you make these Trumps yourself?" I asked. The figures and brushstrokes seemed cruder than those on the cards which Aber and Dad had painted. And yet I could still feel power radiating from them: crudely done though they were, they *worked*.

"No," she said. "I have no talent for making them. Aber painted these many years ago. I have little call to use them, so I never asked him to make nicer ones."

I nodded. These Trumps definitely looked like apprentice-level work.

"Is it safe to contact these . . . people?"

She nodded slightly. "They are relatives. More than that, they are . . . *were* . . . friends. Most are so far removed from Dad and court politics that they should be safe from Swayvil's wrath."

"You're sure they won't turn you in?" I asked.

She smiled. "How can they, if we only talk? I have no intention of visiting the Courts again. The rest of my days will be spent in Amber . . . I am resigned to a life in exile."

"Not exile," I said quickly. That sounded too depressing. "We are colonists."

"I suppose," she said wistfully.

She did have a point, though. If her relatives feared contact with anyone in Amber, they could always refuse to talk to us. And if they willingly chose to talk, they could hardly betray our confidence without incriminating themselves. We could not lose.

"This is the one I wanted." Freda pulled out a Trump showing a round, almost-human woman, only she had two mouths, one on each side of her face where a normal person's cheeks would have been.

"Who is she?" I asked. Despite the extra mouth, she had an almost grandmotherly quality. I could easily imagine liking her.

"Great Aunt Eddarg. She hears everything that goes on in the palace. If anyone in our family knows what happened to Aber, it is she."

"How would she know?"

"She has been head chef at the palace for two hundred years."

"Ah." I'd always found that palace servants had all the best gossip. "Perhaps she has news of our other missing siblings as well."

"I will ask."

Freda raised the Trump, concentrated, and soon got a flickering, uncertain contact with her great aunt. After making sure they could both talk freely, Freda introduced me, then got down to swapping family news. I listened with interest.

"Have you heard anything about our brothers and sisters?" Freda asked. "The ones King Uthor arrested? We don't know if they're alive or dead."

"There are but two of them here."

"Who?"

"Syara, poor thing, and Pella."

"What of Isadora?" I asked. "Or Leona?"

"I don't know where they are."

Neither did we. It was a puzzle. What could have become of them? Hiding, somewhere?

"Is Pella well?" Freda said.

"Yes, dearie," said Eddarg, smiling that horribly toothy smile. "Except for Mattus and Titus, whom the old king executed, all of the prisoners here are well, but thin. I feed them as often as I can. King Swayvil is taking good care of them."

"Is Swayvil torturing them?" I asked.

"Goodness, no! Why should he? They are no threat to Chaos. Now, if he ever gets his hands on that lunatic father of yours, that would be another story!"

Freda sighed with relief. "And Uthor . . . he didn't harm them? They are whole?"

"Yes, yes — just thin, the poor dears." She smiled with one mouth and bobbed her head, saying with the other mouth: "They are strong, yes, like their mothers."

"Why hasn't Swayvil tortured them?" I wondering aloud.

"Goodness," said Great Aunt Eddarg, "why should he torture them? It was King Uthor who hated your father, after all. He's the one who banished that idiot Dworkin and the rest of you poor innocent dearies. The new king is much kinder." Her other mouth echoed: "Kinder, yes, much."

"They also do not know anything of any real value," Freda said to me. "Swayvil must know that. Why waste his time on them?"

"True," I said.

Great Aunt Eddarg cackled a bit. "And the king is more than busy with his own enemies," said one mouth. The other added: "All of King Uthor's immediate family — wives, children, grandchildren, down through a dozen generations, poor dearies — have been arrested." And the other mouth continued, "Those who waive all claim to the throne and swear fealty to King Swayvil are allowed to live. Any who hesitate receive summary execution."

"Let me guess," I said. "Most are swearing fealty?"

The left mouth said, "Of course! Wouldn't you, knowing King Uthor is gone and you have no longer have any hope of ascending the throne?"

"Probably." With King Uthor dead, few would dare stand openly against Swayvil.

"The good news," said Great Aunt Eddarg's right mouth, "is that the *lai she'one* are no longer hunting Dworkin" — ("That idiot!" chimed in the other mouth.) — "or the rest of you. That must come as a relief."

I nodded. "Good news, indeed."

Freda said, "But he has not released any of our family, nor lifted the death sentences on us?"

"No, no," said the right mouth. The left said, "Not yet. Except for your brother, of course." And the first mouth added: "He is a dearie, but thin. We must get him fattened up."

"Do you mean Aber?" I asked.

"Yes," said both mouths at once. "A hero," said one.

"How is he faring?" Freda asked.

"Haven't you heard?" said Great Aunt Eddarg. "He was adopted into House Swayvil two days ago." Her second mouth added: "The king gave him a suite in the palace — though not in the king's own wing — and the dearie has been throwing lavish parties for his friends." The first mouth continued: "He is quite partial to roast piqnar and keeps asking for it." The second mouth added: "Expensive tastes, but King Swayvil does not seem to mind. They dine together now and again."

"Then he is doing well," Freda asked. She shot me an uncertain glance — not sure whether to be happy or dismayed, I guessed. That was my own reaction.

"Thriving, from the sounds of it," I said. For once, Aber seemed to have everything he'd ever wanted: security, a place in a powerful family, and freedom from our father's influence.

"Has he asked King Swayvil to free Pella and Syara?" I asked casually.

"I do not know, dearie. I am not privy to their discussions. Now, I must get dinner ready," said Great Aunt Eddarg. "There is another banquet tonight." Her other mouth added: "Talk to me again soon, dearies?"

"I will," Freda promised with a smile. "I will let you know whenever we have news. And you must do the same."

"Of course, dearie!"

Freda covered the Trump with her hand, and we were alone. We stared at each other for a heartbeat. Aber had certainly landed on his feet.

"We must," Freda said, "find a way to use Aber to our advantage."

"The best way to deal with a serpent," I said unhappily, "is to cut off its head."

THIRTY-ONE

ver the next week, events seemed to hit a strange lull. With the newly crowned King Swayvil concentrating on hunting down the last of King Uthor's followers, no one in Chaos seemed to be paying the slightest bit of attention to us. It was as if Dad, the Shadows, and Amber had suddenly ceased to be important. Perhaps Uthor had been right in his estimation: Swayvil had used us solely as a distraction. Now that he held the throne, he would spend his days consolidating his base of power.

Which was entirely fine by me: while he worked on strengthening his hold on the Courts of Chaos, I would consolidate my own power in Amber.

"King Oberon" still had a very nice ring to it, and I meant to hang on to my title, my crown, and most of all my life.

Weeks passed, a constant blur of non-stop action. I spent exhausting and exhilarating days in the field, reviewing troops or recruiting new ones with Conner. . . fascinating days visiting nearby Shadows and buying or bartering with the native populations for food, supplies, and most important of all, settlers . . . but most especially glorious days exploring our new world of Amber.

I sailed with our fledgling navy as it explored the coastline . . . rode with the cavalry as it mapped the hills and valleys . . . marched with the infantry as they cut roads through the forests and began the lengthy task of setting up watchtowers along our soon-to-be-city's flanks.

When I returned to Amber one evening, I found an unhappy reception committee waiting: my father, Freda, and Conner, all looking angry.

"What's wrong?" I asked.

"What have you done with him?" Freda said.

"I am close to a cure!" Dad said. "Another week, and he would have been free from Suhuy's poison!"

"What are you talking about?" I demanded, looking from one to another. Had they lost all reason?

Sharply, Conner said, "Do you deny releasing Fenn?"

"What — you mean he's gone?" I looked uncomprehendingly from one to another. "I've been at sea all day! When could I possibly have released him?"

Dad let out his breath. "I see Suhuy's hand in this," he muttered. "Another imposter!"

"What! And nobody thought to question him?" I demanded.

"You . . . *he* . . . was in a foul mood," Freda said. "He rode in alone, went straight to Fenn's cell, and ordered the guards to tie Fenn up. Which they did. Then he dragged Fenn out, ordered fresh horses, threw Fenn across the saddle, and left. Dad and I were here, but it happened so fast . . . he was gone before we knew it."

I shook my head. "This must stop. *Now.* Every time someone returns from a trip, one of us must be in the courtyard to greet him. We will have a password system."

"What do you mean?" Freda asked.

"Each time one of us comes home, someone else will say a word or ask a question. The proper response must be given to establish a true identity."

Conner frowned. "When you came home, I would say, 'fish' and then you would say, 'cakes'? Something like that?"

"Something a little more subtle." I frowned. "The first person will say, 'How was the weather?' and the correct reply will be, 'Fire and hail.' That way, if another imposter shows up and gives the wrong answer, he won't know he's been discovered."

"Agreed," Conner said quickly.

"Now, why did Suhuy want Fenn back?" I mused. "We discovered his true identity. Suhuy must know that trick won't work again."

"A better question," Dad said, "is — who was impersonating *you?*"

A month passed since Aber had betrayed King Uthor and me. Freda continued to check with her aunts nearly every day for updates on the political situation in the Courts of Chaos. Sometimes we got word of a friend or family member who had sworn fealty to King Swayvil; more often, however, we got lists of the executed as Swayvil's bloody purges continued.

Always we looked for word of missing family members, but

since Uthor's death, not one had been publicly executed. Of course, they could be undergoing torture in Swayvil's dungeons . . . or, as Conner had been, simply left to rot in a cell. We had no way of knowing. Perhaps, I sometimes thought, the new King of Chaos meant to save them for bargaining chips when he finally moved against us.

Several weeks into the new king's rule, King Uthor's brother Irtar tried to seize the throne. Backed by half a dozen powerful Lords of Chaos, his assassination attempt nearly succeeded. But Suhuy's timely intervention, according to Great Aunt Eddarg, saved the day.

After that, Swayvil rushed many of Uthor's former supporters to trial. Some days as many as two dozen Lords of Chaos met the axe in public ceremonies . . . all to the cheering of the bloodthirsty residents of Chaos. After Irtar's death, Swayvil declared a holiday and gave out refreshments and favors at the palace gates to all who called.

Of course, I recognized none of the names of the dead, though Freda wept several times when men and women she knew fell to Swayvil's purge. I could do little to comfort her.

She spent days working on Castle Amber, organizing the staff, decorating the halls and rooms, supervising all the little niceties that finished off the castle properly. And Amber slowly became a home to us all.

Early one morning I took a stroll along the castle's upper battlements, gazing out across the fields and rolling hills that had begun to sprout the beginnings of a town. It was a gloriously beautiful day, the air tasted crisp and fresh, and I felt well-rested and strong. Below me, the castle guard had turned out for morning drills, and with a wistful little smile I listened to the officers' orders and the beginnings of swordplay. I missed dawn roll-calls and early morning workouts.

Then I felt a light mental contact. Someone was trying to reach me through a Trump . . . probably Conner, who had gone off to explore the southern marshlands with several squads of infantryman. He had instructions to call me if anything went wrong.

When I opened my thoughts, though, I found myself staring at a wavering, uncertain image of Aber. He sat high on a pile of luxurious-looking cushions, and he looked well oiled and well fed.

He had nerve. My rage started to bubble toward the surface, but I held it in check.

"What is it?" I said coldly. He must have something important to say, after all he had done.

"Hi, Oberon."

He smiled with his usual cheerfulness, as though nothing had happened between us. Didn't he realize how much his betrayal had wounded me?

Slowly I dropped one hand to the knife at my belt. It had a good balance, perfect for throwing. I palmed it as subtly as I could. Would it strike him through the Trump if I threw it while we were talking? Somehow, I thought so.

"What do you want?" I said.

"I miss everyone," he said. He frowned a bit. "How would you feel about returning to the Courts on an official state visit, as ruler of Amber? Freda too, of course. And Conner if he wants."

"You must be joking," I said. I couldn't believe he'd just asked me to return to Chaos.

He grinned. "Okay. You don't have to bring Conner if you don't want to."

"Swayvil would kill us all!"

He actually laughed. "Nonsense. I hate to be insulting, but you have an exaggerated opinion of your own importance. The king simply doesn't care about you, Dad, or Amber right now — he has bigger problems."

"I can imagine," I said. "The body count seems to be rising quite fast, from what I hear."

"Ah? Freda's keeping tabs on us, I guess."

"Yes."

He cleared his throat. "Anyway, I'm something of a golden boy right now, you know . . . after all, I single-handedly ended the civil war and probably saved tens of thousands of lives. That makes me quite the hero in certain circles."

"Uh-huh. You're a hero." I let a note of disdain creep into my voice. "Congratulations."

"So, I asked the king if you could all visit, and he agreed. He personally guarantees your safety. When can you come?"

"You're insane," I said. He had to be out of his mind if he thought we would blindly walk into the Courts of Chaos again. "After all that's happened, you expect us to simply show up for dinner, never mind that Swayvil has been killing off our family for years?"

"Well, yes. And it would be more than just dinner — it would be an official state visit. You'll all be quite safe, of course."

"I'd sooner slit my own throat than let Swayvil do it for me. Or you, for that matter."

"How can you say that!" He actually looked hurt. And he managed it with such sincerity, I almost believed him. He had certainly missed his true calling — the stage.

I tightened my grip on the knife. "I don't take betrayal well, Aber. You can't talk your way out of it."

"You ought to be thanking me." He folded his arms stubbornly. "I did you a huge favor."

"Murdering King Uthor? If Swayvil hadn't attacked when he did . . ."

"It *was* carefully timed," he said smugly.

"You left us there to die!"

"Not at all. I had every faith in you. You're a survivor, after all. You'll just have to trust me this time — you were never in any real danger."

I shook my head. He made it sound almost plausible . . . only I knew the truth. He'd been looking out for himself, without a moment's thought for the rest of us.

Trust him? *Never again.*

At my silence, he continued: "You *are* my favorite brother, after all. That's got to count for something, Oberon!"

"Sure it does," I said, reaching my empty hand toward him. "Come on through. We'll discuss it over dinner . . . I know Freda wants to see you, too."

"Ah-ah." He wagged a finger at me and grinned. "Business before vengeance."

I raised my eyebrows. "Business?"

"Well, I *had* hoped to save it for the banquet . . . but what would you say to a pardon from King Swayvil?"

I stared at him. "Impossible!"

"If the king offered you and Dad and everyone else in our family pardons, including the return of our lands and restoration of our titles, would you return to Chaos and swear fealty to him?"

"What about Amber?" I demanded. After all we'd done, I couldn't just leave it.

"Amber will become a principality. You would remain Prince of Amber . . . and continue to rule it, paying homage to King Swayvil of course. An annual tribute, that sort of thing — a token of your allegiance to Chaos."

It all came clear. "So I would become a puppet for Swayvil."

"Of course not."

"Forget it," I said. If he couldn't see through that plot, he was deluding himself. It might take a year — or five years, or ten years — but sooner or later Swayvil would move against me. Whether it came through slow poisons or a hunting "accident" or an a late-night assassination attempt didn't really matter. I knew without the slightest doubt that Swayvil would try to get rid of the Pattern and the Shadows as soon as his attention moved beyond Chaos.

"Think!" Aber said, leaning forward. "Our family could return to Chaos. Our father's lands and titles would be restored. It would be easy. Take advantage of the king's generosity!"

"It's too easy," I said. "What about everyone currently being held by Swayvil?"

"Freed." His voice dropped, low and urgent now. "This is the chance of a lifetime. Think of it, Oberon — it's what you've been waiting for. You'll be a hero."

"This banquet idea . . . who do I have to thank for it?"

"Me." He all but preened.

"Hmm." Of course, I didn't believe him. He had his devious side, but somehow this plan seemed beyond him. And he really seemed to believe Swayvil meant to keep his word.

"First," I said, ticking off my fingers on my free hand, "I don't trust you. Second, I don't trust Swayvil to keep his word and not kill me the moment I set foot in the Courts. And third, I am *king* here . . . and I will never serve anyone else ever again."

He sighed and leaned back in his cushions. "Is that your final word?"

"No. Please give Swayvil a message for me."

In one quick motion, I hurled my knife at his head.

He severed the Trump connection so fast, my throw never had a chance. The wavering window to Chaos vanished. Instead of striking him, my knife sailed over the battlements and disappeared.

Hurrying to the edge, I leaned out and watched it bounce across the ground ten feet from where a small squad of guardsman drilled with swords. They whirled, craning their heads to look up at me.

"Sire?" called the captain of the guard.

"Bring my knife back up, Giras!" I called. It was a nice weapon; no point losing it.

Then I went to find Freda.

THIRTY-TWO

found my sister in the rose garden, overseeing the new plantings. Drawing her aside, I relayed Aber's message.

"What do you think of it?" I asked.

She frowned thoughtfully. "It *is* a tempting proposition."

"*Too* tempting. It's exactly what we need."

"Yes." She sighed, then shook her head. "I advise patience. After all, Swayvil is preoccupied now with tightening his grip on Chaos. Leave him to his problems; we will continue to strengthen Amber. That is our best hope for survival."

"Exactly my own conclusion," I said.

A week passed. I didn't hear from Aber again in all that time — which half surprised me. He wasn't the sort who gave up easily. But I shrugged and went on with the seemingly endless supply of tasks that required my immediate attention. Blueprints for unbuilt sections of the castle . . . street-plans for the someday-soon city surrounding the castle proper . . . land grants for the hundreds of settlers now streaming into Amber, courtesy of Conner's recruitment efforts in nearby Shadows . . . and of course all the regular duties of an army commander, king, lord of the manor, and general administrator - everything from meting out justice in court to simply signing off on military duty assignments.

I wished, for the thousandth time, that I had more lieutenants to whom duties could be passed. King Aslom's sons, though of unquestioning loyalty, needed many more years of seasoning to be left on their own. And Conner had to be in nearby Shadows, buying whatever we needed, bringing in soldiers and mercenaries and artisans and all the other workers we now needed in great number.

Despite my work load, I never forgot about Aber. Perhaps, I thought at times, he would grow content to stay in Chaos and crow about his heroic accomplishments. . . . If it impressed his friends and the women of the Courts, who was I to object? So long as he kept out of my way, I would not pursue revenge.

Overall, life felt good. As the castle crept toward completion, as the population grew and the army took shape, a sense of pride filled me. This was what I had been born to do. Amber would stand forever.

Busy as my days became, I made sure our family managed to gather as often as possible for dinner.

When the banquet hall was finally finished to her satisfaction, Freda set it up magnificently — long and broad, it had twin columns of white marble to either side of a fifty-foot-long table. A pair of crystal chandeliers glittered with the light of two thousand candles. Tapestries on the walls showed cheerful scenes — hunting stags, epic battles, and portraits of family members in handsome poses. Freda had commissioned one of me in kingly robes with a gold circlet on my head, beaming down at the table. I had to admit it was a good likeness.

She had also commissioned portraits of all our brothers and sisters, even the missing and the dead. I walked down the row of them, staring up at the missing and the dead. Locke . . . Davin . . . Mattus . . . Titus. So many . . .

A portrait of Aber hung at the very end, where it could not be seen from my seat at the head of the table. I frowned up at it. No, this would not do at all.

I called one of the stewards over. "This one . . . I don't want to see it."

"I will have it taken down, Sire," he said.

"No. Drape it in black."

"Are we to be in mourning for Lord Aber?" the steward asked, looking puzzled. "Isn't he still alive?"

"Yes . . . and yes."

That night, after dinner, Freda turned to me and said, "I need to speak with you."

"Oh?" I raised my eyebrows and took another sip of wine. Mentally, I sighed. She must have noticed the black crepe over Aber's tapestry; at least she had waited till the end of the meal to bring it up.

"At your convenience, of course."

"Is it about Aber?"

"Yes."

I took another sip of wine, studying her over the rim of my goblet. Somehow, I had known this was coming. I had a sudden premonition that he had contacted her again . . . asked her to intercede with me. She still loved him, I knew. She would certainly prove the weakest link in getting back into my good graces.

Not that I would ever let it happen.

I sighed. "Go on." I could at least hear her out. I owed her that much.

She said, "He wants me to talk to you about Swayvil's offer. I told him I would."

I snorted. "It's a most generous offer, I'm sure. But I'm no one's puppet."

"You should refuse," she went on. "You must never go back to Chaos. And you must never trust Swayvil, Suhuy, or Aber again."

I sat up. "What! I thought you would be in favor of it. A return to Chaos . . . freedom for Pella . . ."

"I know." She shook her head unhappily. "I think the offer was meant as a distraction for us. For *you*."

"How so?" I wouldn't have accepted Swayvil's offer anyway, but I wanted to know her reasoning.

"Swayvil has a history of deception and misdirection. Aber may be my brother, and I love him, but I do recognize his flaws. He is too clever for his own good. Now he has fallen under Swayvil's influence, and none of us must trust him. The words he speaks and the plots he weaves are not his own. They are Swayvil's — and he cannot see the whole of them."

"You can?"

She hesitated. "I . . . suspect things."

Nodding, I said, "I do, too. You said the offer was a distraction."

"Yes. What better way to put us off our guard? What better way to lure you back to Chaos?"

"Possibly." I nodded slowly. "But why? He would not be able to kill me once I got there, if he publicly promised that pardon."

"He can make the terms unpalatable to you."

"Then I would refuse . . ."

"And — ?"

Frowning, I finished my thought: ". . . which is what he wants. If I refuse to swear allegiance to him, he will be free to move against Amber!"

"In the meantime, you will have been in Chaos. Distracted. Cut off from our troops. Everyone here will be unprepared. Perhaps the attack will occur while you are in Chaos . . . and there will be no Amber for you to return to."

I swallowed. "Devious . . ."

She smiled thinly. "You begin to see the nature of politics in Chaos. King Uthor did not play the game well enough. We must."

"If Swayvil is ready to move against us . . ."

"He is," she said firmly.

". . . then we must move against him first. We will fight as we would have fought against Uthor. Nothing has changed."

I rose and paced. We would have to prepare ourselves, and quickly. My army numbered, what - three hundred thousand? And we had been making allies among the neighboring Shadows. If we ran into trouble, we might be able to field as many as a half-million men.

And, of course, Conner had been approaching more of his "special forces," as he liked to call dragons, ogres, trolls, and other nonhuman denizens of Shadow . . . they, too, would join us. We would meet whatever price they demanded.

We would need to dispatch scouts into Shadow . . . begin looking for Swayvil's forces as they marched on Amber . . .

"Please," Freda said. "Bring Aber back? Before Swayvil tires of him and has him killed — for me?"

I swallowed hard. It pained me, but I had to be firm in my resolve.

"I cannot," I said softly. "Do not ask me to." I could never forgive him for what he had done.

"Is that your final decision?""

"Yes." I could not look her in the eye.

She bowed her head. "As you will . . . Sire."

That night, I summoned Conner and my father to a council of war. They listened raptly as I told them of Aber's tantalizing offer . . . and my refusal. Then I repeated Freda's and my suspicions about Swayvil being ready to move against us.

"Was I wrong to refuse to bring Aber back?" I asked them.

"No!" Conner said.

Dad said, "He would only betray you again. Do not be a fool, my boy."

I nodded slowly. Having to make the hard decisions of a king sometimes hurt. I would have to steel myself to them. I would have to think not just of my own selfish pleasures — or Freda's for that matter — but make decisions for the good of all in Amber.

So be it. My decision had been made. It would stand.

To Conner, I said, "Have Aslom and the other generals start bringing in everyone from the field," I said. "We must begin our preparations for war. I want to see the latest troop reports."

"We can have all our forces in the staging area within the week."

"Dad? You must bring the scouts into Shadows. Find Swayvil's army."

"Easier said than done."

I grinned. "I have faith in you. Just don't let them catch you." Then I turned to my brother. "You know what to do."

"Special troops," he said.

"Right."

He grinned. "This is the part I have been waiting for!"

"It's not going to be pleasant," I said grimly. "A lot of people are going to die. Possibly even us."

"I know. But we're going to win, Oberon. I feel it."

"I do, too," I said. A strange calmness came over me. At a time like this, I would have expected to be at least a little nervous. But I wasn't. Everything was coming out better than I'd hoped.

We would field an army unmatched in the history of war. Half a million soldiers marching against Chaos, all under my banner . . . Swayvil could not prevail.

THIRTY-THREE

reda always managed to surprise me. I expected news of King Swayvil's pending attack to come from Dad and the scouts he was scattering through Shadows. But it was my sister who came to me in the library and said simply:

"Swayvil's forces are marching now."

"What! How do you know?"

"Great Aunt Eddarg." She smiled. "We discuss dinner at the palace nearly every day. Apparently the king neglected to tell her that half the court wouldn't be at dinner last night because they had left on a military mission."

"And you inferred from this that his men are marching on Amber." I gave her a kiss on the forehead. "Brilliant!"

She smiled. "Tell Father and Conner."

"What about Swayvil? Is he joining them?"

"No. By tradition, he will remain in the Courts of Chaos while his generals battle. And . . . Aber has also left the palace."

"Why?" It didn't sound like him to pass up life in the palace for a military expedition.

"Great Aunt Eddarg did not know. Our brother is not a fighter; he would not take part in the actual battle. But I do fear another trick ... something to remove you from the battlefield ..."

"I will watch for him."

Between the scouts and our father's knowledge of Shadows and the Pattern, they managed to spot the army of Chaos marching through Shadows. Our outriders paced them, keeping hidden, using Trumps to come and go quickly without being seen. I did not think Swayvil's men even knew they were being observed. Dad and I made sure none of the mistakes he and Locke had made in Juniper would be repeated here. We had all learned our lesson well.

Half a dozen times, I watched from cover on nearby mountainsides as the forces of Chaos marched past, heading down a black road conjured by the sorcerers of Chaos. Dad and Conner — and once even Freda — joined me.

Freda brought a large picnic lunch prepared by Great Aunt Eddarg. The irony of it was not lost on any of us. Although I tried not to look too closely at the food, and I did not ask what might be in the sandwiches, I ate six of them. They were quite tasty if you ignored the crunching and occasional squeals.

Below us, columns of soldiers — so small I could not tell whether they were hell-creatures, men, or something else entirely — marched down that black road in columns twenty abreast.

"Is that Aber?" I asked suddenly leaning forward and squinting.

"Where?" Freda asked. She raised herself up to see.

"Directly across from us now." I pointed to an open carriage drawn by a team of eight slow-moving lizards. Someone sat in the back, high on a pile of golden pillows. Such decadence on the way to war — who else could it be but our brother?

"No . . ." Dad said, peering through a spyglass. "I believe that is General Droth. He must be in charge of this campaign."

"A general? Waging war perched on pillows?" I asked incredulously.

Dad handed my his spyglass. I put it to one eye. On closer examination, it definitely wasn't my brother, but an older, more portly man with horns and a long red tail.

"Why not be comfortable?" Conner said with a small grin. "Maybe I should get us all pillows for the coming battle."

"I could use one now," Freda said. "I am not accustomed to sitting on the ground while I eat."

"Is it worth our time to kill General Droth?" I asked. I tried to estimate the distance between us. A thousand yards . . . an impossible bowshot. But perhaps, using the Pattern . . .

"Patience, my boy . . ." Dad chuckled. "Our army is not so far away now."

"Besides, it would tip them off that we know they're coming," Conner said. "We do have plans, remember."

"We should get back and prepare for our ambush," I said, rising.

"Go on," Freda said. "I will clean up and return to Amber. Good luck to you all."

"Thanks," I said. "We will celebrate our victory tonight."

Dad pulled out a Trump he had drawn the week before. It showed a valley in the next Shadow, lush and green and surrounded by hills now filled with archers. Any of Swayvil's army who made it through the valley alive would find cavalry and foot soldiers waiting, along with more of Conner's "special forces."

If all went as planned, it would be a devastating rout for General Droth and his men.

An hour later, I rode the cavalry line, reviewing the troops. General Aslom and his sons, with their golden war-chariots, would lead the Ceyoldar brigade. They looked splendid in their brightly polished armor. Next came the Mong, somber men, small and wiry, who fought on sturdy little ponies with all the fury of berserkers. They wore hardened leather armor and face-concealing helms. After them came forces from other nearby Shadows Dad and Conner had found: Tir-Na-Gath, Mulvia, Jarvoon, Zelloque, and so many more.

As I rode past, they stood up in their stirrups, swords and lances held high, cheering.

"Keep the banners up!" I cried. "We will sweep them away before us!"

My stallion danced and fought for his head, but I wouldn't let him go. He wanted the coming battle almost as much as I did.

I felt the beginnings of Trump contact and answered. It was Conner.

"The first of them are entering the valley," he said softly. "Prepare yourself, brother. Keep your eyes on the black highway!"

The spikard-ring on my finger pulsed briefly — not so much a warning, I thought, as an acknowledgment.

I raised my hands for silence, and the tens of thousands of men before me grew still. A low wind whistled. Here and there a horse snorted or neighed, or the wheels of a war-chariot creaked as its occupant shifted his weight.

Suddenly, just visible over the top of the hill before us, flashed volley after volley of my army's arrows. A cloud of dust rose. Faintly, far in the distance, came a rumble of noise . . . the mingled stampeding of hundreds of thousands of soldiers who fought to escape the death-trap in which they found themselves . . . the shrieks of the dying and wounded . . . the battle-cries of those who drew their weapons and sought to fight.

"Wait . . . wait . . ." I murmured.

I turned my horse to face the hills. We would hold our position until the archers had done their worst, or Swayvil's men topped the rise — whichever came first.

One, then another, then another hell-creature in black armor appeared on the road before us. They drew up short when they saw the lines of horsemen and chariots waiting scarcely a hundred yards away. But more and more creatures of Chaos swarmed behind them, fleeing the valley, pushing them forward.

"Now!" I screamed, spurring my horse and giving him his head.

Like a demon, he raced for the hell-creatures, his hooves drumming. Around and behind me, I heard the thunder of an all-out cavalry charge.

Screaming in fear, the hell-creatures tried to turn and flee back down their black highway. But it was too late. There could be no flight to safely now. None would escape my wrath.

A bloodlust came over me, terrible and strong. The ring on my finger burned. A roar of blood filled my ears. I rode into the hell-creatures' midst, swinging my sword like a scythe. Heads rolled. Bodies fell. My horse reared and struck with its hooves, crushing skulls, then leaping forward to bite and rend with its teeth.

Together we cut a swath through the onrushing soldiers of Chaos. Those who sought to run were trampled or struck from behind. Those who stood and fought were slashed, stabbed, disemboweled, or beheaded — sometimes all at once.

And still we fought. My horse went down, and I leaped from his back with a savage war-cry, tackling a group of hell-creatures. Their glowing red eyes showed nothing but terror at the blood-drenched monster I must have been. As they scrambled to get away, I laughed and roared and swung my sword like a whip through the air, and so many pieces of them fell to the red-stained grass.

Finally, panting, I drew to a halt, covered in sweat and gore. Around me the battle had begun to wind down. None of the hell-creatures still stood anywhere within fifty feet of me. Men, *my* men, moved among the bodies, stabbing them with swords, making sure they were truly dead. We did not want any survivors or surprises.

Then my ring pulsed once, quick and sharp — a warning? I whirled, scanning the bodies around me, looking for anything unusual or out of place.

Then I spotted a figure standing in the cover of a copse of trees on the next hill. I couldn't see his face, but he seemed to be staring directly at me. A shiver of alarm went through me. Swayvil?

And then the figure raised one arm . . . and waved. *Aber.*

I took a deep breath, glanced around at the mopping-up efforts of my men, and decided they didn't need me for the moment. I had personal business to take care of.

Then I waved back. Might as well put him off his guard, I decided. Let him think I had forgotten or forgiven . . .

I stripped the cloak from a dead hell-creature's back, wiped my face and sword clean, then calmly marched toward my brother's position. I kept my expression carefully neutral . . . showing neither hate nor anger nor the desire for revenge that burned within me.

As I grew near, he seemed to sense something of my intentions, for he suddenly turned and ran off into the trees. I followed, rushing through the tall oaks, catching a glimpse of him now and then.

"Don't run!" I shouted. "Aber! Make it easy for yourself!"

"Then promise you won't hurt me!" he shouted back.

"Do you take me for a fool?" I demanded.

"Yes," he said with a light laugh. "But don't be offended. I'm smarter than everyone in the family. Even Dad, though he doesn't realize it."

"Wait for me!"

We reached a small clearing, and I found him standing there with his arms crossed, a little smile on his lips.

I drew up. "I'm sick of games!" I told him. I raised my sword. I would make his death as quick and as painless as I could, for Freda's sake. "Why did you come here? What did you possibly think would happen?"

He sighed and shook his head. "Look behind you."

"If I do, you'll disappear again."

"If you don't, you'll be dead." He shrugged. "It's my last warning for my favorite brother."

To Rule in Amber

Suddenly I had a very bad feeling inside. I glanced over my shoulder.

And just as suddenly I wished I hadn't.

THIRTY-FOUR

 saw myself standing there. Or, rather, I saw my double. Face, hair, shape of chest, length of legs — I might have been looking in a mirror. And he even held a sword exactly like mine.

This had to be the man who kidnapped Fenn from Amber. We had all assumed Suhuy sent him. Apparently it had been King Swayvil . . . or Aber.

"Who are you?" I demanded of him.

"I am Oberon," he said.

I snorted. "I don't think so."

"I am and *will be* the rightful King of Amber," he growled. "You stole my place. I will take it back."

"You may have my face, but you aren't *me*."

He raised his sword. "I am. I *will be*."

"Incredible," Aber said. He looked from the double to me and back again wonderingly. "You really *are* identical. I didn't quite believe it."

"The difference," I said grimly, "is that *I'm* real. And after I've killed your creature — whatever it is — I'm going to kill you."

"I think not," he said.

"I'm real enough," said the fake Oberon. "Look at me! I am you

304

in every way . . ."

And, as I would have, he leaped without warning, hammering at me with a series of bone-jarring blows. I parried his first attacks, sending our swords ringing, then threw him back and riposted. Again our blades sang and danced, steel on steel, blurring with the speed of our every move. We each strained to throw the other one back. His muscles knotted like mine. His neck corded; his face grew red and veins bulged at his temples.

We both leaped back at the same time too, swords up, panting hard. He looked as winded as I felt.

Slowly, we circled each other, swords up, feeling each other out. Though I hated to admit it, we seemed equally matched.

"I think the Pattern copied you," Aber said casually. I let my gaze flicker over to him for a second. He sat down under an oak tree and crossed his legs, relaxing. For all the care he showed, he might have been attending a picnic.

"Explain!" I said.

"I'm not sure I can." He laced his fingers behind his head. "But, in a way, I think you're both Oberon."

I leaped forward, a whirlwind of thrusting, lunging, slashing. My double gave way before me. Although I could have countered each such attack easily, he seemed to be having trouble keeping up. An advantage? Did he lack my stamina?

We both drew back, panting, glaring at one another.

"Oberon?" Aber continued, "Do you want to know where I found him?"

"Yes!"

"Then I'll tell you. You will find it amusing." He cleared his throat. "I went back to the new Pattern after Dad made it. You thought I didn't know where it was, but I did. I saw Dad start to draw it, and I made a Trump to get back there. It worked. Dad was just finishing when I arrived. He attacked me — I don't know why, since I never did anything to him. He did it without warning — just drew his sword and stabbed me!"

I nodded. "He did the same to me. But I defended myself. He was crazy."

"Yes. I didn't realize it at the time." Aber paused. "Watch out!"

My double came at me again, sword swinging. I parried, then drove him back with an attack of my own, raining down blow after blow.

Still Aber talked. "I wished myself away — anywhere else — and the Pattern sent me outside the pattern. I crawled into the bushes, thinking I was going to die. Dad collapsed, like it had been too much for him. So I lay there, too weak to move, just watching and waiting. That's when you showed up. You walked the Pattern, woke Dad up, knocked him senseless, and then picked him up and disappeared."

Panting, my double and I drew apart again, glaring at each other. I had never fought a man so much like me. He knew all my moves, just as I knew his. Neither of us seemed capable of gaining an edge on the other.

"Go on," I told Aber.

He smiled. "A few seconds after you left with Dad, the whole Pattern kind of flickered. Then *he* appeared. Another *you*. Only he was out of his head, too, like Dad had been. He didn't remember anything — how you betrayed King Uthor, tricked Dad into making a new Pattern for you, how you planned to set yourself up as ruler of all the Shadows."

"That's a rather twisted way of looking at things," I told him.

He shrugged. "The truth is in the eye of the beholder. Anyway, I took him back to Chaos with me, kept him hidden, nursed him back to health. But he wasn't quite like you. He's found it's more rewarding to follow King Swayvil. And he isn't trying to kill me. So, dear brother, I've backed my *other* dear brother."

"You want him to kill me," I said, "and take my place."

"That's right."

"And the two of you will rule the Shadows . . . with Swayvil's kind permission?"

He chuckled. "Something like that. Yes. You're smarter than you look."

I gave a double feint — one of our father's tricks with the sword — and my blade slipped under my double's guard. I put all my weight on my forefoot and lunged, gashing his right arm to the bone.

He punched me in the face with his left fist. I reeled back, stunned for a heartbeat, but he didn't follow up with an attack of his own.

I stared into his eyes. He made no sound, but I could tell he was in pain. He was losing a lot of blood fast. I must have hit an artery. His face went white.

"Yield," I said.

"I cannot," he replied.

"Why? Because of *him*?" I jerked my head at Aber.

"No. Because there can only be one of us."

He switched the sword to his left hand. As I watched, the wound on his arm closed up. It seemed we shared another talent — he could change shape as well as I could. And he'd done it to cover up his wound and stop the bleeding.

I would have done the same thing.

Unfortunately, he would have to use part of his strength and concentration to hold his new form. With all other things between us being equal, that gave me an edge.

My ring pulsed in warning. I dove to the side a moment before I heard the familiar *snick* of a crossbow being fired.

Of course it had to be Aber. And of course he had just fired it at my back.

Faster than I had ever moved before, I whirled and threw my sword at Aber. It struck his right shoulder and pinned him to the tree. He screamed in agony.

Unfortunately, that left me unarmed.

Grinning through his pain, my double stalked forward, sword ready. Quickly I drew a knife. Then I began to back up.

"Kneel," he said to me. "Raise your head. I'll make it quick — a single blow. You fought well. You deserve that much."

"Look behind you," I said, focusing my attention over his shoulder. "You haven't won yet."

He hesitated. There wasn't anything behind him, of course — but he had been behind me when Aber uttered those same words. Could he take the chance?

He knew he had me outmatched. It only took a second to check. When he glanced over his shoulder, I threw my knife at his head. He batted the knife away with his sword, but in that instant, with his arm up and out of position, I closed with him. So close, a sword would do him no good.

I drove him back with my fists. He fell, helmet flying off, and I landed on top. Then I hit him in the face as hard as I could, again and again. He did not scream, and he only flailed for a minute as I pounded. I stopped when the shattered bits of his skull began to shred my knuckles.

Panting, I rose unsteadily to my feet. I felt exhausted suddenly, like I'd been fighting for hours. Slowly, I turned.

Aber had managed to get the sword out of the tree and his shoulder. He couldn't hold it, though, much as he tried. It fell as his fingers spasmed open.

Standing there sullenly, dripping blood, a gaping wound in his shoulder, it struck me how pathetic he truly was. He had never matched our father's expectations. He had murdered King Uthor. And I knew now, without a doubt, that he had sent assassins after me at least twice.

And, despite all that, I still liked him. It wasn't a spell. I actually *liked* him — which made killing him all the harder.

He fell to his knees and grinned his slightly lopsided grin. "I suppose it's too late to explain?"

"Yes," I said. I picked up my double's sword.

"I can still be useful," he said. "You need me, Oberon."

"What happened to Fenn?" I asked.

"The other Oberon was . . . a little rough in his questioning. Didn't believe Fenn's story about a slow poison."

"He's dead, then."

"Yes. See? I can be useful. You *need* me."

"And Isadora? Leona? Davin?"

"I don't know. I can find out, though. If anyone can, it's me."

"You're right," I said slowly. "I do need you."

He sighed with relief. "Good."

"Unfortunately," I went on, "I need to stay alive a lot more."

With a single quick, clean blow, I parted my brother's head from his shoulders. His body flopped and lay still. The head rolled a few feet before coming to a stop facing me. The eyes blinked several times, then went glassy.

I sagged under the oak tree and wept. Of all my family, I had loved him the most. I would miss him. Not the traitorous Aber, but the Aber who had befriended me in Juniper. The Aber who had made me feel like part of the family. The Aber whom I had trusted and in whom I had believed . . . even if it had been due to a charm-spell.

Finally, after I finished mourning, I buried him in that unnamed Shadow, in an unmarked grave, alongside my double. Hopefully they would both find peace now.

Rising, finding new strength, I went to see what had become of my father, my brother Conner, and all the Shadows I was destined to rule.

THE END

ABOUT THE AUTHOR

JOHN GREGORY BETANCOURT is an editor, publisher, and bestselling author of science fiction and fantasy novels and short stories. He has had 37 books published, including the bestselling Star Trek novel, *Infection*, and three other Star Trek novels; a trilogy of mythic novels starring Hercules; the critically acclaimed *Born of Elven Blood*; *Rememory*; *Johnny Zed*; *The Blind Archer*, and many others. His fantasy novel *The Dragon Sorcerer* was released by ibooks. He is personally responsible for the revival of *Weird Tales*, the classic magazine of the fantastic, and has authored two critical works in conjunction with the Sci-Fi Channel: *The Sci-Fi Channel Trivia Book* and *The Sci-Fi Channel Encyclopedia of TV Science Fiction*.

ROGER ZELAZNY authored many science fiction and fantasy classics, and won three Nebula Awards and six Hugo Awards over the course of his long and distinguished career. While he is best known for his ten-volume *Chronicles of Amber* series of novels (beginning with 1970's *Nine Princes in Amber*), Zelazny also wrote many other novels, short stories, and novellas, including *Psychoshop* (with Alfred Bester), *Damnation Alley*, the award-winning *The Doors of His Face, The Lamps of His Mouth* and *Lord of Light*, and the stories "24 Views of Mount Fuji, by Hokusai," "Permafrost," and "Home is the Hangman." Zelazny died in Santa Fe, New Mexico, in June 1995.